Anna Bradley lives with her husband and two children in Portland, Oregon. *A Wicked Way to Win an Earl* is her first novel.

Visit Anna Bradley online:

www.annabradley.net
www.facebook.com/annabradley472
www.twitter.com/annabradley472

ANNA BRADLEY

A WICKED WAY to WIN AN EARL

The Sutherland Scandals

piatkus

PIATKUS

First published in the United States in 2015 by Berkley Sensation,
an imprint of Penguin Random House LLC, New York
First published in Great Britain in 2015 by Piatkus

1 3 5 7 9 10 8 6 4 2

A CIP catalogue record for this book
is available from the British Library.

ISBN 978-0-349-41048-7

Printed and bound in Great Britain by
Clays Ltd, St Ives plc

Papers used by Piatkus are from well-managed forests
and other responsible sources.

 MIX
Paper from
responsible sources
FSC
www.fsc.org FSC® C104740

Piatkus
An imprint of
Little, Brown Book Group
Carmelite House
50 Victoria Embankment
London EC4Y 0DZ

An Hachette UK Company
www.hachette.co.uk

www.piatkus.co.uk

TO MY THREE INSPIRATIONS:

My husband, Brad.

My daughter, Annabel,
queen of all she surveys,

And especially to my son, Eli,
who loves stories, and thinks like a writer.

My deepest thanks to my agent, the divine Marlene Stringer, my wonderful editor, Cindy Hwang, and all the talented staff at Berkley. Special thanks to those readers who took a chance on a new author, and, of course, my very first reader, my sister Jennifer.

Prologue

"Hurry, Caroline! Oh, please do hurry!" Millicent Chase cast an uneasy look over her shoulder as she rushed down the empty corridor.

Caroline Swan placed a firm hand on Millicent's arm to keep her from breaking into a run. "Millie! Someone will notice if we dash about. They won't be looking for you. Not yet."

Click. Click. Click. The heels of Millicent's elegant silver slippers made a distinct patter on the marble floors. Despite Caroline's warning, the patter only quickened. Millicent lowered the hood of her black velvet cloak as she hurried down the hallway. It was an unusually deep one, and the luxurious black jet beadwork sewn lavishly around the hood's edges glittered even in the dim light of the corridor.

The young ladies ducked into a shallow alcove just off the main passage. It was a servant's passageway, but as it didn't lead directly from the kitchens to the ballroom, it would be deserted tonight. Better yet, it let out right into the dark mews at the back of the town house.

"Just here, Caroline." Millicent pulled her friend into the alcove and turned to face her, glancing over Caroline's shoulder to make sure they hadn't been followed. She put her hands up to her flushed cheeks. "Goodness, I'm nervous!" She reached for the black mask that hid her face, which was sewn with some of the same jet beads that adorned the hood. Her fingers shook.

Caroline took Millicent's hands gently in her own and lowered them to her sides. "Let me." She removed the mask and unbuttoned Millicent's cloak. Millicent stood as docile as a child as Caroline freed her from the enveloping garment.

"Millie, I . . ." Caroline hesitated, the cloak clutched in her hands. "We may not speak for some time, and I . . ."

Millicent's eyes misted with tears. She reached down and grasped Caroline's cold fingers. "You're my dearest friend, Caroline, and I won't ever forget what you've done for me tonight. I'll miss you terribly. But surely we'll see each other again." Her voice rose hopefully. "The *ton* has a short memory for scandal."

But a long memory for insult and social humiliation.

Caroline didn't say it. There wasn't any point. Millicent had made up her mind, and things had gone too far for her to turn back now. There would be consequences for her actions tonight. Millicent knew it. She'd accepted it. Caroline studied her friend's face and smiled. She saw no regret in Millie's dark, famously blue eyes.

Caroline squeezed the slim fingers that clutched her own and smiled. "Here, give me the mask and help me tie it."

Millicent handed her the mask and helped Caroline tie the silken cord at the back; then she held out the cloak and Caroline slipped her arms into the voluminous folds. The black velvet billowed around her, easily concealing her gown.

Millicent arranged the hood over her friend's fair hair, then stood back and studied the effect. The girls were a similar size, both of them tall and slim. The hood came down low over Caroline's face and completely disguised her hair. The domino mask didn't hide the hazel eyes that could never be mistaken for Millicent's blue ones, but it didn't matter. There was no one to notice.

Millicent grasped Caroline's shoulders. "It will do very well. Do the best you can not to draw attention to yourself and no one will be the wiser for at least several hours."

"What about Lord Carlisle?" Caroline asked, suddenly nervous. "What shall I do if he engages me in conversation? Won't he notice if we dance together?"

Millicent shook her head, but she didn't answer, and after a moment Caroline nodded. Lord Carlisle wouldn't attempt to engage his fiancée in conversation. He wouldn't look into her eyes and wonder why they were no longer blue. He wouldn't look into her eyes at all.

Caroline straightened her shoulders and smiled. "Well," she said, making a valiant attempt at merriment. "I'm the luckiest girl at the ball. Every young lady here wishes she were Millicent Chase."

But Millicent didn't smile. Instead, her mouth twisted bitterly. For the past few months she'd been the most sought-after young lady in London. Every debutante dreamed of being the belle of her season, but Caroline knew they hadn't been two weeks into the season before Millicent felt like a fox cornered by hounds.

"That will be true for approximately three more hours. When the truth is revealed, Caroline . . ." Millicent began, but then she stopped, as if she weren't sure what to say.

But Caroline was under no illusions about her part in the

drama that would unfold at midnight. One didn't betray Hart Sutherland on a whim. Not under any circumstances. Still, she brushed Millicent's concern aside with a wave of her hand. "I'll manage it, Millie. Please be careful yourself. But I'm not too worried for you, for I know Captain Somerset appreciates the value of his burden."

Millicent pressed her damp cheek against Caroline's. "Good-bye." The click of her slippers echoed in the dim hallway as she disappeared around the corner.

Caroline's heart gave a painful squeeze. Tonight would live forever in the memory of Millicent's family and friends as the night she gave up everything for the mad adventure of a lifetime.

Lady Hadresham gazed down at the ballroom from her vantage point on the balcony, a satisfied smile on her face. Mrs. Gisborne's peacock plumes wilted in the heat. Ladies young and old clutched their glasses of champagne as though a drought had descended upon London. They fluttered their fans to and fro in a fruitless effort to cool their cheeks and dry their faces. Couples twirled gingerly on the dance floor, aware one missed step would send them all atilt and they'd scatter like a line of dominoes tweaked by a careless finger.

As usual, it was an intolerable crush. No one wanted to miss Lord and Lady Hadresham's annual masque ball. It was the *ton*'s last chance to strut and preen before they scurried off to their country houses, rats abandoning the sinking ship that was London after the season ended.

Behind gloved hands and painted silk fans the gossip flowed steadily, buoyed along by wave after wave of French champagne. Lips to ear. Lips to ear.

That gown! Whatever made her decide to wear that shade of green with her sallow complexion?

It curled and drifted, clinging to the smoke that lingered over the billiards table:

You might have a chance with her, old boy, for I hear Lord Weymouth is tiring of her . . .

It was delivered in whispers and snickers by the debutantes and traded like currency at the card tables:

Another season and still no offer for poor Miss Chatsworth. My dear, this is her sixth season! How sad . . .

Lady Hadresham's eyes moved over the crush of people and the smile at the corners of her pretty mouth grew ever more complacent.

The Chase family was here. They stood near the terrace with Anne Sutherland, Lady Carlisle, and her eldest son, Hart, now Earl of Carlisle. Even masked, they were unmistakable. They weren't inconvenienced by the crush of people. The cool air coming through the door wafted over them as if on command. It was without a doubt the one comfortable spot in the entire ballroom, but no one questioned their right to it. They were the Chases and the Sutherlands, after all. It was as it should be.

The engagement of the season would be announced at midnight. At the moment of unmasking, Lady Hadresham would be immortalized as London's premier hostess.

The light from the ballroom chandeliers drifted out onto the stairs leading up to Lord and Lady Hadresham's town house, but it was no match for the dense London fog. The night swallowed the light a few steps from the doorway. Had anyone been watching the mews, they would have caught only a glimpse of a young lady, hatless and without a cloak, before she melted into the shadows.

Like the young lady, the carriage was unobtrusive. Black, with no crest. It could have been any carriage on any street in London. As the young lady approached, a tall silhouette leapt from the open door and wrapped a cloak tenderly about her shoulders. The two figures melted together until no light or shadow was visible between them.

As one, they ascended the carriage. The door closed with a quiet click, and the driver brought the ribbons down over the horses' backs.

Chapter One

KENT, 1814

The spring mud seeped through the thin soles of her leather walking boots and began to creep into her stockings. This was no ordinary mud. Before long it would be tickling her garters.

"Blast it," Delia muttered halfheartedly. She'd known it was a mistake to come here. A mudslide would certainly prove her right, wouldn't it? There was a sort of grim satisfaction in being right, though at the moment she'd settle for being dry. And clean. And home, instead of stranded on a deserted road in Kent, with the sky turning dark over her head, at grave risk of being buried in a freak mudslide.

At the very least she should have listened to her sister Lily and stayed with the carriage, but no, she'd insisted on finding help, and now here she was in an awful predicament—

Delia stopped suddenly, one foot in a puddle. Was that . . . Yes! She crossed her fingers and sent a quick prayer up to heaven the noise she'd just heard was not a bear or some other wild animal.

Were there bears in Kent?

Delia strained to hear, and waited. No, it wasn't a bear. That was, unless the bears in this part of England were prone to high-pitched giggling. She pulled at her foot with some force to dislodge it from the puddle. The sound was coming from farther up the road, around the other side of a bend.

She staggered forward as quickly as her sopping skirts would allow. It was odd to hear giggling on a lonely road at dusk, but she was in no position to be choosy. All she wished for in the world was one single person who could help her find a conveyance. One human being. Was that too much to ask? Anyone would do. Anyone at all.

She trudged around the bend, dragging her hems.

Oh, dear. One did need to be careful what one wished for.

She squinted into the dusk, trying to make sense of the two shapes leaning against a tree. It was a woman, and she was . . . The squint turned into wide-eyed shock. Delia froze, as if the mud at her feet had become quicksand and she was sunk up to her neck in it.

It was a woman, indeed, and she wasn't alone. She was engaged. With a man. A very large man. He was at least a head taller than his companion. If the woman hadn't been giggling, Delia would have missed her entirely, hidden as she was by a pair of impossibly wide shoulders. The man had discarded his coat, which hung carelessly over a wet tree branch. Without it, his white shirt was just visible in the dusk, and under it what appeared to Delia to be miles of muscled arm and long, sinewy back.

Well, he wouldn't need his coat, would he? Not for what he was doing. It would only get in the way. For instance, it might prove difficult for him to trap the woman against the tree. His arms were stretched on either side of her and his palms rested on the trunk beside her head. Delia swallowed. If he wasn't right on top of her like that, his lips might not be able to reach her throat and neck so easily. And his hands . . .

Delia held her breath as one of the man's hands dropped away from the tree and slipped inside the gaping neckline of the woman's dress to caress her breast.

A hot flush began deep in the pit of Delia's belly. She looked behind her, then back at the scene in front of her, her eyes darting wildly. Was it too late to turn back the way she'd come? She'd decided in favor of the mudslide and the bears, after all. But her feet refused to move. She was rooted to the spot, unable to tear her eyes away from this man with his muscular back and his bold, seeking hand.

"Alec! Stop that!" The woman let out a little squeal and slapped playfully at the man's hand.

Oh, thank God. Delia breathed a silent sigh of relief. This reckless young woman was coming to her senses at last. Any moment now she'd push the man away.

Any moment now.

But then the man gave a low chuckle and murmured something in the woman's ear. Delia watched, appalled, as the woman giggled again and snaked her arms around the man's lean hips to pull him tighter against her. Once he was there, the woman sighed. And oh, it was such a sigh! Delia had never heard one like it before, and it made her ears burn with embarrassment.

And he was . . . *Oh no!* One large hand slipped down to fumble at the fall of his breeches while the other caught a handful of the woman's skirts and began to raise them up, up, and higher still . . .

Delia clapped her hand over her mouth but some noise must have escaped, some cry of distress or outrage, because suddenly the man's back stiffened. The woman peered over his shoulder, saw Delia, and with a quick, practiced tug, she freed her skirts from the man's grip, batted them down,

jerked her neckline up, and disappeared around the side of
the tree. Within seconds it was as if she'd never been there
at all.

Delia blinked. Well, that was over quickly, wasn't it? Now
that it was, she had two choices. She could ask the man for
help, or she could flee back to Lily and the safety of the
carriage and pretend she'd never been here, either.

Then again . . . she'd never seen a real debauchery before.
Since there was no longer any danger of this one coming to its
final embarrassing conclusion, Delia found she was curious.

What would he do *now*?

She watched, rapt, but for a long time he didn't do anything. He didn't turn around. He didn't speak. He just stood
there, inhaling deeply, the muscles of his back rippling with
each breath. *In. Out. In. Out.* He tipped his head back and
for several minutes he concentrated on the tree branches
swaying above him.

She was just about to conclude this was the dullest debauchery ever when he let out a frustrated groan, grabbed
his coat from the branch, and turned to face her.

"Who the *devil* are you?"

Delia's mouth dropped open and she stumbled backward
a few steps, her curiosity evaporating. His tone was inexcus-
ably rude, and he was even bigger and more intimidating
from the front, but the real trouble here was that . . .

He was naked.

Well, not naked *really*, but more naked than any man
she'd ever seen in the flesh, and he had a great deal of flesh.
His loose white shirt was open at the neck, revealing a gen-
erous expanse of his muscular chest. Delia stared, her face
flaming even as her eyes moved helplessly over the bounty
of bare male flesh.

He pinned her down with penetrating dark eyes that
sported lashes long enough to satisfy even the vainest of
women, and crossed his arms over his chest.

"Miss?" he barked. "I asked you a question."

Yes—he had, hadn't he? Yes, of course—who the devil *was* she? "Delia Somerset?" She cringed when it emerged as a question.

A glint of lazy humor flashed in the black eyes. "Well, are you or aren't you? You don't seem to be sure."

Delia didn't trust that glint. Her married friends sometimes whispered about men like him. Men who became crazed with lust and were swept away by their animal passions. All manner of wicked behavior followed.

This one looked more savage than most.

"Let's assume you are indeed Miss Somerset," he drawled, when she still didn't speak. "Now that I know *who* the devil you are, may I suggest you tell me what the *devil* you're doing here?"

Why, of all the offensive, bullying . . . All at once Delia's embarrassment faded under a wave of indignation. Even an intriguingly bare chest didn't excuse profanity.

"And may *I* suggest, sir," she snapped, "that you don your coat?"

One dark eyebrow shot up in acknowledgment of this show of temper. "Forgive me, Miss Somerset." He put on his waistcoat and began buttoning it with an air of complete unconcern, as if he spent every day half-naked on a public road. He shrugged into his coat. "I didn't mean to offend your delicate sensibilities."

Delia stared at him. "It's a bit late for that, isn't it? My sensibilities were offended, sir, when you unfastened your *breeches*."

She'd meant to give him a firm set-down, but instead of looking ashamed or embarrassed as a proper gentleman would in such disgraceful circumstances, this awful man actually *laughed*.

"I fastened them again before I turned around," he pointed out, as if this were a perfectly reasonable argument.

Delia pressed her lips together. "I see that. Are you expecting applause? A standing ovation, perhaps?"

"No, just pointing out you should be grateful for it, as it was damned difficult to do under the circumstances."

Delia sniffed. "I'm sure I don't know what you mean."

The man studied her face for a moment, noted her baffled expression, and all at once he seemed to grow bored with her. "Of course you don't. Now that we've discussed my clothing in more detail than I do with my valet, you will answer my question."

Delia huffed out a breath. "My sister and I have come from Surrey to attend a house party at the home of the Earl of Carlisle. We're friends with the earl's sisters."

No reaction. Delia stopped and waited, but not even a flicker of recognition crossed his face. For pity's sake. He must know who Lord Carlisle was?

"The coach we were traveling in broke an axle about a mile down the road." She pointed in the direction from which she'd just come. "My sister and the coachman—"

"You should have stayed with the coach. What possessed you to go scampering around the countryside like a curious little rabbit?"

Annoyed by his condescending tone, Delia decided to overlook the fact she'd been thinking the same thing only minutes ago. "Believe me, sir, I've come to regret that decision most bitterly. But I thought it best in this case because—"

"Why didn't you just send the coachman to the inn for a carriage?" he interrupted again, looking at her as though she were simple.

"I couldn't, because when the axle broke—"

"The Prickly Thistle is in the opposite direction," he said, as if she hadn't spoken. "Didn't you ask for directions?"

"Would you kindly stop interrupting me?" Delia nearly shouted the words.

There was a pause, then, "Why should I? You interrupted *me*."

For a moment she wasn't sure what he meant, but then she felt her cheeks go hot and she knew they'd turned scarlet. "I'm sorry to have interrupted your"—she gestured with her hands—"your fornication, but that's no reason to—"

"Fornication?" He found this very funny indeed. "Did you just call it *fornication*?"

"Well, yes. What of it?"

"Oh, nothing. It's just very, ah, biblical of you."

Delia crossed her arms stubbornly over her chest. There was *no way* she was going to ask. He was mad indeed if he believed she would. If she asked, he might just tell her, and she didn't want to know the answer.

"Well, what do you call it?"

Drat.

He smirked. "Something far more descriptive, but I'd rather not repeat it now. Tell me. Precisely how much of my fornication did you witness?"

"Far more than one generally expects to see on a public road," Delia snapped. "In short, a shocking amount."

"I see. That would explain why you stood there for so long, gaping. The shock."

Delia glowered at him. "I didn't have much choice, did I? I heard a noise and so I followed it, and there you were, right in plain sight." *Pressing against each other, sighing, kissing, caressing . . .*

"You heard a noise. What kind of noise was it?" he asked, as if he were humoring her.

"At first I thought it was a wild animal," she said, then added in an undertone, "and I wasn't entirely wrong."

His eyes narrowed. "I beg your pardon, Miss Somerset?"

Delia bit her lip to keep from laughing. "I said, can't we move this along? My sister is waiting for me to return with a conveyance. She's been ill, and I would rather not leave her in the cold any longer than necessary."

He waved his hand imperiously, as if he were the lord of the manor and she a lowly servant. "Very well. Go on."

She took a deep breath and recited the facts quickly, before he could interrupt again. "The axle broke, the coachman suffered an injury, they're stranded on the road, and night is coming on. I need to find the inn, procure a conveyance, and fetch them both at once."

"The coachman is injured?" Now she had his full attention. "How badly injured?"

"Badly enough. He fell from the box when the axle broke and twisted his ankle. It's either sprained or broken. That's why he couldn't come for help. He did describe where I could find the Prickly Thistle Inn, but I must have missed a turn, for I didn't see it."

"The turn is difficult to spot from the road." He thought for a moment and came to some kind of decision. "Come." He turned and started back down the road, splashing casually through the mud puddles, clearly expecting her to follow without question, as if she were a dog or a sheep or some other kind of dense livestock.

Delia hesitated. She was in no more danger alone with him here than she'd be a mile down the road, and she didn't have much choice, but the idea of putting herself under this man's sole protection seemed, well, unwise.

When she didn't immediately follow, he jerked around. He must have read her thoughts on her face because his arrogant gaze moved deliberately from the top of her bedraggled bonnet down over her muddy traveling dress, and came to rest at last on her ruined boots. "Believe me, Miss Somerset, *you* are perfectly safe with me."

Delia gasped in outrage. He was insulting her? She didn't need him to remind her she looked a perfect fright. "Such a gallant thing to say." She had to struggle to keep her temper. "But perhaps you're not accustomed to the company of ladies who are fully dressed."

He shrugged, then turned again and started back down the road, leaving her no choice but to stagger behind him. "Let's just say I prefer the company of ladies who are fully *undressed*."

Delia supposed he meant to shock her, but she was beyond shock at this point, and hardly turned a hair at this scandalous comment. She followed behind him, scrambling to keep pace with his long-legged stride. "I see. Well, that explains why you felt compelled to undress your friend on a public road. How terrible it must be, to be so at the mercy of your animal passions."

She was glaring at the back of his head when she noticed he'd begun shoving a hand through his thick dark hair. The crisp waves curled and caught a bit against his long fingers. Did that mean he was nettled, then? Oh, she hoped so. She'd be immensely gratified to have annoyed him.

She had just begun to enjoy that idea when he whipped around to face her. She was so surprised she crashed right into him. Strong hands reached out to steady her, but when she was upright again, he didn't release her. Instead he pulled her just a bit closer—not so close his body touched hers, but more than close enough to completely unnerve her.

"I *was* carried away by my animal passions," he murmured in a low, seductive voice. His velvety dark eyes caught and held hers. "I'm an impatient man, you see, Miss Somerset. Especially when it comes to"—he dropped his voice to a whisper—"*fornication*."

For one moment Delia was mesmerized, staring at him as if he were a snake charmer and she were rising from her basket after languishing there for decades. But then she noticed a hint of a smirk on his lips and jerked free from his grasp.

Goodness gracious. Her face heated yet again. "Perhaps it would be better if we didn't speak."

Another careless shrug. "If you choose."

Awful, teasing man.

They walked along the road for a while, the only sound now the soft, wet thud of boots against mud. After a half mile or so he turned off the road and pulled back some overgrown bushes. "The inn is on the other side." He gestured for her to walk in front of him.

As soon as Delia passed through the thick brush, she could see the path, and there at the end was the Prickly Thistle Inn. She'd walked right by it earlier without noticing, as it was impossible to see the squat stone building from the road. She glanced resentfully at her silent companion. She had cause to regret her inattention now, didn't she?

Delia breathed an immediate sigh of relief when they entered the inn. It was almost dark outside and growing colder, but there was a massive stone fireplace at one end of the main room that threw out considerable light and heat. A grizzled little man was running a damp cloth over the scarred wooden surface of the bar. "A pint fer ye, me lord?" he called, when he caught sight of Delia and her companion hovering in the doorway.

"Not this time, thank you, George," Delia's companion replied, but he wasn't looking at the gray-haired man. He was looking at her, a smug grin lifting the corners of his wide mouth.

Delia stared back at him, aghast. *Oh, no, no, no!* But even as her brain worked frantically to deny it, she began to remember certain little details. His lack of reaction when she mentioned the earl's name. His concern over the injured coachman, a coachman who had been sent by the Earl of Carlisle to convey them to Kent. The fine quality and fit of his clothes—that was, when they were fastened.

And who else but an arrogant earl would *dare* . . .

Delia wanted to stamp her foot with ire. It couldn't be!

Her mind struggled to think of anything that would prove her dreadful suspicion wrong.

Yes! The woman. The one he'd been groping. The giggler. She'd called this man *Alec*. That wasn't right, because Charlotte and Ellie's brother was named . . .

Delia closed her eyes in despair. Charlotte and Ellie's brother was named Alexander. Alexander Sutherland.

Alec.

The fornicator. The debaucher. The lifter of women's skirts and the unbuttoner of breeches.

He was Lord Carlisle.

Chapter Two

"Miss Somerset." Alec swept her a low, mocking bow. *"As* you may have deduced, I am Carlisle. You'll be my guest at Bellwood for the next several weeks."

He watched with detached interest as a series of expressions flickered across her mud-streaked face. Doubt. Denial. Fury. Finally, resignation. It had been a nasty trick to play on her. Childish, too. Alec almost felt guilty. *Almost.* But a man was not responsible for his actions when his bollocks were aching.

They weren't likely to stop aching anytime soon, either, thanks to Delia Somerset. He wasn't exactly proud to be caught with one hand in a village wench's bodice and the other raising her skirts, but things had become a bit more heated than he'd intended. That did tend to happen with Maggie. He was a man, after all, and Maggie had a spectacular bosom.

"My lord." Alec jerked his attention back to Miss Somerset, who'd dipped into a very low, very deferential curtsy. He was impressed, despite himself. He'd never seen a young lady curtsy *sarcastically* before.

He knew who she was, of course—had known before she said her name. Few things happened at Bellwood without Alec knowing about it. If his mother chose a new china pattern or one of his sisters broke a nail, he knew.

He'd expected Delia Somerset.

His sisters had revealed the information the previous evening. They'd been giggling over something for days, batting it between them like two kittens with a ball of yarn, repeating Robyn's name and the phrase "yellow gown" so often Alec had at last grown curious.

"Who is Robyn chasing now?" he'd asked idly.

"Delia Somerset," Eleanor replied. "You remember we told you we became intimately acquainted with two young ladies during our stay in Surrey, Alec? Robyn was quite struck with Delia, the elder sister. I think yellow is his new favorite color."

Somerset. Of course Alec knew the name. Millicent Somerset, formerly Millicent Chase, had been a legend during her London season. Trust Robyn to find a Somerset in the wilds of Surrey and deem her worthy of chasing.

"He couldn't take his eyes off her," Charlotte added, breathless with the romance of it. "He teased and teased until we invited her to the house party."

Alec froze. *Invited her to the house party?*

"Charlotte, Eleanor, I wish to speak with Robyn in my study. Please tell him."

The girls turned and stared at him, surprised by his grim tone. "Um, I think Robyn has gone out for the evening already . . ." Eleanor began.

Alec raised one black eyebrow. "At once, Eleanor."

His sisters weren't about to sacrifice themselves to the big bad wolf on Robyn's account. They must have decided Alec looked decidedly wolfish, because both girls turned without another word and hurried out the door, before he could catch their little red hoods in his teeth.

Alec walked into the study, moved behind his desk, and unstopped the decanter of whiskey. He had a feeling he was going to need a drink.

"Alec." A few minutes later Robyn breezed in and threw his long body into a full sprawl in front of the heavy mahogany desk. He nodded when Alec held up a second glass. Alec poured a measure and pushed it across to him.

Mincing words seemed pointless, so he didn't. "What will you do with the Somerset girl if you catch her, Robyn?"

There was a pause. "Delphinium," Robyn said with a faint smile.

Alec gave his brother a blank look. "I beg your pardon?"

"Her name is Delphinium."

Alec was speechless for a moment, then, "You're joking."

"No. Charming, isn't it? Her friends call her Delia."

"Is this really all about a damned yellow gown, Robyn?"

"The color of the gown isn't important, Alec. It had more to do with the cut. It fit her nicely. Very nicely indeed."

Alec didn't leap across the polished surface of the desk and seize his brother by the throat, so he had cause to marvel at his own restraint. "Let me understand you, Robyn. You have invited Miss Somerset—*Delphinium*, if one can credit it—to Bellwood because she fills out her yellow gown?"

Robyn crossed his legs. "No, of course not. I didn't invite her here. That wouldn't be proper, would it, Alec? Charlotte and Ellie invited Delia and her sister Lily."

"We wouldn't want you to overlook propriety," Alec muttered.

He often played this game with Robyn these days. Alec pretended to be calm while his knuckles turned white from his grip on his whiskey glass. Robyn affected casual indifference, but he watched his brother with the wariness of a hare hiding in the shadows from a hound. If Alec lost his temper before Robyn could escape the study, Alec lost the game.

"Tell me, Robyn—the Somerset girl. What level of scandal are you planning? Should I send word to London? Or will you confine yourself to the country this time?"

An angry flush rose above Robyn's collar and surged into his cheeks, but then he recalled his role in the game, and with a visible effort, he gave a careless shrug. "Who can tell?" There was a brief pause, then, "Perhaps I just enjoy her company, Alec. She's clever and amusing, and . . . *alive.*"

Alec stared at his brother. Something about Robyn's inflection on that last word stopped the retort on Alec's lips. Was that *longing* in Robyn's voice? Christ, he hoped not. Before he could decipher it, however, Robyn reverted to the lazy, bored tone that never failed to push Alec's temper to the boiling point. "As to warning London, I suppose you should do just what you please, Alec. You always do."

Alec wrapped his fingers tightly around his glass. *Losing the game.* It was time for Robyn to leave. He gave a short nod. "Enjoy your evening, Robyn."

It was a dismissal, and Robyn knew one when he heard it. He unfolded his long frame gracefully from the chair and bowed to his brother. "I always do. Good evening, Alec."

Alec hadn't seen or spoken to Robyn since then. Not surprisingly, there had been no sign of him when Alec left Bellwood at midday. Robyn was likely even now still snoring off the remainder of last night's debauchery. Or maybe Robyn was just avoiding him. Robyn generally did avoid him these days.

Nonetheless, Alec made it his business to know if his scapegrace brother was contemplating a new liaison. He didn't object to Robyn *having* liaisons—he wasn't quite such a hypocrite as that. His brother could tup whomever he wished, with Alec's blessing. The trouble was, Robyn wasn't discreet. Far from it, and he'd spent the past year honing his gift for causing scandal.

Well, not this time. Alec wouldn't tolerate another scandal. Not with Lady Lisette and her mother attending the house party.

Hard to believe it to look at the girl, but Delia Somerset was another explosive scandal waiting to happen, for all she looked like a London street urchin. Alec couldn't tell whether she was pretty or not, and it made him uneasy. Robyn appreciated tangible qualities in a female, starting with a lush, obvious kind of beauty and concluding with a devastating bosom.

Delia Somerset didn't make sense, and Alec didn't like it when things didn't make sense. How had this plain chit captured Robyn's fickle, roving eye? Was it possible Alec had overlooked a devastating bosom? He lowered his eyes to her chest for a quick inspection. Her dark traveling cloak was so practical and modestly cut, her figure in general remained a mystery. Perhaps another sneaky glance would reveal—

"Lord *Carlisle*!" she snapped, crossing her arms firmly over her bosom.

Damn it. Not sneaky enough. Alec raised his eyes from her breasts to find her glaring at him.

"Before you start unbuttoning your breeches," she said acidly, "perhaps you'd care to speak to the innkeeper about a carriage?"

Alec grimaced. Sharp-tongued chit. "Have you a carriage about, George?"

Mr. George shook his head. "'Fraid I don't, me lord. Not today. Mrs. George took the inn carriage off to her sister's house. I lets her take it, ye see, me lord, on account o' otherwise her sister comes to visit us here, and I'd just as soon she didn't." Mr. George grinned. "Not much in life worse than an irascible female, if ye take my meaning, me lord."

Alec glanced at his silently fuming companion. "I do, George."

"We has the hay cart." There was a brief pause; then George added doubtfully, "Yer welcome to it, me lord."

Damnation. It would be pitch-dark by the time they returned to Bellwood and fetched another carriage. Alec hated to leave William on the side of the road with an injury, not to mention a potentially hysterical female, but he'd pushed Miss Somerset about as far as she'd—

"We'll take the cart," she said. Then she smiled. "Thank you, Mr. George, for your kindness in offering it to us."

"Of course, miss." George, obviously charmed, beamed at her. "I'll have the lad bring it 'round fer ye."

Alec stared at her. Just when he'd made up his mind she couldn't possibly pose any real threat, she'd smiled, and there went George, scurrying off to the back room, almost tripping over his short legs in his haste to accommodate Miss Somerset. If she smiled at Robyn that way, spoke to him in that soft, husky voice . . . Well, even Alec had forgotten for a moment she was covered in mud and her bosom remained a mystery.

The mystery wouldn't be solved tonight, however. She wasn't about to agree to remove her cloak so he could inspect her bosom. She wasn't Maggie, after all. Still, if he exerted himself to be charming, who knew what he could wheedle out of Miss Somerset on the drive to Bellwood?

"The cart is ready for ye, me lord." George bustled back into the main room and took up his place behind the bar. "I wish you a good evening, miss," he added, with a nod and shy smile for Miss Somerset.

Alec rolled his eyes. It was time to get her out the door before George tried to kiss her hand.

"It won't be a comfortable ride," Alec said, once they were outside. He eyed the cart. "Or a clean one."

Miss Somerset shrugged and made a move as if to spring into the cart.

"Allow me, Miss Somerset." Alec offered his hand. She looked at it as if it were a snake about to strike, but he seized hers anyway, determined to be charming, whether she liked it or not.

Her hand was fine-boned, her fingers long and slim. He could feel her chill even through her glove. Surprisingly, Alec felt a stab of conscience when that cold, delicate hand slipped into his. He swung up next to her on the seat, and after a silent apology to Weston, he shrugged out of his coat and placed it around her shoulders. The mud would ruin it, but if she caught pneumonia, she could be at Bellwood for months, languishing. Even a plain country mouse could snare Robyn if she languished seductively enough.

"No! I mean, no thank you, my lord. I mean, it's not necessary to . . ." she stammered.

Damn it. What was wrong with the girl this time? She looked aghast, as if she thought she could catch the pox from his coat. He was about to reassure her that he was as spotless as a newborn babe when it occurred to him it was *not* charming to discuss the pox with gently bred young ladies. "Your hands are cold," he said gruffly instead. "It will be a chilly ride to Bellwood."

He took up the reins. "My sisters were grateful for your company during their stay in Surrey," he began politely after a moment.

There was a brief silence, then, "They were relieved," she allowed. "They seemed to be under the impression the neighborhood was restricted to maiden aunts and elderly widowers."

"That's the company their aunt usually keeps. They were

fortunate to find such delightful young ladies in you and
your sister."

There. That should do. It couldn't be that difficult to
charm a rustic like Miss Somerset.

But if he'd been expecting simpering and cooing, he was
disappointed. She gave a short, disbelieving laugh. "Are we
to have compliments now, my lord? Ah yes, I remember.
The Mirror of the Graces does say after a gentleman exposes
his unmentionables to a lady, he should flatter her and pretend to admire her."

Alec chuckled. Did she really think she'd seen his *unmentionables*? "I only meant any company would be more
engaging than their aunt Matilda's. She's not exactly viva-
cious, though Charlotte and Eleanor don't need more of that."

She pounced at once. "Why is that? Do you disapprove
of your sisters showing spirit, my lord?"

"Not in the proper time and place," Alec said, then
cringed. He sounded like a prig. Prigs weren't charming.
This conversation wasn't going at all the way he'd planned,
and it was her fault. Talking to her was like having a thorn
stuck in his boot. Every time he took a step forward, she
pricked at him.

"That rather defeats the purpose of having spirit in the
first place, doesn't it?" she asked, trying to stifle a laugh.
"But truly, how unfortunate lively young ladies like Charlotte
and Ellie should have such a disapproving brother."

She was *laughing* at him? "They have only one disapproving brother, at least." He'd started to lose patience. "My
brother Robyn detests disapproval, especially when it's directed at him. No doubt you found *him* charming, Miss
Somerset."

Christ. Now he sounded like a petulant child. Again, it
was her fault. He felt like he was trying to charm a stick of
furniture.

"Oh, I did," she replied without hesitation. "He has such gentlemanly manners."

Her implication was clear. *Not like his elder brother.*

Robyn? *Gentlemanly?* Miss Somerset may be clever, but she was also hopelessly naïve if she hadn't recognized Robyn for the rogue he was. Alec doubted she'd spent much time out of Surrey. There was one way to find out. "Did you spend the entire winter with your family in Surrey?"

"Yes. We had a quiet winter. Some find the country a bit dull, I suppose. It's not exciting, but it's peaceful."

If she'd come to Kent for excitement, she was off to a promising start. "Have you seen much of the English countryside?"

"No. I haven't had much opportunity, my lord. We did have a chance to see some of Kent while the light held today."

"I see. Then you only go to London for the season?"

There was a short silence. He glanced over at her. A faint frown had appeared between her brows.

"I've never been to London, Lord Carlisle."

"No London season?" He managed just a touch of aristocratic horror. "How extraordinary."

"It's grievous indeed, Lord Carlisle," she returned dryly.

Alec paused, as if still absorbing this shocking piece of information. "You have no relations in London?"

She shrugged. "We have no relations in London who wish to host us for a season, my lord."

She'd phrased it so it wasn't quite a lie. Alec already knew, of course, she did have relations in London. Her maternal grandmother was even now terrifying the *ton* from her town house in St. James's Square.

Lady Chase didn't receive her granddaughters, then. If so, neither would anyone else. "So you and your sister don't spend time in society?"

"I have four sisters, my lord. We don't spend time in

society and not one of us has been to London. Nor are we likely ever to go."

Despite himself, Alec was momentarily distracted. "*Four* sisters?" Millicent Chase had been busy after her exile from the *ton*. Five girls. No money to speak of. Plenty of scandal attached to the family name, though. He had to give his brother credit. Robyn couldn't have chosen a more spectacularly bad prospect than Delia Somerset.

"Why did your other three sisters not accompany you to Kent?" he asked. *Why not drag the whole penniless, scandalous lot along?*

"My youngest sister is just fifteen years old, and the next one in age to Lily isn't yet eighteen. A house party isn't appropriate for them." She made the words *house party* sound like *den of iniquity*.

"How kind of your parents to trust you and your sister Lily among us," he bit out. At some point during this conversation, he'd started gritting his teeth.

As soon as the words left his mouth, he felt it—a surge of such sudden and intense emotion he nearly dropped the reins. She'd gone still, as though she could keep it all inside her if only she didn't move.

"My parents are dead, my lord." Her voice was expressionless. "They were killed in a carriage accident last spring."

Chapter Three

She couldn't get her breath. Grief closed over her head, a relentless, sucking tidal wave of it. She gasped a little, panicking. If she could just get her breath. *Breathe.* Breathing would stop the welling pressure behind her eyes and the torrent of painful words that rushed to her lips. Stop them before they spilled over and drowned Lord Carlisle.

She bit her lip. Hard.

Delia focused on the sky and concentrated on the fading light until the choked feeling began to ease. The afternoon dusk had long since faded into evening, but it was not entirely dark yet. Not dark enough for a sky full of stars. The faintest glimmers had begun to appear here and there in the deep blue above her, as though tiny pinpricks had been made in the dark canvas to let the starlight peek through.

She took another deep, cleansing breath and silently exhaled. Her parents' sudden death last spring wasn't a secret, but it was private. She didn't want to present it for Lord Carlisle's dispassionate inspection. Or anyone else's. Certainly not anyone high enough in the instep to attend this house party. She'd imagined the death of a disgraced London belle and her provincial spouse would be beneath their notice. The *ton* hadn't bothered with Millicent Chase since she'd become Millicent Somerset. Why should Lord Carlisle ask about her family now?

She glanced at him out of the corner of her eye. He had high cheekbones and firm, sensuously sculpted lips. It was an arrogant face. An aristocrat's face. Now that she knew who he was, she could easily trace a likeness to his sisters in his features. Charlotte and Ellie were both beauties, with dark hair and merry black eyes.

Lord Carlisle didn't look merry at the moment. He looked grim. His large hands gripped the reins and he'd fallen silent after her last disclosure. She looked away. What did she care if he were grim? She cared only that he was silent.

And really, what was there to say? *I'm sorry you and your sisters are orphans? What an unspeakable tragedy?* She was oddly rather grateful he said nothing. It saved her the effort of having to manufacture the empty words required when someone expressed their condolences. *Thank you, my lord. Indeed it is a tragedy, my lord.* No one wanted to hear the truth. *My life as I've known it is over, my lord. My sisters are awash in grief, my lord. I'm not sure we'll survive, my lord.*

Delia closed her eyes and listened to the soothing sounds of night. The deepening sky disguised her surroundings and for a little while she could imagine she was still in Surrey. The spring sunlight would have sunk below the roofline of the cottage by now, plunging the long narrow walkway and the modest front entry into darkness. Her sisters would be squabbling cheerfully as they prepared dinner—all except Hyacinth, who would muck about in the gardens for as long as possible, dirt caked under her fingernails, ignoring Hannah's orders to come indoors.

Delia had been gone for less than a day, and already she longed for home with an ache that left her breathless again. An entire fortnight in Kent seemed impossible, an eternity—

"The carriage is just ahead," Lord Carlisle said. His voice was low but it startled her. She'd all but forgotten he was there. He pulled the cart up beside a bulky dark shape at the side of the road, barely discernible in the dusk.

Delia was out of the cart almost before it stopped. "Lily!" Her voice trembled. Her sister had been stranded on the road for hours, in the cold and the dark. Lily's health was precarious at the moment. What if she—

Before Delia could become truly alarmed, however, a slim figured appeared in the doorway of the carriage. "Here, Delia," Lily replied in her soft voice. "We're all right."

"Thank goodness for that." Delia rushed toward her sister, removing Lord Carlisle's coat to drape it around Lily's shoulders. "I'm sorry it took such an age to return for you both. I was delayed by—"

She stopped. What could she say? That extra time was required for Lord Carlisle to fasten both his shirt *and* his breeches? "That is, Lord Carlisle was engaged with—"

Alec stepped forward and bowed smoothly to Lily. "I apologize for the delay. I was on the verge of satisfactorily concluding an urgent affair when Miss Somerset interrupted me with word of your distress. It took a few moments to disentangle myself."

"Oh, dear," Lily said with concern. "I'm sorry to interrupt such important business. I do hope the intrusion didn't cause irreparable damage."

"You're very kind." He gave Delia a diabolical smile. "No serious damage was done. I'm certain to achieve a gratifying conclusion at the next opportunity."

Delia stared at him, her mouth open in astonishment. She remained silent until Lily delicately cleared her throat and raised her eyebrows meaningfully.

"Lord Carlisle, this is my sister, Miss Lily Somerset," Delia said sullenly, squirming with the indignity of making a formal introduction under the circumstances.

Lily, as elegant and inexplicably as neatly attired as if she'd been out for a leisurely stroll, dipped into a curtsy that would have done justice to a London ballroom. If she thought it odd Lord Carlisle himself had come to fetch her in a hay cart, she gave no sign of it. She smiled graciously at him. "It's indeed a delight to meet you, my lord, though William's pleasure at your arrival must exceed even mine. He hasn't uttered a word of complaint, but I'm afraid his ankle pains him."

A voice spoke up from inside the carriage. "Yer very kind, miss, but there's no need to take on so on account of me. I've 'ad worse." There was a rustling inside the carriage and then William limped to the door. He bowed awkwardly to Lord Carlisle. "My lord, I beg yer pardon—"

"It's all right, William." Lord Carlisle's voice was rough, but not unkind. He stepped forward to help William down from the carriage. "Lean on me." He offered his arm. William hobbled over to the cart and heaved himself into the back with the earl's assistance.

Then Lord Carlisle turned to Lily and offered her a hand. "I apologize for the roughness of the accommodations. Miss Somerset chose expediency over luxury. The inn's hay cart was the quickest means of fetching you."

Lily smiled. "That doesn't sound like Delia." She placed her tidily gloved hand in Lord Carlisle's and joined William in the back of the cart. "She isn't usually that practical."

"Is that so?" Lord Carlisle ran his eyes over Delia's mud-splattered gown. "I find that difficult to believe."

Delia crossed her arms defensively over her chest. "I'm sure Lord Carlisle isn't the least bit interested in discussing this, Lily. Shall we go, my lord?" She nodded at the cart. "It grows late. Your sisters will have expected us hours ago."

"A practical reminder," he replied dryly, and turned back to the disabled carriage. He placed one booted foot on the intact rear wheel and swung easily up to reach the trunks strapped to the top of the coach. He unsnapped the straps, heaved the nearest trunk over his shoulder, and jumped nimbly down from the wheel. Delia stepped back as he lowered the trunk into the cart and returned for the second one.

Oh, my.

That trunk was heavy. She'd stood by yesterday and watched Lily attempt to squeeze yet another pair of slippers into its depths, to no avail.

So, the taut, muscular body she'd seen in such embarrassing detail was not simply decorative, then. No, it was *practical.* Instead of sending servants to fetch the trunks as a typical nobleman would do, this one tossed them over his shoulder as though they weighed no more than a corset, or a lace shift, or a pair of silk stockings.

Good heavens. Why was she thinking of women's undergarments at a time like this? *Stop it, Delia.*

But it was too late. Every salacious image from earlier in the day rushed into her brain in tormenting detail. A fine white linen shirt opened to expose a smooth, hard chest. A low, laughing murmur and an answering sigh. Such a sigh! His teasing hand slipping into the woman's bodice, the other hand lifting her skirts . . .

Suddenly panicked, Delia rushed toward the front of the cart and scrambled clumsily into her seat before Lord Carlisle could return and offer to hand her up. She couldn't touch his hand. Not now. Not ever. Not his hand or any other part of him. He had entirely too much . . . too much . . .

He had too much *skin.*

The cart sagged as Lord Carlisle stepped up and took his seat next to her. Delia felt his quizzical gaze on her face, but she kept her eyes straight ahead. After a moment the cart lurched forward. At last, they were on their way to Bell-wood.

They had jostled along for a few miles in silence when a happy thought occurred to Delia. Why, once they arrived and the house party was under way, she'd see little of Lord Carlisle. She sighed with relief. Indeed, it would be the easiest thing in the world to avoid him entirely. She and Lily were far beneath his notice, after all. He wouldn't spare her another glance, and she could forget all about him and his unbuttoned breeches and his overabundance of flesh.

After another mile or so they crested a hill and all thought fled from Delia's mind as a burst of blazing light lit up the night sky. Bellwood had appeared through the bare branches of the trees that lined the long road leading up to the estate. The cart had come upon the house from the north side, which was unlit and not noticeable from the road. But the front of the house! Delia caught her breath in pleasure. She'd expected a grand house, but there were plenty of grand, ugly country estates in England.

Bellwood wasn't one of them. "Oh," Delia exclaimed. "It's exquisite."

She wasn't aware she'd spoken the words aloud until Lord Carlisle startled her with a reply. "Yes. It is. It's been in the Sutherland family for centuries."

It was striking, not least because of the long row of stately ash trees that led to the entrance of the house. The branches of the trees seemed to reach for one another, entwining like slender silver arms to protect the road beneath. It was almost a tunnel of trees, even now, before they'd set all their leaves.

"It must be lovely to walk here in the summer," Delia whispered. Somehow with the night and the light pouring from the windows and the skeleton of tree branches above, whispering seemed appropriate.

Lord Carlisle turned the cart onto the long gravel drive.

They were under the trees, and he and Delia both looked up at the latticework of branches above them. "It is. To ride, as well," he agreed casually, not bothering to lower his own voice. "The trees have been that way for as long as I can remember."

"They look like they've partnered for a dance," she murmured.

He glanced at her, darkly amused. "What a whimsical notion, Miss Somerset." His tone mocked her, but then he added, as if to himself, "They do, rather."

Delia watched as the house drew closer. It was built of a cream-colored stone that had at one time likely been a pale shade, but it had mellowed over the years to a stately gold. There was a low gate at the end of the drive that separated the massive double front door of the house from the approach. The gate, which looked as though it had been added later, created an enclosed courtyard that ran the entire width of the center wing. It softened the front of the house a bit and lent a more welcome aspect to the entrance, yet the overall impression was of a grand and imposing estate.

They were close enough now Delia could see a white-capped head peeking out through a crack in the huge front doors. The head disappeared and a minute later a stiff-backed butler opened the door. Charlotte and Eleanor Sutherland shot past him like two overeager puppies and tumbled down the steps into the courtyard just as the cart pulled up.

"Delia! Lily! We've been waiting for you this age! Whatever happened?" They stopped short when they saw the cart.

"Alec!" Charlotte looked at her brother, aghast. "Where is the carriage? Tell me you didn't . . . Is that a *hay cart*? At night, in the cold . . ."

Charlotte was so flabbergasted she was unable to string together a coherent sentence.

Lord Carlisle lifted one bland eyebrow, unmoved by his sister's sputtering. "The carriage broke an axle about a mile from the Prickly Thistle. William twisted an ankle. I could have left your friends on the side of the road, Charlotte, but I thought they'd prefer a ride in a cart to a night outdoors."

Charlotte and Eleanor both gasped, the cart forgotten. "Broke an axle? My goodness, are you both all right? You could have been . . ."

You could have been hurt. Or killed.

Delia felt the panic begin to close over her again, but then a warm, gloved hand squeezed her shoulder gently. Lily. Delia closed her eyes and reached up to squeeze Lily's fingers in return. *It's all right, Lily.* After a moment, it was.

But when she opened her eyes again, she found Lord Carlisle's dark, penetrating gaze on her. "Your friends are no worse off from a ride in a hay cart, Charlotte," was all he said, however. He jumped down and offered Lily his hand. "I may take you and Ellie for a ride in it, as well. It would do you both good to travel in a cart."

Charlotte snorted.

"How can you say they're no worse off, Alec?" Eleanor asked. "Why, the mud alone is . . . Delia! Is that a piece of hay stuck to the front of your dress?"

"No doubt it is," Delia replied, a little unsteadily.

She looked down at her dress, but she didn't bother to brush off the hay. It was far, far too late for that. "But we can't hold the cart responsible for the mud or the hay, I'm afraid," she continued, thankful her voice sounded normal. "Look at Lily. She looks as fresh as a spring flower still."

Eleanor and Charlotte rushed forward to embrace Lily as soon as she descended from the cart. "Lily! I'm afraid you're frozen nearly to death," Charlotte said, with another reproachful glance in her brother's direction.

But Lord Carlisle only shrugged and handed Delia down

from the cart. Charlotte and Ellie rushed forward and embraced her warmly, as well, though Delia noted with amusement they were careful not to get any mud on their spotless gowns.

"Rylands?" Eleanor said to the butler. "You will see Miss Somerset and Miss Lily's things are sent to the blue bedrooms, please?"

The butler bowed. "Of course, miss." His expression was respectfully stoic, despite the mud and the deplorable hay cart.

"My dears, we had thought to have a light supper together this evening," Charlotte began as she led Lily and Delia into the entrance hall. "But given the late hour and Alec's disgraceful hay cart—"

Eleanor interrupted her sister. "It's best if you go straight to your rooms so you can recover from the shock and cold. It would be too bad if one of you took a chill and became ill. It would spoil all our fun." Eleanor turned back to the butler. "Rylands, our guests will need baths and trays with a light supper."

Rylands bowed again. "Yes, miss."

Alec followed the ladies into the entrance hall. "Where's Robyn? I would think he'd make an effort to greet his guests."

Delia turned to him in surprise. Eleanor was surprised by this comment, as well. "Don't be absurd, Alec. They're *our* guests. Robyn is off somewhere." She waved her hand vaguely.

Lord Carlisle bowed. "Miss Somerset, Miss Lily. I hope you both recover enough from your alarming journey that you are able to enjoy your stay. If you'll excuse me, I need to send a servant back to the inn with the hay cart, and find someone to tend to William."

When he straightened from his formal bow, his eyes found Delia's face and lingered there, as if he were trying to solve a puzzle. She couldn't quite read his expression, but there was something in it that sent a surge of warm color into her cheeks.

He narrowed his eyes on her in surprise, blinked, but said nothing. Then he bowed again and disappeared.

Chapter Four

"It's just like a cloud." Lily *peeked around the door that* connected her room to Delia's, a dazed expression on her face.

Delia stood motionless by the door that led from her room into the hallway. She hadn't moved since the maid had shown them up to their rooms. "What is?"

"My room. It's . . ." Lily paused, gesturing with her hands, as if words failed her. "It's fluffy. It's creamy white with the softest blue accents. It's . . . it's frothy, Delia. It looks like a cloud. It *feels* like a cloud. You can't imagine . . ." Her voice trailed off as she took in Delia's room. She stepped toward the bed and ran a hesitant finger across the pale blue damask coverlet, closing her eyes in bliss at the feel of the rich fabric.

"I don't need to imagine it," Delia said shortly. She still stood stiffly by the door.

Maybe it was the cold, or the ordeal with Lord Carlisle, or the broken axle and the hay cart, but all of a sudden she felt like crying.

Lily opened her eyes. "Delia!" she exclaimed, noting her sister's stricken expression. "What's the matter?"

Delia gathered the folds of her ruined cloak in her fists. "I can't touch anything! I'm afraid to move. I'll get mud and hay all over this beautiful room!"

"Oh, my dear." Lily hurried to Delia's side and began to work on the tangled strings of her sister's bonnet. She made sympathetic noises in her throat, but Delia was sure she was stifling a smile.

"There. That's better." Lily held the ruined bonnet pinched between the tips of her fingers and hesitated, looking for a safe place to set it down. Finally she balanced it on the edge of the washbasin. "The bath will be here soon, and you can . . ." She stopped in the middle of unbuttoning Delia's cloak. "My goodness, Delia! Is there any mud left in Kent, or is it all on your cloak?"

Delia scowled. "There seems to be plenty for everyone, but Kent could be awash in mud, Lily, and *you* would still manage to remain spotless."

Lily rolled her eyes. "Let's not start with that again. What was your first impression of the estate?" she asked instead, changing to a subject she knew her sister would be unable to resist.

"Exquisite. Most of the *ton*'s country estates are grand and impressive, of course, but few are as truly lovely as this one is. At least it seemed so from the brief look we had. If the weather holds, perhaps we can walk in the garden tomorrow, or ride around the park."

"If you wish to see the gardens and park, Delia, I'm certain Mr. Robert Sutherland would be very pleased to escort you." A provoking little smile lifted the corners of Lily's mouth.

Lily's expression was so comical Delia couldn't prevent a laugh. "Oh, what nonsense, Lily."

"He did pay you rather marked attention at the Mainwarings' party the night before he escorted Charlotte and Ellie home."

"I believe you mean he paid rather marked attention to my cleavage. Had I not been forced to borrow Iris's yellow gown, I daresay Mr. Sutherland would have completely over-looked me. Perhaps if you had worn a gown a half size too small, Lily?"

The cleavage-baring yellow gown had become a bit of a legend in the Somerset household after the Mainwarings' party. Delia and Lily had regaled their wide-eyed younger sisters at length with exaggerated stories of the effect the tight yellow gown had had on Robyn Sutherland.

"Your underestimate your own charms, Delia," Lily said, still giggling.

"Not at all." Delia forgot all about the mud as she began to warm to her subject. "You overestimate Mr. Sutherland's attention span. He's a member of the *beau-monde* and has doubtless been distracted by another plunging neckline by now. The Mainwarings' party was nearly two weeks ago! If you didn't bring Iris's gown with you, Lily, then perhaps you have a shiny object? For I imagine that will do almost as well."

"Oh, you are too cruel," Lily said, wiping her eyes.

"Perhaps I am. Besides, I found Mr. Sutherland quite charming. He's easy and friendly—not at all what one would expect from a fashionable young man of the *ton*."

His brother, on the other hand . . .

But Delia kept that thought private. Lily didn't need to know about Lord Carlisle's bare chest and unbuttoned breeches. It would worry her, and Delia was determined to let nothing worry or vex Lily in her current precarious state of health.

After their parents' deaths, Delia had emerged from her own dark abyss of grief to find her sister hollow-cheeked, with black-shadowed, dull eyes. Nothing seemed to rouse

Lily from her lethargy. She grew paler and thinner with each passing day until Delia became frantic with worry.

Then Charlotte and Ellie Sutherland had arrived in Surrey and they'd chased away the worst of the demons with their high spirits and contagious laughter, and Lily had begun to show signs of life again. Nothing less than a hope for her sister's full recovery could have induced Delia to come to this house party. She much preferred their quiet little corner of Surrey to a fortnight with the *ton*.

"Robyn is very handsome." Lily raised one eyebrow suggestively.

"Yes, quite. But, Lily"—Delia took a step closer to Lily and lowered her voice to a whisper—"there's been some scandal about Mr. Sutherland and the plunging bodices. Gossip has it he's had his hand in his share of—"

A sharp rap sounded on the door and they jumped guiltily apart. Delia opened it to find a fresh-faced maid in a white cap.

"Good evening, miss." The maid curtsied. "I've come to stir up the fire. Your baths will be up straightaway. I hope you don't mind, Miss Somerset, but I asked the cook to hold your supper tray. I thought you might wish to bathe first." She cast an eye over the muddy bonnet on the side of the washbasin.

"Oh, yes." Delia stood away from the door so the maid could enter. "Very wise of you, um . . ."

"Polly, miss. I'm to help you ladies while you visit." She crossed the room and poked the fire into a satisfying blaze, then gathered up the muddy cloak and bonnet. "May I take these down for a cleaning?"

"Well, I'd thought I would just throw them away," Delia confessed. "They look to be beyond redemption."

Polly ran a practiced eye over the garments. "I may be able to do something with them. Shall I try, miss?"

"By all means. Though I'll be overjoyed if I never see

either of them again," Delia said to Lily in a low voice as
Polly left the room.

Lily giggled. "Don't give them up for lost yet, Delia. The
staff in a grand house like this one must have some launder-
ing secrets far beyond the wildest imaginings of our meager
household."

"I suppose so," Delia agreed, but she braced herself as
another wave of homesickness washed through her. Perhaps
their home was meager compared to this majestic estate,
but it was theirs.

"What do you suppose the girls are doing right now?"
Lily asked.

Delia smiled. Lily was thinking of home, too. "Oh, I
imagine they're running about in their usual disorganized
fashion, pestering Hannah to within an inch of her sanity."

Hannah was the Somersets' housekeeper and second
mother. She'd been with the family since Delia was in pin-
afores. None of the girls could imagine their home without
her, now more than ever, when they missed their parents so
desperately.

"How I would have loved to have Hannah come with us
on this trip." Lily sighed. But it was unthinkable that Iris,
Violet, and Hyacinth should be left alone, and there wasn't
anyone else to accompany Delia and Lily to Kent.

"I wouldn't," Delia said, trying to lighten the mood.
"Then both of you would have scolded me about the mud."

"Indeed we would. Do you suppose Mr. Downing will
continue to pursue Iris while we're away?"

The Downings were local gentry in the neighborhood.
Mr. Edward Downing was the eldest son. Over the past few
months he'd begun to show an interest in Iris, who, at not
quite eighteen years of age, had blossomed into a notable
beauty. "I think if he pursues her too ardently, then Hannah
will pursue him, with a broom over her shoulder."

Hannah was a staunch defender of virtue.

"You did say you left the yellow gown with Iris, didn't you?" Lily asked. "Perhaps that was unwise, Delia?"

"Not at all. The gown fits *her*!"

Their peals of laughter were interrupted by another brisk knock on the door. Delia opened it to find two footmen carrying a large tub followed by a line of maids with steaming pitchers of water. Polly hurried in at the end of this impressive parade with a stack of thick, soft towels.

"Here we are, miss. Place the tub by the fire, now, James. Yes, yes, that'll do." Polly pulled a chair up next to the tub and placed the towels and a luxurious-looking cake of violet-colored soap on it.

Polly nodded to Lily. "Your bath is ready too, miss. I have a supper tray for you as well."

"Delightful. Night, Delia," Lily said, hurrying off to her own room without a backward glance. "You'll feel more yourself when you've bathed."

"Do you need help with your dress, miss?" Polly asked.

Delia shook her head. "No, thank you. I can manage."

Polly curtsied and followed Lily, pulling the connecting door closed behind her.

"Well, that's Lily for you," Delia mumbled to herself. "Not a speck of dirt or mud to be found on her anywhere, but ready to sacrifice a limb to get to her bath."

She couldn't blame Lily, though. The bath looked like heaven. Polly had poured some kind of subtly scented oil into it. Delia picked up the pretty cake of soap and sniffed at it. Yes, it was the same scent. Jasmine perhaps?

Scented swirls of steam rose temptingly above the water and beckoned to Delia, who nearly ripped off her dress in her eagerness to get into the bath. She did take the time to wipe the worst of the mud off her body with a damp towel beforehand, however. She had no desire for a second mud bath today.

"Ahhhhh." She could not restrain a moan of pleasure

when she was up to her neck in the scented water. It was bliss to be surrounded by the pure, delicate fragrance of the oil. Even the water felt softer. Did the scented oil make it so? Or did the aristocracy enjoy better water than the rest of England?

Delia lingered in the bath until the warm water had soaked into every one of her sore muscles. When it started to cool, she ducked her head under to rinse the worst of the mud from her hair; then she washed it with the cake of soap and rinsed it again.

She'd changed into her white cotton night rail and was drying her hair by the fire when there was a knock on the hall door. "Yes?"

Polly entered the room with a supper tray. "Your supper, miss," she began, but stopped when she saw Delia. "Oh my, you look ever so much better!" Polly clapped a hand over her mouth and turned bright red. "That is . . ."

Delia smiled. "It's all right, Polly. I know I looked a fright when I arrived."

"Will you be needing anything else tonight, miss?"

"No, I don't think so, thank you. I'm off to bed. Good night."

"Good night, miss."

But Delia didn't go to bed. She rose and crept to the door that connected her room to Lily's and listened. Silence. She eased the door open and peered in. She assumed the lump in the center of the bed was her sister. All she could see of her under the thick coverlet was a tangled mass of curling dark blond hair, but the lump snored like Lily.

Delia backed out of the room and closed the door with a quiet click. Good. Lily needed to rest. Now if she could convince her own body to succumb to sleep, all would be well. She should be exhausted. She glanced at the supper tray Polly had left. She should be ravenous, too, but instead of eating, she retrieved the goblet from the tray and left the food untouched. Maybe the wine would help her sleep.

Today's coach accident had been minor, but Delia had been terrified when the axle broke. The coach had lurched and shuddered and skittered madly across the road before it at last staggered to a stop. How must her parents have felt when they realized their carriage was careening into a ditch? Delia heard the terrified screams of the horses and the sound of splintering wood in her nightmares as if she'd been there.

Their mother wouldn't have wanted them to come to Bellwood. Oh, Millicent Chase hadn't been bitter about being shunned by the *ton*. She'd never regretted her decision to marry Henry Somerset. Delia's parents had been madly in love.

But Millicent knew every unsavory truth of the life she'd left behind. The posturing. The idleness and vanity. The arrogance and vindictiveness. The cruelty. She hadn't hidden these truths from her children. Her mother wouldn't have wanted two of her beloved daughters tangled up in such a world.

Lord Carlisle's world.

Delia drained the glass of wine. "It's only for two weeks. We'll just stay away from him," she comforted herself as she crawled under the covers. "It won't be difficult. Far beneath his notice . . ."

She dropped off to sleep, dreaming of a bare chest, unbuttoned breeches, and bold, seeking hands.

Lord Archibald leaned against his cue. A cheroot dangled from his mouth and his eyes were trained on the billiards table. Alec leaned across the green baize and lined up his shot.

"What was the outcome of that business with the rustic chits from Surrey?" Archie asked, just as Alec drew back his cue. "Bloody awful shot, Carlisle," he crowed when Alec's ball veered far left of his target.

Alec scowled. Archie hated to lose at billiards. "It remains to be seen." He took up his own cheroot from a tray on the side table. "The matter bears further investigation."

"Come, now, Carlisle—at least tell me if she's pretty or not."

Alec drew on his cheroot. "I don't know."

"You don't *know*? Why the devil not? This isn't a difficult question."

"I didn't notice a devastating bosom." He thought of the angry glare Miss Somerset had given him when she'd caught him sneaking a look.

Archie grinned. "Yes, well, perhaps if you'd started with her face, Carlisle . . ."

"I couldn't see it properly. She was covered in mud and it had grown dark. And before you ask," he added, "I couldn't see her hair, either. Not one strand. Her bonnet appeared to be nailed to her head."

"Not a promising start," Archie said. "Or a very promising one, depending on how you look at it. Robyn's attention span is shorter than most. It doesn't sound as though she's the sort to hold it for long."

"Where is Robyn? I haven't seen him all evening."

Archie shrugged. "Shepherdson."

Nothing further needed to be said. If Robyn was out with Lord Shepherdson, they wouldn't see him again tonight.

"Robyn wasn't here to welcome her to Bellwood," Archie pointed out. "That's a good sign, isn't it? He can't be *that* enamored of her."

Alec snorted. "You assume Robyn remembers what day she's arriving. I'd be surprised if he even remembers what day of the week it is today."

"Still, a silly little country lass may be just what you need, eh?"

"She's not silly. Just the opposite. She's clever. Sharp-tongued, too."

Archie grimaced. "Clever, sharp-tongued, and plain? Dreadful combination."

"I never said she was plain." *That blush that had stained her cheeks right before she retired this evening* . . . "I said I couldn't see her well enough to tell."

"Oh, she's plain. Or at least she doesn't have the legendary Chase beauty. You'd have noticed *that*. What color are her eyes? Does she have *des yeux de feu bleu*?"

Alec stared blankly at his friend. "What the *devil* are you on about?"

"Come, now, Carlisle. Surely you've heard of 'the eyes of blue fire'? Who was that Greek chit? The one with snakes for her hair?"

Alec wasn't drunk, but this conversation made him feel as if he were. Still, he'd known Archie since they were lads. The best course of action was to follow along. "Medusa."

"Right. That's the one. Back when Millicent Chase was the toast of the *ton*, the gentlemen swore her eyes were such a beautiful, perfect blue, they could turn a man to stone."

"Part of him, anyway," Alec said dryly.

Archie laughed. "They used to take bets at White's on who would be the next to fall under the spell of *des yeux de feu bleu*. I recall my father falling into raptures about Millicent Chase's eyes. He was one of her suitors, you know."

Alec grinned. "Your father was a scandal and a rogue, Archie."

"Yes, well, like father like son, and the apple and the tree, and all that nonsense."

Alec's grin faded. He hated those expressions, probably

because his own father had been a cold, manipulative bastard.

"I didn't see the color of her eyes, either," Alec said. "They were dark."

"Dark blue? Like blue fire?"

"Blue fire," Alec snorted. "What nonsense. Bloody hell, Archie. Why not just wait and see for yourself? I'm sure she'll be at breakfast."

Archie shook his head. "I must remain in suspense until dinner tomorrow night. I have to leave early in the morning. I'll return to Bellwood in the evening."

Alec smothered a laugh. "Ah, yes. I forgot. Aunt Bettina is visiting."

Archie nodded glumly. "She's Lady Humphries now, and she's dragged old Humphries along with her on her visit. Poor sod. Why in God's name they felt compelled to marry, I'll never understand. She's almost as rich as King George. What need has she of a husband?"

Alec shrugged. "She did gain a title from the marriage."

"What would induce Humphries to wed again, then? He doesn't need Aunt's money."

"Perhaps they had certain, ah, physical needs—"

Archie cringed. "Not another *word*, Carlisle. She's sixty-five if she's a day, and Humphries is at least seventy! It's too hideous to contemplate."

"You say the same about every marriage."

"Quite right, too. I have no wish to be leg-shackled. You must be mad to even consider it." He frowned darkly. "Do you have an understanding with Lady Lisette yet?" Archie sounded as if he didn't want to hear the answer.

"No. Not yet. But I expect the business will be concluded by the end of the house party."

"Business, eh? What a romantic way to put it. What about the other matter?"

"As I said, it bears further investigation, but I doubt Delia Somerset will prove to be a serious problem."

"Too bad," Archie said with a disappointed sigh. "Think how amusing it could be if she did."

Alec took one last draw on his cheroot. "Sorry, old boy. You'd better prepare yourself for another long, dull, tedious house party."

Chapter Five

By the time she became aware of the sound of hooves behind her, it was too late.

Delia turned in time see a very tall rider on an absurdly large black horse galloping toward her through the trees. The huge hooves sent up a spray of gravel with each pounding stride.

Drat.

It had been such a promising start to the day, too. It was early yet, but the sun was beginning to emerge from behind some wispy low-lying clouds, and the air was fresh and cool. She'd just reached the middle of the long walkway that led up to the estate and she'd stopped to admire the view of the house from there. She cocked her head. Even the ivy that climbed up the outside corner of the left wing looked perfect, as if a giant hand had draped it just so for maximum artistic effect.

Now her walk was spoiled. For one wild moment she considered running in the opposite direction. Ridiculous, of course—it would be unspeakably rude to flee, not to mention cowardly. Well, she was no coward. Delia straightened her shoulders and pasted a polite smile over her gritted teeth. Perhaps he was in a tearing hurry to be somewhere.

Somewhere *else*.

"Miss Somerset." Lord Carlisle reined the horse to a halt beside her. "I'm surprised to see you up so early this morning."

Delia had to crane her neck to look up at him. If he didn't dismount, it might mean he wouldn't linger. "Good morning, my lord. I do tend to rise early. I suppose I keep country hours."

He dismounted and Delia suppressed a sigh. He had nowhere else to be, then. He took the horse's reins in his hand and walked over to her.

He intended to join her on her walk, then. *Drat.*

"I'm surprised to see *you* up this early, my lord. Not very fashionable, is it?" Delia cringed a little when she heard the bite in her voice. She'd promised Lily she'd do her best to keep her tongue in check.

But he didn't answer. The uncomfortable silence continued to stretch between them until at last Delia peeked at him from the corner of her eye. He was staring at her. In fact, he was studying her with such furious intensity she felt a flush begin to rise from her chest into her cheeks. She jerked her gaze away.

What in the world was he staring at? She raised a hand self-consciously to her hair. The pins had come loose. She'd woken this morning longing to get a walk before breakfast. She hadn't expected to see anyone, so she'd simply twisted the heavy locks into a knot at the back of her neck and slipped into a dark blue walking dress. She hadn't even worn a bonnet.

For heaven's sake! Was the missing bonnet so shocking? At least her clothes were *buttoned*!

He cleared his throat. "Ah, I see you've rid yourself of the mud."

He actually had the nerve to sound shocked! Had he imagined she wouldn't *bathe*? "Yes, my lord. Imagine my relief when I discovered it wasn't permanent."

Delia bit her lip. Her tongue seemed to sprout barbs whenever she spoke to Lord Carlisle. Instead of the swift retort she expected, however, there was another silence. She turned to him in surprise. "Lord Carlisle?"

He'd stopped walking and was standing in the middle of the path. He went still as his dark, dark eyes wandered over her face and figure. He started at the top of her head, taking in the loose strands of hair. He lingered on her eyes, on her mouth, and on the open neck of her gown, and then moved leisurely over her plain blue walking dress.

Delia was speechless, both at the intense perusal and the expression in his eyes. She couldn't quite put her finger on it, but his expression was strange, familiar . . .

Oh! A furious blush stained her cheeks. Yesterday.

I'm an impatient man, especially when it comes to . . .

Dear God. *Fornication.* She'd seen a hint of that same look in his eyes during their ill-advised argument about fornication.

Delia glanced up, as if fascinated with the trees above them. She looked down and studied her feet. She fidgeted with the skirts of her blue walking dress. Anything to avoid meeting those assessing black eyes.

"You look completely different. I wouldn't have recognized you from yesterday." His tone was faintly accusing.

Delia narrowed her eyes. "Well, then, my lord, it's fortunate for both of us I couldn't fail to recognize you. You're forever burned into my memory."

Blast it! She clenched her fists in frustration. It had sounded like . . .

"Is that so?" He grinned. "Well, I'm flattered."

Like she was paying him a compliment. Judging by his smug grin, he'd decided to take it as one. Delia huffed out a breath and crossed her arms over her chest. "If you choose," she said, struggling to keep her tone bland.

"Tell me, Miss Somerset," he said in a low voice. "In what way am I burned into your memory?"

She blinked. His tone sounded almost suggestive. Surely not.

"In every way," she snapped back without thinking, and then she wanted to bite her tongue out. *Again.* What was the matter with her? She'd been known to carry on reasonable conversations with gentlemen before, all without blushing and stammering like a schoolgirl.

Lord Carlisle threw back his head and laughed. "The reason I ask," he said, taking a step closer to her, "is you've seen more of me than most young ladies."

Ha! Delia doubted it. Surely his female companion from yesterday had seen far more of him than she had, and more than one time, too, she'd wager. Not that it mattered to her, of course. One time had been more than enough for her. It was one time too many, in fact, even if he did have intriguingly smooth skin on his chest.

Besides, there was something odd going on here. Was he *flirting* with her? No! It was impossible. It was ridiculous. Why would he bother to flirt with her? It was out of the question he'd single her out for any particular attention.

And yet . . . that had sounded like an innuendo, and he was watching her now as if he were a spoiled child and she a sugary sweet. Delia pursed her lips into a thin, disapproving line.

She was *not* going to flirt with Lord Carlisle.

She didn't flirt with aristocrats. Flirting with an aristocrat was about as wise as poking a bear with a sharp stick. One might escape unscathed, but the odds were against it. Aristocrats were vain. They were idle and arrogant and generally untrustworthy. Gentlemen of the *ton* were shiftier than most. At their worst they were downright dangerous.

"I did see more of you than I wanted to. I'm sorry to have embarrassed you." Her voice dripped with acid sweetness. "Perhaps it would be wise for you to limit the exposure of your parts in the future? Especially in public."

"Oh, I'm not embarrassed, Miss Somerset." He held her eyes. "Merely curious. Which of my *parts* did you find the most memorable?"

Delia placed her hands on her hips. "I found your disregard for propriety the most memorable, my lord."

He chuckled. "Come, now, Miss Somerset. There's no need to be coy." He stared down at her, his eyes glinting with amusement. Lord Carlisle was teasing her, all right, and not innocently, either. *But why?* It didn't make sense.

Whatever the reason, he seemed to be enjoying himself. How irritating. *Coy indeed.* Well, if he wanted to see coy . . . "Very well, my lord." She lowered her eyes demurely. "There was one thing."

He leaned just a little closer. "Yes?"

She had his undivided attention now. "Well," she said, struggling to keep the amusement out of her voice. "I did notice your . . ." She paused strategically. "Your back."

"My back?" He sounded puzzled.

"Yes. It's very broad, isn't it?" She peeked up at him through her lashes. Should she twirl a lock of hair in her finger? No. That might be a bit too much. "Your shoulders are very wide, too, and your arms are long and muscular. I noticed them, as well."

"Did you?" He seemed to find this far more promising, if she could judge by the intrigued look on his face.

"Oh, *yes*. When I first came upon you, I couldn't even see your, ah, companion. You towered over her and your . . ." Heat surged into her face. "Your, um, body is so large, you obscured her completely." She shook her head as though she couldn't quite believe a mere mortal man could have such amazing physical attributes. "I confess at first I wondered what you were doing to that tree. Then I spied her up against it. I believe you were *holding* her against the tree, in fact." She fluttered her lashes.

His eyes were rapt on her face. "You noticed a great deal, didn't you?" He seemed to be having a bit of trouble catching his breath.

"Oh, I'm very perceptive, my lord," she purred. "But there is one thing that caught my attention more than anything else."

"What was that?"

Delia bit her bottom lip to smother her smile. He sounded almost painfully curious. "I noticed, my lord, even given your superior height, your broad shoulders, your long arms, and your impressive musculature, your friend managed to get away from you quite easily."

Lord Carlisle blinked at her.

"I mean, one minute she was there and the next she was gone." She tapped her finger against her bottom lip, as though she couldn't quite account for it. "I almost thought I had imagined her. She was at such a disadvantage, too. Physically, I mean. She *was* pinned to the tree, was she not?"

There was a silence; then Lord Carlisle straightened and stepped away from her. Delia choked back a laugh. Oh, his expression! It looked as if a reluctant smile and an annoyed frown were fighting a duel on his face! At last, one corner of his mouth lifted. "She was not pinned against her will, if that's what you're asking."

"Of course not, my lord. Still, she vanished so quickly. One quick tug to pull down her skirts and she was gone. Do you think she wanted to get away from you?" Her eyes were wide and innocent.

"Ah, well. She wanted something, at any rate," he replied, grinning when her blush deepened. "What do you think it was? Because I think I know. I think she wanted me to pull her skirts *up*."

Delia's mouth dropped open in shock. Oh, the wicked man! She was gathering her wits together to deliver a scathing reply when all at once her thoughts scattered like billiard balls at the cue strike. An image rose in her mind, startlingly clear. Lord Carlisle's hand, lifting the woman's skirts. Higher, then higher still . . .

Her eyes darted to his hands. He still held the horse's reins. He hadn't felt the need for riding gloves this morning. Bare, tanned skin stretched taut over large, capable hands, lightly dusted across the back with crisp dark hair.

Delia swallowed. A memory nagged at her, a kaleidoscope of images. Had she dreamed about his hands last night?

She heard Lord Carlisle draw in a quick, sharp breath, and her eyes flew back to his face. He was gazing at her, riveted, and his own eyes had darkened. He'd noticed her staring at his hands. She was sure of it. She'd given herself away.

A second ticked by. Another.

Delia's heart began to thump wildly in her chest. She must be mad to play with him like this. He was an earl, for pity's sake. *Bear, Delia. Sharp stick.*

Lord Carlisle wasn't one of the shifty ones. He was one of the dangerous ones. "Isn't it time we return to the house, my lord?" she asked a little desperately. "Surely they've held breakfast for us?"

He brushed the questions aside. "Shall I tell you what I find most memorable about you?" His rough, silky voice brushed across her nerve endings.

"No! That is," she said, striving for a calmer tone, "I would rather you didn't."

"Your eyes," he said, as if she hadn't spoken. "They're remarkable. I can't think how I didn't notice them last night."

Delia just resisted the urge to squirm. "Are you trying to flatter me, my lord?"

He shrugged. "No. I'm simply stating the truth. I can't be the first person to remark upon your eyes, Miss Somerset? They're an unusual color. They're your mother's eyes, aren't they?"

Delia stiffened. "Yes." She did have her mother's eyes, and he wasn't the first person to remark on them, but she had no wish to discuss either her eyes or her mother with Lord Carlisle.

"I thought so. I never saw her, but I believe she was famous among the *ton* for her startling blue eyes."

"She was famous among the *ton* for any number of things, my lord," Delia replied tightly. "But I'm sure you're far above paying attention to idle gossip."

"It's only gossip if it isn't true, Miss Somerset."

"It's neither here nor there now, is it?" She tried to keep the bitterness out of her voice. "My mother is dead, and as far as the *ton* is concerned, she's been as good as dead for many years now. It's an old story. I'm sure there's more diverting gossip to be had."

"That depends. Do you look like your mother? Aside from your eyes, that is."

Delia had begun to hasten back to the house, but now she stopped and turned to glare at him. "What difference does that make?" Her voice was cold.

He stopped as well. "I should think it was obvious."

His tone was so reasonable it made Delia want to scream.

"If you favor your mother," he went on, "there will be more than one person at this house party who recognizes you as Millicent Chase's daughter."

Oh, no. Delia stared at him, and a cold shiver darted down her back. She'd planned to fade into the background like any respectable wallflower, but now that option was evaporating before her eyes. She hadn't even considered the possibility the other guests might recognize her or Lily as members of the Chase family. Not that they were, really. At least, not in any way that mattered to these people.

He was waiting for a reply. "I look just like her. Both Lily and I do."

"Ah." He nodded. "Then your appearance at Bellwood will be a new chapter in the old story, and doubtless the most diverting source of gossip for the next several weeks. You and your sister should prepare yourselves."

What an awful prospect. Delia's shoulders slumped just thinking about it. Gossip, snide comments, whispers, and she and Lily caught right in the center of it. The next two weeks couldn't pass quickly enough for her.

Lord Carlisle's casual laughter interrupted her thoughts. "You look glum, Miss Somerset. Come, now. It won't be as bad as you imagine."

"Oh, I'm certain it will be far worse than I imagine," she replied, trying to sound as if she didn't care. "I must say you don't seem at all concerned, however. Remember, my lord, this story began with my mother publicly jilting your father. The gossips will linger over that as if it were a fine wine."

There. It was out in the open now. There was no way to take it back. Delia bit her lip and wondered whether she'd gone too far.

But to her surprise, Lord Carlisle only lifted a shoulder in a careless shrug. "Yes, I imagine that's true. Perhaps this house party won't be as dull as I feared."

Delia felt a tirade coming on, but for Lily's sake she struggled to keep calm. "Then this is a fortunate occurrence, my lord. For you, that is. It would be terrible indeed if you were *bored*. But won't your mother find it difficult?" He might find it easy to bear, even amusing, but no one would be gossiping about *him*. "It will, after all, be her name on the lips of every gossip."

And my name. And Lily's. And my mother's. Delia felt a little stab at her heart when she thought of it.

"You haven't met my mother yet, have you, Miss Somerset? I think you'll find she tolerates the gossip very well. She's weathered worse."

Delia didn't doubt she had. As members of the *ton*, the Sutherlands were accustomed to the sniping and whispering that took place behind fans and over billiard tables. Perhaps they even participated in it themselves. It was likely.

But she and Lily? No. It would be far more difficult for them. Difficult enough, in fact, it was best if Lily knew nothing about it. With a little luck and some maneuvering on Delia's part, she wouldn't have to know. Delia sighed. They'd been here less than a day and already she was keeping secrets from her sister.

"Well, then." She resumed her brisk pace back to the house. "It's settled. Let the scandal and gossip commence at your pleasure, my lord."

"Not a moment too soon." A satisfied smile played around his lips. "Scandal and gossip are much more diverting than chess."

Chapter Six

She turned on her heel and marched, stiff-backed, in the direction of the house. He strolled after her, leading Ceres beside him. A shadowy, hazy memory drifted just at the corner of his mind, but he couldn't quite drag it to the surface.

The sun had come up over Bellwood, and it was as if it shone for no other reason than to highlight the thousands of threads of gold in the rich brown tendrils that escaped her hairpins. He watched as the light sifted lovingly through the heavy locks and lit up strand after strand.

Then he remembered.

He'd been ten or eleven years old and out for a ride with his father. Alec didn't recall what they'd been doing, though spending any time with his father had been a rare enough occurrence during his childhood. Perhaps they'd been checking the fencing around one of the far-flung fields that surrounded Bellwood. Hadn't his father's steward been with them?

Alec, a victim of youthful high spirits like most young

lads at that age, had taken it into his head to jump one of the fences. He'd circled in front of it a few times to calculate the height and the required speed and distance at which he should initiate the jump. He smiled a little now, thinking of it. He'd been very serious about it, in the way only an eleven-year-old contemplating a foolish trick can be serious.

But he'd miscalculated. Badly. And he'd fallen. Hard.

One minute he'd been gleefully charging the fence, and the next he'd been flat on his back, stunned and gasping for breath as he watched the tree branches above his head move in and out of focus. He'd staggered at last to a standing position, but he'd been unsteady on his feet for some time afterward, the wind knocked out of him.

That was just how he'd felt this morning when he'd gotten a good look at Delia Somerset. As though he'd miscalculated. Badly. As if he'd had the wind knocked clean out of him. Today, however, he felt none of the sick dizziness he'd experienced when he was eleven. No, it was more like . . . He paused, trying to think of a way to describe how it felt. Ah, yes. It was like he'd drunk too much of an old, fine Scotch whiskey. He might be dizzy and shaky the next morning, but it was difficult to regret the overindulgence.

He shook his head, amazed at himself. Had he actually just imagined the sun shone only to set fire to the gold in Miss Somerset's hair? Oh, that was pure poetry, much along the same pathetic lines as *les yeux de feu bleu*, in fact.

He traced the slim line of her back as she marched in front of him like a soldier on parade. He couldn't imagine now how he'd ever thought her features were unremarkable. Had it been too dark? Had it been the mud? Or had he been so intent on punishing her for interrupting his liaison with Maggie that he'd willfully overlooked it? Alec didn't overlook things, particularly not potentially explosive things like uncommonly fetching, unsuitable young ladies. He'd known beforehand she was the second. He should have been on the alert for the first.

God, that blush. He'd seen a hint of it yesterday evening. It had startled him then, but watching it wash over her cheeks and her slim, pale neck and throat this morning had aroused him to the point of pain. Did she blush like that everywhere? She was vivid everywhere—the rich golden brown hair, the wide eyes, such a deep blue they were almost indigo. The pale, creamy, translucent skin. And her figure . . . Today's plain blue dress looked to Alec just like yesterday's plain blue dress, but Delia Somerset was mistaken if she thought her Surrey camouflage would fool him. He ran a hand over his mouth. It was best if he didn't think about how her body would look awash with that tantalizing blush, but Alec couldn't deny he deeply regretted not having seen her in the infamously snug yellow gown.

One thing was clear. There was no way he could overlook Delia Somerset *now.* It made the situation so much more complicated. He could have dismissed a plain, country rustic. Even a calculating fortune hunter was easily dealt with. Robyn could simply take a new mistress. Problem solved.

But this girl? No. He was a cynical bastard, and even he'd been moved to spout inane drivel about the sun and golden strands of hair. Robyn was *not* a cynical bastard, and he'd chase Delia Somerset until he gasped for breath and his legs buckled beneath him. She'd have Robyn stamping, panting, and sweating like an overbred stallion before the first case of champagne had run dry at the house party.

Something would have to be done. Robyn wouldn't want to give her up, though.

Robyn. *Christ.* Alec didn't know what to expect from Robyn anymore, and Robyn didn't confide in him, not since Alec had become the earl. What had once been a warm brotherly affection seemed to have cooled and hardened into an icy detachment, one that grew icier by the day.

Ever since their father died, Alec had been chasing his own tail like a rabid dog, trying to keep his brother in line. There hadn't been anyone to manage Robyn during that first year after their father's death. Not long after Alec had inherited the title, the extent to which the estates had been mismanaged had become painfully clear. The responsibilities had fallen on Alec's shoulders with the force of an anvil dropped from the roof of Bellwood.

Robyn had taken up with a fast crowd of wild London bucks. He had the family's dark good looks and deep pockets, and though he was merely a second son, he was still a Sutherland. That was as good as hard currency among the *ton*. The ladies adored him, particularly those ladies who teetered on a fine line of respectability, one scandal away from toppling headfirst into the *demimonde*. Worse, Robyn fancied himself very sophisticated. In truth, he was almost as inexperienced and naïve as Delia Somerset.

Alec stole another glance at that straight back. She hadn't turned around once since they'd begun walking back to the house. He chuckled, thinking of her disapproving stare when he'd so boldly mentioned his *parts*. It was obvious Miss Somerset was not often in the company of gentlemen who dared to mention their . . . What had she called them? Their *unmentionables*. Could it be the lovely lady was a prude?

Yet there'd been that one moment. Alec wouldn't call it flirting, because young ladies flirted in order to pique a man's interest, and Miss Somerset had flirted only to teach him a lesson. It was a little morality play disguised as flirting, which was droll of her, he admitted. It had piqued his interest. Not only his interest. One other thing had been *piqued*. So she was a clever, lovely prude with a latent trace of wicked? How titillating. Of all Robyn's scrapes, this one could prove to be the most amusing. For the first time in recent memory, Alec was beginning to look forward to a house party.

"Miss Somerset!"

Alec jerked his head up and came to an abrupt halt. He watched, dumbfounded, as Robyn bounded across the court-yard, his eyes fixed on Delia Somerset.

Alec glanced up at the sky. The sun had just crested the roofline of Bellwood. It couldn't be later than nine o'clock. In the *morning*. That meant it was before three o'clock. In the *afternoon*.

Never mind the poetry and the sun and the strands of delicate golden hair wafting on the breeze. He was witness-ing a full-fledged miracle right before his eyes. Robyn was awake. He was, against all odds, alert and standing in an upright position. He was dressed. He was *outdoors*.

"Miss Somerset." Robyn came to a halt in front of her and took both her hands in his. "I'm very happy to see you again." He smiled into her eyes and raised one of her hands to his lips. Then Robyn glanced behind Delia and noticed Alec. "Oh. Good morning, Alec," he said with far less en-thusiasm.

"Robyn." Alec kept his voice neutral, but behind his bland expression, he was astonished.

Alec studied his brother. Robyn's eyes were bloodshot and his valet had clearly shaved him in a hurry. His clothes were rumpled. *Ah*. So it wasn't a true miracle, then. Robyn hadn't awoken early. He'd just returned home from last night's entertainment. If Alec cared to look, he'd doubtless find Shepherdson skulking about the hallways of Bellwood, cravat askew and reeking of spirits.

Still, for Robyn to appear at breakfast in a lucid condition was a miracle of sorts, and that was bloody disconcerting enough, since this astounding attentiveness was no doubt for Delia Somerset's benefit.

For her part, Miss Somerset seemed a bit taken aback at Robyn's effusive greeting, but pleased nonetheless. "Thank you, Mr. Sutherland, and good morning. Lily and I are de-lighted to be here."

"I heard from my sisters you had a rough journey," Robyn said. "Something about a broken axle and a hay cart? My apologies that I wasn't here to greet you last night. I was detained at a previous engagement."

Alec snorted. Which of Robyn's *engagements* had kept him this time, he wondered. Tossing dice perhaps? Tossing back tumblers of whiskey? Tossing a barmaid's skirts over her head? Likely all of the above.

"Have you been out for a walk this morning?" Robyn asked Delia, offering his arm to escort her into the breakfast room.

"Yes." Delia took his arm. "The idea of exploring a bit of the park proved too tempting to resist."

"Of course." Robyn guided Delia toward the front entrance. "And you, Alec? I see you've also been out this morning." Robyn swept his gaze over Cerus and Alec's muddy riding boots.

Alec smiled pleasantly at his brother. "I often ride early in the morning, Robyn. But perhaps you weren't aware of that."

"I wasn't aware of it, no." Robyn shrugged. "I don't track *your* every move, Alec. This way, Miss Somerset," he added before Alec could reply. "My mother is anticipating meeting you. Miss Lily and my sisters are awake, as well."

Delia looked from one brother to the other with a puzzled expression. No doubt she could feel the tension, just as she could feel the sun on her face. The sun in reverse, that was. The dark thing that surged between him and Robyn could devour the sun.

The whole family was assembled in the breakfast room. Charlotte and Eleanor were yawning over their morning chocolate. Lily Somerset sat next to them wearing a pale lilac-colored morning gown and looking none the worse for her adventure the night before. His mother was seated across from them, sipping tea and looking as placid as ever.

"I found Miss Somerset." Robyn presented Delia with the kind of flourish usually reserved for royalty. "She was taking advantage of the fine day with an early morning walk."

Alec watched Delia with interest. Another pink blush rose in her cheeks, as though she was embarrassed by Robyn's fanfare. He wished she'd stop blushing. It was damned distracting.

"Mother," Alec said, dragging his attention away from Delia. "May I present Miss Delia Somerset? Miss Somerset, this is my mother, Catherine, the Countess of Carlisle."

Lady Carlisle smiled at Delia and nodded politely. "Miss Somerset, it's a pleasure to meet you. You and your sister are welcome at Bellwood."

Delia dipped into a graceful curtsy. "Thank you, Lady Carlisle, for your kind invitation. I'm happy to meet you."

Alec's mouth twisted. Under all that propriety and politeness he knew his mother burned with unladylike curiosity about Millicent Chase's daughters. His mother had known Millicent—they'd been debutantes together. Though any of the ladies who sat around the breakfast table would die of mortification before admitting it, each of them was thinking the same thing. If Millicent Chase hadn't fled headlong into a dark London night, Catherine Grey would never have married Hart Sutherland.

That was reason enough not to like the chits. If they had any sense at all, meeting his mother should have Delia and Lily Somerset quaking in their half boots. Still, Lady Carlisle could be boiling with rage or overcome with joy at meeting Millicent's daughters, and her expression would remain smooth and unruffled either way. In fact, an entire troop of baboons dressed in the Carlisle livery could seat themselves at the breakfast table and help themselves to toast and tea, and Lady Carlisle wouldn't turn a hair.

His mother was a bit like an exotic species of animal that had adapted to an intensely stressful environment by developing a new appendage. Lady Carlisle's ability to appear placid no matter what kind of chaos erupted around her had served her well during her many years of marriage to Hart Sutherland.

"You put me in mind of your mother, Miss Somerset," Lady Carlisle said gently. "You look very much like her." She paused. "I was sorry to hear about your parents' passing last spring."

It had to be said, and it was just as well it was said now rather than later. "Thank you, my lady," Delia murmured. Her voice was steady, but a shadow passed over her suddenly pale face. Unlike his mother, Delia Somerset hadn't developed the art of affecting indifference. Alec watched dispassionately as the emotions flitted across her face. It was fascinating—almost like watching an artist painting on a canvas, except it was both beautiful and awful at once.

What must it be like, to reveal so much? To be at the mercy of every casual observer? That kind of transparency was a disadvantage. He doubted Miss Somerset was good at games, especially those that required a certain coldblooded strategy.

Games like chess, for instance.

"It's fine out this morning," he said, breaking the silence. He took a seat next to his mother and signaled one of the footmen for coffee. "Will you take advantage of the day to show our guests around the grounds?" Alec addressed this question to Charlotte and Eleanor.

Both of his sisters gaped at him.

He did not usually appear at the breakfast table. When he did, he didn't make idle chitchat, or offer suggestions about how his sisters might spend their day. Both Charlotte and Ellie appeared to be stunned into silence, but after a moment Charlotte gathered herself together. "Is it fine?" She looked vaguely toward the window.

"It is," Robyn said with a teasing grin. "Think of what

you can accomplish today, Charlotte. The day is much longer than your usual, since you're up so much earlier."

Eleanor lowered her cup of chocolate daintily to her saucer. "You're one to talk, Robyn. You're up so much earlier today, by noon you'll think it's tomorrow!"

Charlotte, Lily, and Delia laughed. Even Alec and Robyn grinned, and Ellie seemed to rouse from her morning stupor. "There's a fine prospect of the lake at the end of the south lawn," she said, "and a lovely little folly where we can sit and sketch today, if that sounds agreeable."

"We should have plenty of time for a sketching party, given how *long* the day is. A walk to the east lawn won't be too taxing." Charlotte stretched languidly and darted a teasing glance at Robyn. "Mama, what time do you need us tonight? We'll be back for luncheon, of course."

"Six will be in plenty of time," their mother said. "Our guests will arrive a little later."

His mother had planned a small family dinner party for that evening, so Delia and Lily could be introduced to their nearest neighbors before the house party got under way in earnest the following day.

"Splendid." Ellie sipped her chocolate. "Robyn, will you accompany us?"

"Yes, please, if I may."

"Of course. You can carry our sketching supplies. Alec, will you come, as well?"

The table went quiet for a moment. Heads swiveled in Alec's direction. He was surprised to be asked, but not as surprised as they'd be if he accepted. He was tempted to accept for that reason alone. He glanced at Miss Somerset, who was quietly drinking her tea.

"No, I'm afraid I can't. I have some business to take care of this morning. I'll see you all this evening at dinner."

Alec could almost hear Robyn's sigh of relief.

Chapter Seven

Delia stood at the foot of the stairs, sketchbook under her arm, tapping the toe of her half boot on the elegant black-and-white-checkered marble floor.

Tap, tap, tap.

Rylands stood stiffly by the door, watching her from under his bushy gray eyebrows. "We *are* embarking on a simple sketching party, aren't we, Rylands?" she asked, turning to him. "I did hear correctly, didn't I?"

"Yes, miss. I believe so."

Tap, tap, sigh. "Because with this much fuss, one would think we were being presented at court."

"Yes, miss."

First Charlotte had deemed her pink bonnet "a fright." Then Eleanor declared her half boots "pinched her dreadfully," and Lily realized she'd forgotten her blue ribbon. Each of them had scurried back up the stairs in turn to address these fashion *faux pas*, which left Delia alone in the entrance hall, rolling her eyes and tapping her toes.

Tap, tap, grumble, sigh.

At this rate they would have to sketch in the dark.

"Ready, girls?" Charlotte called gaily at last, skipping down the stairs and into the foyer. They were just about to sail forth when Eleanor came to an abrupt halt. "Wait. Where's Robyn? I thought he was going to carry our sketching supplies."

Charlotte snorted. "Robyn disappeared back up the stairs a half hour ago to bathe and change." She tied the ribbons of yet another pink bonnet under her chin. "He promised to join us later. James will carry the supplies." She gestured to a footman so burdened with bundles and baskets he looked like a camel about to embark on a journey across the desert.

"I should have known," Eleanor said. "I can't recall the last time Robyn *carried* anything. No doubt he needs to bathe. He was out all night. He didn't return home until just before breakfast this morning, you know."

"Oh, dear!" Lily's face was a picture of dismay. "Surely that's not true?"

"Oh, yes. I'm afraid so," Ellie said. "Robyn is very wicked."

"I wouldn't call Robyn *wicked*," Charlotte protested. "How can you say so, Eleanor?"

"Well, not precisely wicked perhaps." She glanced at James and then lowered her voice to a whisper. "But Lady Audley, Charlotte!"

Charlotte shrugged. "All gentlemen of the *ton* have mistresses."

Lily's mouth dropped open and Delia felt her own face flood with heat. As the eldest of the young ladies, she should be the one to put a stop to the conversation, but she remained silent, half-ashamed, but also burning with curiosity.

"Oh, it's not the *having* of a mistress," Eleanor continued airily, shocking both Delia and Lily again with her cavalier air. "It's the antics, Charlotte. The drinking, the gambling, and the bordello, you know."

The bordello! This time even Delia gasped. But unfortunately Charlotte cut her sister off at this interesting point in the conversation. "Robyn behaves like all fashionable young men. Though of course, being a Sutherland, he pushes it rather farther than is wise."

"He's going to push Alec right off the edge of sanity if he continues," Eleanor said.

Charlotte grinned. "Poor Alec! But he's had mistresses of his own, you know, Ellie. Maybe he still does."

Indeed he does! Delia bit down on her bottom lip so she wouldn't shout the words aloud.

"But Alec is discreet," Eleanor objected. "One doesn't hear of carriage races and wagering and bordellos in relation to Alec."

"Did you say something, Delia?" Lily asked.

Three bonneted heads turned to look expectantly at her.

"No, no," Delia replied, trying to hide the strangled noise that had escaped her with a violent cough into her gloved hand. "I, ah, had something stuck in my throat, that's all."

The *truth*—that was what was stuck in her throat. One may not hear of plunging bodices and mistresses in relation to Lord Carlisle, but one could see it with their own eyes if they happened along the road at the right time. Discreet indeed! He was about as discreet as a blow to the head.

"Perhaps not anymore," Charlotte said, interrupting Delia's thoughts. "But before father died, there were rumors about Alec, you know. He was a rake," she whispered delightedly. "I once overheard Lady Connelly say Alec was *such a delicious rogue.*" Charlotte frowned. "In fact, that was the precise phrase she used. Delicious rogue. She sounded rather disappointed he wasn't one anymore."

Delia didn't know the difference between a rogue and a rake, but she was sure Lord Carlisle qualified as either. Or both. But she hadn't time to consider it.

"Lady Connelly is such a scandal," Eleanor said with relish. "I'm sure she *was* disappointed."

"I think it rather unfair on Alec," Charlotte said then. "He was only twenty-eight years old when Father died. He hadn't the time to sow his oats after he inherited the title."

Delia just managed to stifle an indignant snort. *He's making up for lost time now!*

"No. He's never been the same since Father died, has he, Charlotte?" Eleanor's voice had gone rather quiet. "Alec never said anything to us, of course," she said, addressing Lily and Delia now, "but I believe some rather appalling financial difficulties accompanied the title."

"I overheard Lady Connelly say Father would have ruined the Sutherlands," Charlotte said.

"Lady Connelly again!" Eleanor's voice was scathing. "She certainly has plenty to say, doesn't she?"

"Yes," Charlotte replied. "And none of it is pleasant."

"Did your father gamble?" Lily hesitated. "Keep, ah, mistresses?" She stumbled a little on the last word.

"Lily!" Delia cried, appalled she'd ask such a question.

"It's all right, Delia," Charlotte said. "No, Lily, father didn't gamble or keep a mistress. Not that we know of anyway."

Eleanor waved this away with a flick of her fingers, as though it were unthinkable. "If the gossip can be believed, he made bad investments. I'm not sure of the details, though I believe he considered most business ventures beneath his dignity."

"Well, Alec has as much family pride as Father did, but apparently he has as much interest in profit as dignity. I've heard it whispered among the *ton* he's utterly ruthless. Not unscrupulous, of course. Well, not entirely," Charlotte added, reconsidering.

Delia thought of his cold black eyes when he'd discovered her on the road yesterday, and a nasty shiver darted down her spine. It was easy to believe Lord Carlisle was ruthless. "Does Lady Connelly approve of this?" she asked archly, attempting to shake off her uneasiness.

Her companions laughed. "Indeed," Eleanor replied. "Let us by all means seek Lady Connelly's approval!"

There was a brief silence; then Eleanor laughed again. "Do you remember when Alec collected all of the small statuary from the house and built an obstacle course, Charlotte? We ran races until Alec cracked Bacchus's wine chalice with the heel of his boot. We had to hide the statue behind the large rose arbor. It's still there, you know."

Charlotte smiled. "There was that little foal, too. Do you remember, Eleanor? The poor thing was born sickly," she said for Delia and Lily's benefit. "Small, too. Father wanted to have her shot, but Alec fed her by hand and walked and groomed her until she grew strong and healthy. He spent every day that summer in the barn with that foal. He named her Athena."

"I remember. Alec was such fun back then!" Eleanor frowned. "I doubt he will recover his good humor once he's married. Lady Lisette isn't the sort who enjoys playful antics. There will be no oat-sowing for Alec once he's married to her."

"*Married!*" Delia bit her tongue for all she was worth, but nothing could keep that shocked exclamation from escaping her mouth. She came to an abrupt halt and turned to stare at Eleanor, a torrent of questions frozen on her lips.

"Is Lord Carlisle engaged?" Lily asked.

"There is no official proposal yet," Eleanor said. "But he's courting Lady Lisette Cecil. We expect them to be engaged by the end of the house party."

"But that's not—" Delia began.

"Oh, look, Delia and Lily!" Charlotte interrupted, pointing. "Is this not the perfect place to sketch?"

Delia pressed her lips together for a moment, then turned to Charlotte. "It's lovely, Charlotte." She gave her friend a wan smile.

What else could she say? That it wasn't possible for Lord Carlisle to be engaged because he'd been debauching a young woman from the village just yesterday? It was more than possible. It was probable. Charlotte was right. Gentlemen of the *ton* regularly kept mistresses. Why should a trifling thing like an engagement, or indeed a marriage, interfere with a gentleman's pleasures? Delia felt a surge of pity for this Lady Lisette, whoever she was. Eleanor's lip had curled with distaste when she'd said the lady's name, but to be shackled to such a husband? No woman deserved such a fate.

"Shall we stop here?" Eleanor asked. "The prospect is beautiful. We have a perfect view of the folly and down the lawn to the lake."

The ladies agreed and James spread out the picnic blanket for them. Delia accepted her sketching supplies from him and took up a perch on the blanket. She turned to a blank page in her book and attempted to focus on the picturesque view in front of her.

The folly was charming, small and dainty, like a doll's toy. The lake was visible just beyond it, flashing in the sun and winding gracefully through the trees like a length of blue satin ribbon. Her companions fell silent, each absorbed in creating a masterpiece. The only sound was the faint scrape of pencils against paper.

Delia gripped her own pencil in her fingers and stared blindly ahead, her hand motionless on the page. How could she focus on her sketch when a libertine like the Earl of Carlisle roamed the estate like a hungry tiger among timid gazelles?

One of the few advantages of social inferiority was invisibility, drat it. She shouldn't have to feel like a gazelle. She should feel like a chameleon or another one of those odd little lizards that lived in Africa. She'd read all about how they could change color with their environment. So why did she feel hunted, as if Lord Carlisle were ready to snap her fragile bones between his greedy jaws?

Delia placed the tip of her pencil against her paper and began to sketch a series of delicate vertical lines. Before long the slender legs of a gazelle emerged in the center of her page.

She couldn't shake the suspicion he'd been hoping to catch her alone this morning. It was too coincidental he'd appear in the exact same place not five minutes after she left the manor for her walk. Had he been waiting for her?

Delia made a few more quick strokes on the page. Her gazelle now had a face, a bow around its slender neck, and a lush meadow under its feet, but it still didn't look pleased. It looked nervous, as if it expected a predator to pounce upon it at any moment.

Then Lord Carlisle had been so determined to walk with her! And not just talk to her, but flirt with her. Oh, she may be innocent by *ton* standards, but she knew when a gentleman was flirting with her, especially when he did it as audaciously as Lord Carlisle had. He'd asked her to comment on his *parts*, for heaven's sake. He'd stared into her eyes as if he could drown in their depths. It was ridiculous.

Delia clutched at her pencil as she remembered. Ah, now she could see why the gazelle was so nervous. The poor thing. A fiendish predator had crept up behind her. This hideous creature looked like a man, with a man's body and a man's face and distinctive wavy dark hair, but it had a tiger's claws and hideous razor-sharp teeth in its gaping mouth.

It wasn't just the flirting, though. Gentlemen flirted. It

meant nothing—even less than nothing with a man of Lord Carlisle's ilk. No, it was the way he'd seemed to relish the idea of the *ton* reviving the old gossip about her mother. Why should that please him when his own mother was a player in that ugly little drama? Then he'd seemed downright gleeful to find she so strongly resembled her mother. What difference should it make to him?

Delia ran her pencil furiously across the page. The horrid tiger man had crept up behind the gazelle now, a frightening leer on his face. The awful paws with their jagged claws were mere inches from her neck, poised for attack.

Was it, as he'd said, that he found house parties a bore, and the gossip would prove entertaining? Of course, a spoiled aristocrat like Lord Carlisle would be accustomed to being entertained at all times. Hadn't he said something about chess?

Delia moved to a blank section of her page and drew a chessboard. A white queen faced off against a black king across the checkered expanse. The king was leering in much the same manner as the tiger man.

Well, a ruthless man like Lord Carlisle would appreciate chess, wouldn't he? Even his own sisters admitted he was ruthless, and from what Delia could tell, they didn't know about even a fraction of his sins. They thought *Robyn* was wicked! She'd been a little shocked to hear of Robyn's antics, but they paled in comparison to Lord Carlisle frolicking in the woods with one woman while he was as good as engaged to another.

Delia supposed his affianced bride was the belle of her season. Nothing less would do for Lord Carlisle, she was sure. Charlotte and Eleanor had said he had as much family pride as their father had, if fewer scruples.

The pencil skittered down to the bottom left corner of the page. Delia drew a huge black horse rearing back, its enormous hooves pawing at the air. The horse was attached to a shiny black lacquered traveling coach with the Carlisle crest emblazoned on the door. The carriage had a broken axle.

Delia stopped sketching and studied her page. A quiet laugh escaped her. Oh, it was a sketch worthy of Rowlandson himself! She'd have to burn it, of course, since the dreadful tiger bore far too recognizable a resemblance to Lord Carlisle.

She was busily adding a bushy tiger's tail when all at once her amusement turned to uneasiness. She stared at the tiger and the gazelle. Something was wrong . . .

Her eyes darted over the chessboard with the battling queen and king, down to the sketch of the horse and carriage and then back to the center of the page. The gazelle stood trembling in the middle of her meadow, the man tiger approaching her menacingly from behind. Delia drew a box around them, like a frame around a picture.

Suddenly all of the blood drained from her face. Oh, no. It couldn't be! Gentlemen of the *ton* were idle, vain, and selfish, but even Lord Carlisle couldn't be as wicked as that—

"May I see your sketch, Delia?" Lily had laid aside her own sketchbook and was holding out her hand for Delia's, a sweet smile on her face.

Delia slammed her sketchbook closed. "No!" Her voice was a shriek, and she slapped her hand over the cover of the book protectively.

Lily stared at her. "Whatever is the matter, Delia?" She started to rise to her feet.

"Nothing!" Delia squeaked. Making an enormous effort to remain calm and lower her voice, she said, "Nothing is the matter, Lily. I'm only embarrassed because I haven't gotten very far with my sketch."

Lily settled back onto her corner of the blanket. "Very well," she replied after a moment. "You don't have to show me." She eyed her sister with concern. "Are you tired from yesterday, dear?"

Delia nodded, relieved to have an excuse for her bizarre behavior. "Yes. I believe I am, Lily. I beg your pardon. I didn't mean to snap at you."

Charlotte closed her sketchbook and stretched her arms over her head. "I've exhausted my artistic inspiration for today. Shall we return to the house for luncheon? I believe I'll have a nap and a bath before the dinner party this evening."

"Yes, I am for the house, as well," Eleanor said. She closed her own book and rose from the blanket.

"Are you coming, Delia?" Lily asked.

"No. Not yet. You go on without me." Delia pasted a smile on her face. "I believe I'll take a few more minutes and see if I can't finish my sketch."

"Don't stay too long," Lily said. "I think you need a nap before dinner, as well."

"I won't. I do feel rather weary," Delia said meekly, trying to look exhausted.

She didn't open her sketchbook again until the others were out of sight; then she raised the cover carefully, as if the tiger man were lying in wait for his chance to leap from the page and sink his deadly claws into her neck.

Then again, it wasn't her *neck* she needed to worry about. It was her virtue and her reputation in danger of being torn to bits.

It was as clear as the page in front of her. Lord Carlisle was going to attempt to seduce her. Not because he desired her, of course, but to amuse himself and put the Somerset family in their place once and for all. It would be nothing at all to him to ruin an innocent for sport, and what better way to relieve his boredom than to add a final chapter to the scandalous tale of Millicent Chase and Hart Sutherland? Wasn't it fortunate for him she looked so much like her mother? It added just the right finishing touch to his fiendish scheme.

Her mother. For one horrible moment Delia felt so alone tears gathered behind her eyes, but then she was gripped by a surge of fury so intense she had to struggle to catch her breath. She frowned at her sketch, the tears evaporating along with all the pity she'd felt earlier for the delicate gazelle. Was the foolish thing just going to stand there, a useless bow about its neck, while a predator threatened to devour her?

She'd be *damned* if she'd be the gazelle in this scenario.

An awful, foolish, delightful plan was taking shape in her head. It was a mad scheme, and Delia had promised Lily she'd be the soul of propriety for the duration of the house party. Now here she was, letting her temper lead her into just the kind of mischief that would infuriate her sister.

But then, Lily didn't have to know, did she? What difference did one more secret make?

No, no, no. She'd best put it out of her mind. It was reckless in the extreme to play games with Lord Carlisle. He was an earl, for goodness' sake, and he was her host, so she was technically under his protection at the moment. He was also haughty, arrogant, and dismissive—not a man who'd take kindly to being toyed with.

But that was exactly what made it so irresistible. The great Lord Carlisle, bested at his own game! How satisfying it would be to show him that even an aristocrat with wealth and a title could be humbled, and by an insignificant girl from some obscure village in Surrey, no less! Oh, it was too delicious.

"Am I late?" a deep male voice asked.

A shadow fell across her sketchbook and Delia's heart leapt into her throat. "Oh!" She closed her sketchbook and scrambled to her feet.

"I apologize, Miss Somerset. I didn't mean to startle you.

Where have the others gone? I thought we were having a sketching party?"

Delia smiled up at Robyn Sutherland, relief weakening her knees for a moment. "We are. That is, we were. It's been hours. The others returned to the house to rest before dinner. I'm just about to return myself."

"Ah. I see." Robyn shook his head with mock regret. "I'm afraid my sketching will never improve at this rate."

Delia looked into his twinkling black eyes and couldn't help but return his crooked grin. Perhaps Robyn Sutherland *was* a little wicked, but he was also so pleasant and charming it was impossible not to like him. "No, I'm afraid it won't. I'm sorry for it, Mr. Sutherland. A gentleman who can't sketch is shocking indeed."

"At least let me escort you back to the house. It will be a kindness on your part to save me from utter disgrace." He held out his hand to carry her sketchbook.

Delia hesitated briefly, but then handed over the book.

"May I take you through some of the formal gardens close to the house on the way back?" He tucked her hand into the crook of his arm. "It's too early for the roses to be in full bloom, but it's still a pleasant walk."

"By all means," Delia said. "I would be delighted."

Chapter Eight

Alec spent the morning and part of the afternoon in his study working on estate business. He'd just dismissed his steward when there was a knock on the door. His mother entered and took a seat in front of Alec's massive mahogany desk.

"Well?" He leaned back in his chair. "What are your initial impressions of our guests?"

"Miss Somerset looks very much like her mother," the dowager said.

"Yes. She mentioned there is a strong family resemblance. What was her mother like?"

"She was a diamond of the first water, of course, labeled an Incomparable less than two weeks into her season. She also had some of the noblest blood in England running through her veins, being a Chase. That's why your father wanted to marry her, of course. He began courting her as soon as she was out."

Alec began to wish he'd poured himself a glass of whiskey.

That sounded just like his father. He'd always insisted on the best of everything, and believed without question he was entitled to it. Alec looked at his mother and his face softened a little. Even when his father had the best in his hand, he'd not appreciated it.

"To be truthful," she said, "I always thought Millicent Somerset rather intriguing."

Intriguing. Bloody hell. He was beginning to suspect that was a family trait, too. "Interesting choice of word. Go on."

His mother lifted one elegant shoulder in a shrug. "Millicent and I were friends after a fashion. But we were rivals, too, and young ladies of the *ton* who are competing for social supremacy aren't encouraged to be intimate. Her family was certainly unimaginative enough, but she was not much like the rest of the Chases."

"Yes, I think that's a safe conclusion." Alec crossed over to a crystal decanter on a side table and poured a finger of whiskey into a glass.

The countess paused. "She was brave," she said unexpectedly.

Alec lowered his glass from his lips and studied his mother. "Brave?"

Lady Carlisle looked up into her son's dark eyes. "Of course, Alec. She was exceptionally so. You must see what she did took tremendous courage."

Alec took a swallow of whiskey. "I can see what she did was tremendously foolish." His tone was harsh.

"Perhaps," his mother replied, as though considering it. "Her family certainly thought so. The *ton* did, as well, though a few of her friends stood by her, the Countess of Donegall, for one."

"What, the Irish countess?"

"She married an Irish earl, but she's English—the Earl

of Dunclare's daughter, formerly Lady Caroline Swan. She helped Millicent escape that night. The *ton* shunned Caroline for her part in the debacle. We all believed her ruined, but Donegall married her before the end of the season. By all accounts, he dotes on her still."

Alec gave his mother a bland smile. "A happy ending for all, it seems. Do you think Millicent Chase was foolish?"

His mother gave another shrug. "I think it hardly matters now. This all happened years ago. Millicent is dead. What difference does it make if she was brave, or foolish, or both?"

Alec had been staring out the row of French doors that opened into the gardens, but now he turned and faced his mother. "Charlotte and Eleanor tell me Robyn is enamored of Miss Somerset. It was his idea to invite her here. He teased the girls into it."

Lady Carlisle paused for a moment, her eyes fixed on him. Then she nodded. "Ah. I see. You object to Miss Somerset's presence here on Robyn's account?"

"Yes, I do."

The countess folded her hands in her lap. Alec had the distinct impression she was going to choose her words with care. "You are concerned because she has no fortune? Or because of the scandal?"

Alec frowned. "The scandal. The lack of fortune isn't desirable, but it could be overlooked."

"The scandal is decades old, Alec," his mother said. "Certainly a marriage between our family and the Somerset family would revive it, but is this a reason to prevent a match if there is true affection between them?"

Alec was struck dumb for a moment. *Was* there true affection between them? He hadn't even considered that possibility. He'd assumed this was just another one of Robyn's scandals. When had he stopped taking Robyn's feelings into account? He felt a pang of conscience at the thought, but he shoved it back down. His one concern here was to protect the family and the Sutherland name.

"Have you forgotten what it was like, Mother?" he asked softly.

Catherine stiffened.

She hadn't forgotten, and neither had he. They couldn't forget those last few years before his father's death, when the family had been on the brink of ruin.

The girls hadn't understood what was happening, and Robyn had been away at school for most of it, but Alec remembered every single awful moment. Constant threats from creditors. His father hiding in his study with a bottle of whiskey at his elbow, snarling at the servants he was "not at home" to the business associates who called, day after day, demanding to speak to him. There had even been talk of selling Bellwood.

His mother's "friends" had anticipated her downfall with delight. On the surface the countess had maintained her placid calm, but the ordeal had drained her. Alec had seen the effort it took for her to hold her head up amid the gossip and the whispers. Robyn, Charlotte, and Eleanor would have been required to make the same effort had they been ruined. The family had been drowning in debt, the Sutherland name was fodder for the worst kind of gossip, and his mother had been on the brink of collapse.

Alec had been helpless to prevent any of it.

Then his father died. Alec would call his death fateful, but it was nothing as romantic as that. Alec wanted to believe that before death came some sort of understanding, but his father had died very much as he'd lived. Selfishly. Hart Sutherland had drowned himself in whiskey, and left his wife and elder son to pick up the pieces.

Alec had picked them up. Shilling by shilling. Pound by pound. Through sheer force of will and iron determination he'd rebuilt the Sutherland fortune. As was usual with the *ton*, once the fortune was secure, the Sutherland name was promptly resurrected.

He wasn't helpless now. He was the Earl of Carlisle, and he would be *damned* if a mere three years later he'd allow this family to suffer again. His sisters were now at marriageable ages. Their prospects would be damaged by another scandal. Delia Somerset might be brave and intriguing, but she was a scandal waiting to happen. She was disgrace. Disgrace with a beautiful face this time, but disgrace nonetheless. And Robyn—well, he might think he knew what he wanted, but Robyn and Delia Somerset came from different worlds. A marriage between them would lead to nothing but regret and misery.

His mother sighed. "Does Robyn have serious intentions toward Miss Somerset?"

Alec shrugged. "I haven't the vaguest idea. Robyn doesn't confide in me."

"No, he doesn't. Not anymore."

A hollow feeling filled Alec's chest at her words, but he let them pass. "The more pressing question is whether Robyn will do whatever is necessary to secure her if he *is* serious."

He stared hard at his mother.

She went still. "You don't mean . . ."

"That if he truly wants her and I object to the match, he'll seduce her?" Alec shook his head. "As recently as a year ago I would have said there was no chance. That Robyn would never do anything so cruel or dishonorable. But now? I'm not sure. I don't know Robyn anymore."

There was such profound sadness buried in those last few words, and his mother must have heard it, for her face softened as she looked at her elder son. But she didn't reply. They fell into a deep silence, each lost in their own thoughts. Finally, she roused herself. "What do you intend to do?" She searched Alec's face.

"Keep them apart as much as possible until the end of the house party, then send Miss Somerset right back to Surrey," Alec said. "It won't take long for Robyn to move on to some other diversion once she's out of his way."

Lady Carlisle shook her head. "You can't mean you intend to trail after Robyn for the next two weeks? You'll both go mad."

"Not Robyn. Miss Somerset. The girl has barely been out of Surrey. She's never been to a house party like this one, and she's not accustomed to the attentions of gentlemen. A little charm and some harmless flirtation will keep her out of Robyn's way."

He didn't mention to his mother that so far Miss Somerset appeared to find him as charming as a steaming pile of horse dung. Or that he was far more distracted by her than she appeared to be by him. *Or* that even the thought of matching wits with her made his groin tighten.

But Lady Carlisle was frowning nonetheless. "I don't like it, Alec. What about Lady Lisette? You've invited her to the house party, and it's my understanding you intend to propose to her by the end of it. She's accustomed to being the center of attention. I doubt she'll be happy to share yours with Miss Somerset. No." She shook her head. "It's best if you don't interfere with Robyn's business. You can't expect to control every . . ."

Her voice trailed off as something outside the window caught her eye. Alec turned toward the French doors to see what had distracted her, and froze.

Robyn and Miss Somerset were walking together in the garden. One of her hands was tucked cozily into his arm; the other swung a bonnet by the strings. She was laughing up at Robyn, and he was gazing down at her with frank admiration, his lips quirked in a smile.

One afternoon. Alec had spent one short afternoon in his study, and already Robyn looked like a bear with his leg caught in a trap. Alec fixed his gaze on Miss Somerset's laughing pink lips and felt his face harden into a cold, stiff mask. He'd expected to find them together. It wasn't a shock.

The shock was that he was so furious about it.

The countess cleared her throat and Alec turned to her in surprise. He'd forgotten she was there. She wasn't looking out the window anymore. She was looking at him, a strange expression on her face. "I'll leave you to it, then, Alec." She slipped out the door, leaving it open behind her.

What the blazes should he do now? He couldn't just tear across the garden and physically separate them, though every one of his instincts urged him to do something savage, like grab Miss Somerset, throw her over his shoulder, and run off with her. Straight back to Surrey, of course.

No, this situation called for something more subtle. But what?

Just then Alec heard a shuffling noise in the hallway and turned in time to see Lord Shepherdson attempting to mount the stairs.

"Shepherdson!" Alec called, struck with a sudden inspiration. "A word?"

Shepherdson turned, baffled to be summoned by Alec, who did his best to ignore Shepherdson entirely. He shuffled through the door. "Afternoon, Carlisle." He eyed Alec with suspicion.

"Robyn tells me you and he had quite a time of it last night," Alec began, resisting the urge to take a step backward. Shepherdson still reeked of spirits. He probably hadn't been to bed at all yet.

"Damn right. Bloody good time, too," Shepherdson slurred.

"I'm sure. Still, fifty pounds is a lot of money. I'm happy to see you so reconciled to your loss."

"Damn right it's a lot of money," Shepherdson agreed

happily. A few seconds passed while he struggled to process the rest of that sentence, but then his face darkened. "What loss?"

Alec pretended to look surprised. "Why, the fifty pounds you lost. Robyn told me you bet him fifty pounds he couldn't best you in a race from the Prickly Thistle back to Bellwood. You lost. You owe Robyn fifty pounds. He says you're cleaned out."

Shepherdson gaped at him. "The devil you say!"

Alec shrugged as if he couldn't care less. "Ask him yourself."

"Damn right I will!" Shepherdson swayed a bit on his feet. "Have you seen him?"

Alec rolled his eyes. Shepherdson was about as bright as a snuffed candle. "Why, yes, Shepherdson, I have. In fact, he's right outside there." Alec pointed in the direction of the garden.

Shepherdson was able to focus just long enough to spot Robyn through the French doors. "Damn right he is!" he squawked, starting forward.

Alec could pinpoint the exact moment when Shepherdson noticed Miss Somerset. "I say, Carlisle." He elbowed Alec in the ribs. "Who's the tempting armful with Sutherland? Damn fine-looking girl."

Alec just managed to restrain himself from hauling that elbow up behind Shepherdson's back and throwing him out the doors himself. He smiled coldly. "Better hurry, Shepherdson. It looks like they're leaving."

Shepherdson lurched through the French doors. "Sutherland!" he bellowed.

Alec followed him. Miss Somerset looked appalled when she saw Shepherdson barreling toward them, and she immediately dropped Robyn's arm. Robyn looked disgusted, but he bowed to Miss Somerset and hurried off to intercept

Shepherdson before he was forced to make introductions. Miss Somerset was left standing awkwardly in the garden alone, looking as if she didn't know quite what to do next.

Alec felt an unexpected thrill shoot through him. "Alone again?" he asked, joining her. "Why is it I always seem to find you wandering around by yourself?"

"I was just wondering the same thing. Why do *you* always seem to find me?"

Her tone was civil enough, but she couldn't quite disguise the quick spark of temper in her deep blue eyes. Alec realized with surprise he'd been waiting for that spark. Anticipating it.

"I didn't find you yesterday," he reminded her softly. "You found me."

Ah, there it was. That blush. Alec watched it tint her neck with pink and then steal into her cheeks, and his mouth went dry.

"So I did." She met his eyes and held them.

There was something different about her. The hectic color blooming in her cheeks wasn't simply embarrassment, and her chest rose and fell rapidly as she struggled to suppress some strong emotion. She seemed excited, or angry. She still wasn't flirting with him. Not really. But her whole attention was fixed on him, as if she were studying his every move, assessing his every breath. It was far better than flirtation. It was almost as if she were touching him, or as if he were being consumed by that intense blue gaze. *Les yeux des feu bleu* didn't seem so ridiculous to Alec now. The gaze that turned a man to stone.

Alec felt like he was turning to fire.

"You'll allow me to escort you through the rose garden." It wasn't a question, but not quite a demand, either. He held out his hand to her.

She didn't take it. She offered him a half smile instead.

"In your case, my lord, the escort may prove riskier than the solitary wandering."

His eyes dropped to her mouth. That smile was a tease. A torment. He waited, both fascinated and inexplicably angry at the same time. She was going to deny him the other half of that smile. Maybe she was saving all of her smiles and laughter for Robyn.

"Come, Miss Somerset," he said, dragging his eyes away from her lips. "Don't you like roses?"

She shrugged. "Every lady likes roses, don't they, Lord Carlisle?"

"I haven't the faintest idea what every lady likes. At the moment I'm only concerned with what pleases *you*, and you are not *every lady*."

The blue eyes narrowed. "No, but then, one lady is very much like another. We're all rather interchangeable, are we not, my lord?"

She was *daring* him. Was that what was different about her? He wasn't sure, but the look in her eyes made Alec's breath stop in his chest. He didn't know what she expected him to do or say, but the dare hung between them like a glove slapped across his cheek.

"No," he answered at last, opting for the truth. He had to make an effort to keep his voice steady, when every single cell in his body leapt to rise to her challenge. "They're not. Both ladies and roses come in infinite varieties."

Her eyes widened a bit skeptically at this comment, but the smile that had been banished to one corner of her mouth broke free at last and took full possession of her face. The deep pink lips curved upward. She'd never truly smiled at him before. Not with her mouth and her eyes, as she was now. No. He would have remembered the way his stomach tightened in response.

She accepted his hand then. His fingers closed gently around the tips of hers. "I think, my lord, that you enjoy a wider variety of ladies than most gentlemen of my acquaintance."

Alec gazed at her in amazement. Now the cheeky little chit was *teasing* him? It was the last thing he'd expected her to say, and he was startled into a sudden laugh. "Now the word *enjoy*—" he began, leading her back through the French doors and into the garden.

"I'm rather surprised to find the estate has formal gardens at all," Miss Somerset interrupted quickly, as if she regretted her teasing and was now determined to keep him from teasing back. "The grounds leading down to the lake are in the natural style."

They were to discuss landscape gardening now, were they? That was safe enough. Much safer than discussing ladies and roses, and the many different ways one night *enjoy* both. Now, that was a topic that could easily be nudged into more titillating territory.

Alec glanced down at her walking beside him. Her head came nearly to his shoulder. If he pulled her close, it would fit under his chin. The sun caressed the golden brown strands and he thought, absurdly, of warm honey.

She was looking up at him expectantly, waiting for his answer. "I had the formal gardens rebuilt last year." He tried to focus on her conversation instead of the wisps of hair that brushed against her neck or the feel of her fingers resting against his arm. "My father had them torn out when I was young, when Brown's designs were in favor."

"Was your father a man who admired the natural landscape?"

Alec stiffened. He hated talking about his father. "My father was a man who believed he deserved the best of everything. Getting it was what concerned him. I don't believe admiration ever came into it. I doubt he ever considered whether he admired the landscape or not."

He was astonished to hear these words leave his mouth.

Christ. He'd imagined they would make some predictable comments about the beauty of the roses or the fineness of the weather, but instead he'd blurted out that ugly truth as if they were in a confessional, and not a bloody rose garden.

He half expected to find her gaping at him in dismay, but instead she was considering his answer. "And you, my lord?" she asked after a moment. "Did you reinstate the gardens because you admire the formal lines, or because Repton's designs are now the fashion?"

Alec raised one dark eyebrow. He couldn't recall ever being asked to explain himself before, particularly not by a young woman he hardly knew, who was so far beneath his notice. She should be attempting to charm him. At the very least she could pretend to show some of the usual modest confusion he expected when he flattered a woman with his attentions. He was a bloody *earl*, for God's sake, and she was . . . nobody.

But her question was an intriguing one, and worthy of an honest answer. "Are you asking, Miss Somerset, if, like my father, I follow the fashion without any thought or understanding of my own desires?"

She darted a quick glance at him from under cover of her thick lashes. "Yes. I suppose I am."

Her glance was not so quick that Alec couldn't see the spark of challenge was back in the blue depths of her eyes. He stared at her, mesmerized again by the flash of spirit he saw there. She was goading him, but carefully, in the same way one might try to ride a horse that threatened to throw them at any moment.

She was right to be cautious. She was insignificant, his social inferior. As a guest in his house, she was also under his sole protection. One might even say she was at his mercy. Alec was half-ashamed of the desire that shot through him at the thought.

Yet she was toying with him. *Why?*

He didn't realize he'd stopped walking. He took hold of her upper arm and turned her to face him, but resisted the urge to tip her chin up with his finger so she couldn't look away from him. "I'm nothing like my father, Miss Somerset. If I admire something, I know why I admire it. If I desire something, I know why I desire it, and I have it."

He felt a slight tremor pass through her slim frame, but she continued to hold his eyes. For a brief, charged moment the rose garden, the sky, and even the sun faded away until he was conscious only of his hand, wrapped around her arm, the closeness of her body, her eyes searching his face.

At last she nodded, as if he'd told her what she'd expected to hear. "Never mind the consequences?" Her voice was so soft he had to lean forward to catch her words. "That's just what I thought you'd say, Lord Carlisle."

Chapter Nine

With those glittering black eyes holding hers, Delia felt more like a timid gazelle than ever.

"Is it?" he asked. "I'm sorry to be so dull and predictable, Miss Somerset." His tone was pleasant, but Delia detected a subtle, underlying warning. She'd almost call it a growl. Predators growled. Tigers, for instance.

So, she was back where she'd started. Which was unfortunate, since it rather defeated the purpose of this encounter. Unless . . .

She looked pointedly at the place where he still clasped her arm. He took her meaning at once and removed his hand as if he was astonished to find it there in the first place.

Well, that was interesting. He seemed a bit uncomfortable. Perhaps he imagined she'd collapse into hysterics because he'd taken her arm. Discomfort was a promising sign. She may be able to rely on his gentlemanly instincts after all, deeply buried as they undoubtedly were.

"I beg your pardon." He ran a hand roughly through his hair.

She'd thought his hair was simply black, but out here in the bright sun she could see it was shot through with shades of rich chestnut and even a strand or two of auburn. It was longer than it should be. The dark waves just brushed the collar of his shirt. It wasn't quite gentlemanly, that hair. And why did the man always seem to be half-clothed? He wore a coat, but it was open, and he'd shed his waistcoat and cravat, as well. The open top of his shirt revealed a strong, tanned throat and a few stray dark, curling hairs.

Oh, dear. She'd gone a bit breathless. Breathless wouldn't do at all—she needed to keep her wits about her. She forced her gaze away from his throat and those fascinating hairs and peeked at his face.

Say something!

"Oh, don't apologize, my lord." She forced a casual note into her voice. "That is, you're right to beg my pardon for grabbing my arm, but not for being dull or predictable."

You're neither. You're too thrilling by half. Apologize for that.

"I'm pleased to hear I'm right about something." A smile tugged at his lips. "Though I believe this is where you're supposed to reassure me I'm neither dull nor predictable."

Delia stared at him. Was the man a mind reader in addition to possessing a devastating smile? It was unfair that a genuine smile could alter his face so dramatically. She wished he'd offer her the same mocking twist of his lips from this morning, because this new, playful smile scattered her wits like rose petals caught in the wind. Even the dark brown eyes she'd thought so cold yesterday had gone warm and liquid. He didn't look much like a ruthless seducer *now*.

Not that it mattered. Delia tried to suppress the quiver of awareness. She was supposed to focus on his conversation.

What had he just said? Oh, yes! That he'd feel better if she reassured him. What a good idea! That was what one did when one flirted, wasn't it? Reassured. Flattered. Simpered. Batted eyelashes.

"Never, my lord," she declared, but then stopped, puzzled. He stared skeptically at her, his eyebrows disappearing into the dark waves lying across his forehead.

Drat. "What I mean," she hastened to clarify, "is you're neither dull nor predictable."

She beamed at him. *There. That was very good!*

"Such effusive praise, Miss Somerset. You'll mortify me."

But he didn't look mortified. He looked amused. Delia eyed him uncertainly, trying to think of what to say next. She should be gushing, shouldn't she? A simper wouldn't go amiss, either, but she wasn't sure she knew how to simper. Best to stick to what she knew.

Aha! She had it now. "Surely you're accustomed to effusive praise from young ladies, Lord Carlisle?"

You're actually accustomed to quite a bit more than that from some young ladies, aren't you?

The traitorous thought rang in her head but she sealed her lips closed, determined to sever the connection between her brain and her mouth before any unpleasant truths could escape. After all, she didn't need a brain to flirt, did she?

His low chuckle brushed across her nerve endings like a stroke of velvet. "Yes. I have occasionally been flattered by young ladies."

That explains your arrogance. But this didn't seem quite the thing to say, either, so Delia stayed silent and settled for batting her eyelashes at him instead.

His mouth twitched. "But never so *delicately*, or with such touching sincerity."

Delia bit her lip to hide her smirk. *She was much better at this than she'd thought she'd be!* "Of course, certain young ladies do tend to fawn over wealthy and titled gentlemen of the *ton*. That's why such gentlemen are so arrogant and intolerable. They take the flattery to be truth."

Oh, no! For goodness' sake, no!

But it was too late. The words had tumbled out of her mouth before she could stop them. Delia's experience with flirting was limited to the gouty old men and married farmers who attended assemblies in Surrey, but even she knew the last thing one should do when flirting with a gentleman was tell the truth.

This was a disaster. How could she excuse herself? She had drawn breath and was hoping for the best when Lord Carlisle threw back his head and gave a shout of genuine laughter. Delia nearly jumped out of her skin, but her astonishment turned to exasperation as he continued to laugh. She crossed her arms over her chest and waited, fuming.

"I wondered how long you'd be able to keep it up," he gasped at last. The awful man was actually wiping his eyes! "Not very long at all, it seems."

Delia huffed out an irritated breath. "I'm afraid I don't know what you mean, my lord."

"Of course you do, Miss Somerset. You were attempting to flirt with me. You're awful at it, you know. I knew you were lying the entire time, even before you blurted out that last part."

"So you've been laughing at me all the while?"

"You weren't being truthful with me. I simply returned the favor."

It seemed she couldn't rely on his gentlemanly instincts, after all. "I forgot the *ladies* you keep company with are much more accomplished flirts than I could ever hope to be. My own modest skills must pale in comparison to theirs."

"They do." He said it so cheerfully, Delia considered kicking him in the shin. "But don't give up now, Miss Somerset. Why don't you practice some more?" He grinned down at her. "I'll even let you practice on me."

Delia put her hands on her hips and glared at him. She didn't like that wicked gleam in his eye. Not one bit. "I don't think that's a good idea."

"Of course it is. Now," he began, just as if he were a tutor and she a thick-skulled student. "Your mistake is in thinking flirtation is about what you *say*. It isn't. It's about what you *do*."

Delia gave him a sullen look. "That wasn't my only mistake." She hated to admit it, but he was far more clever and perceptive than was convenient.

"Well, you got the setting right. A rose garden is an excellent place to conduct a flirtation. You could start by asking the gentleman which is his favorite rose, or by showing him yours."

"I didn't choose the setting, Lord Carlisle. You did."

"Yes, well, *I* am very good at flirtation, but in this case, for the sake of discussion, let's assume you lured me out into the rose garden for your own licentious purposes."

Her licentious purposes? Despite herself, Delia laughed. She couldn't help it. It was so silly, and he looked so much like a naughty little boy. "All right, we'll imagine, for the sake of discussion, I'm the licentious one in this scenario, and I lured you into the rose garden with evil intent."

She *had* been trying to lure him, but only to find out whether he'd take advantage of a little innocent flirtation on her part. It was what a man bent on seduction would do. Surely *that* didn't make her licentious?

It hadn't worked anyway, so it didn't count.

"Very good. Now, as I said, the rose garden is a perfect setting for a flirtation. It's private, but not so secluded it's improper."

Delia nodded gravely. "I'm glad to hear we're observing the proprieties, Lord Carlisle. I thought you might insist we move this lesson to a deserted road somewhere."

She couldn't have explained why she said it—perhaps to

see that smile twitch at the corner of his mouth? Whatever the reason, she couldn't resist.

He looked amazed, but then an appreciative smile took slow possession of his face. "What you saw on that road was *not* a flirtation, Miss Somerset. I shudder to think where you'll end up if you don't know the difference."

Right where you want me, no doubt.

She'd do well to remember that, but in the meantime she was beginning to enjoy herself. "Please, Lord Carlisle." She waved her hand dismissively. "Even I know the difference between a flirtation and . . ." She hesitated, trying to find a ladylike way to say it.

"Fornication? You have no idea how relieved I am to hear it. Now, you won't catch the gentleman's attention by flattering him, especially a gentleman who's used to receiving female attentions."

"And of course they're the only gentlemen worth flirting with."

"Very good, Miss Somerset." He grinned like a boy again. "You're an apt pupil so far. Everything you say should be pleasant, of course. That may prove challenging for *you*." He raised an eyebrow at her. "But true flirtation comes from your body, not your conversation."

"My body?" Delia swallowed nervously. Surely she shouldn't be discussing her body with Lord Carlisle?

"Yes. You look a little flushed, Miss Somerset. Shall I stop the lesson?" There was an unmistakable flash of challenge in his dark eyes.

"Certainly not." Delia stubbornly met his gaze. She wasn't going to back down *now*.

"Very well. It starts with your eyes."

Delia breathed a silent sigh of relief. Eyes. That seemed harmless enough. "Indeed?"

"Yes. That is particularly good advice for you."

What in the world was that supposed to mean? That she

must rely on her eyes because she had such a sharp tongue? "Why is that, my lord?" she asked, irritated.

"Because your eyes are so unusual, and so extraordinarily beautiful."

Oh, my. Delia's breath stopped in her chest. She opened her mouth to reply, but no words emerged. She hadn't been expecting a compliment, especially not one so lovely.

"Speechless, Miss Somerset? It's true, you know." He laughed softly, but he didn't appear to be amused anymore. "Your eyes could move the most jaded rogue to poetry. Eyes such a dark blue they're nearly indigo. Eyes like glimmering sapphires. Eyes like pools of water, endlessly blue, and endlessly deep." He drew in a sharp breath and continued almost angrily, as though the words were dragged out of the depths of his body against his will. "Hold a man's eyes with your own, or dart teasing glances at him from under your eyelashes. The poor devil won't even be able to remember his own name."

Delia was astonished and mesmerized at once. Had he moved closer to her? Or had she taken a step toward him? She waited, breathless and wide-eyed, for him to continue.

"And your mouth," he said huskily. His eyes dropped to her lips and lingered there. "Your lips. Draw his attention to them. Smile. Laugh."

For one wild moment Delia thought he was going to touch her mouth, could almost feel his thumb brushing gently across her lips. She parted them just slightly in unconscious invitation, and her tongue darted out to wet her bottom lip.

"Yes," he hissed softly, the word ending on a near groan. "That's it. Just like that."

Delia's heart gave a painful thump in her chest. It occurred to her they were very much alone in the rose garden, and somehow what had begun as a jest had turned dangerously intimate. She needed to stop this, to stop him before he said anything else. But she didn't. She couldn't, not when everything in her strained toward him, both anticipating and dreading what he'd say next.

"Use your hands." His voice had gone hoarse. "Touch him. Walk just a little too close beside him so your shoulder brushes against his. Put your hand on his arm, or stroke your fingertips against his palm when he takes your hand in his. Light, teasing touches are the most exquisite torment, for they leave a man aching for more."

His silky, coaxing voice felt like fingertips trailing across her skin, leaving a flush of pink in their wake. His gaze touched her, too, his lids heavy over eyes gone black. An image arose in her mind then, of the woman from the day before, of his hand, slipping into her bodice, seeking and finding her breast. Caressing. The woman had sighed, as if his touch was exquisite torment.

What would his fingers feel like against her heated skin? Visions of his knowing, teasing hands had haunted her ever since she'd heard that fevered sigh. If he touched her, would she ache for more?

Delia waited, trembling, desperate for him to touch her. Her eyes dropped involuntarily to seek his hands.

His arms were rigid at his sides, his hands clenching into fists and then unclenching, as if he exerted the most unbearable restraint over them. A low, pained sound tore from his throat when he noticed her gaze on them.

She wanted him to touch her.

"Will he . . ." she began, but the words were trapped in her throat. She took a deep breath and tried again. "Will he touch me?" Her voice was the barest whisper.

"He'll want to." His voice was low, rough. "He may kiss your hands. But a true gentleman will not—"

He broke off then, and shook his head from side to side as if to clear it. There was a long pause while he stared hard at her, his expression lost somewhere between amazement and fury. When he spoke again, it was as if he'd awakened from a spell. "A true gentleman won't touch you unless he's courting you. At least, that's what I've heard. As you know, Miss Somerset, I'm no gentleman."

His voice had gone cold.

His sneering, sarcastic tone hit Delia like a physical blow. She instinctively staggered back several steps to get away from him, away from a cold fury she didn't understand. She was stunned, much as she'd been a day ago when the coach had thrown an axle. One minute she'd been admiring the scenery outside the window, and the next she was thrown to the floor, her bones rattling as the coach screeched to a violent stop.

He either didn't notice her dazed expression, or he didn't care. "The secret to flirtation is to keep the illusion intact. Once it's shattered"—his icy gaze locked on her face—"the gentleman may be forced to ask himself some unpleasant questions." He closed the distance she'd put between them with one long stride. "For instance, I might ask myself why you'd want to flirt with me in the first place."

His voice was calm, but Delia heard the trace of menace.

To teach you a lesson. This time she didn't have to struggle to keep the truth to herself.

"You've made it plain you don't like or trust me," he said when she didn't reply. "You despise the *ton* in general. I must conclude, then, you have your own private reasons for trying to engage my attentions."

"Why should I like or trust you, Lord Carlisle?" she shot back.

There was a tense pause, then, "You shouldn't."

"You're full of advice today, my lord." She struggled to keep her voice from shaking.

He stared at her, his eyes hard and accusing. "What is your game, Miss Somerset?"

"Game?" Her hands fluttered nervously, like a moth too near a candle flame. She shoved them behind her back to hide their trembling. "I don't know what you mean, my lord."

It was a lie. She *was* playing a game—the very same game he was playing, except she was on the opposite side of the chessboard. If he won, the *ton* would leave this house party whispering in scandalized delight that the Earl of Carlisle had seduced Millicent Somerset's daughter and avenged the insult offered to his father all those years ago. They'd say the Somersets were no better than they should be, that they'd been sent back to the depths of Surrey where they belonged.

Oh, she'd let him think she could be seduced, that she was swooning with desire for him. He'd believe she was ripe for the plucking, right up to the point when he reached up a hand to grasp the fruit. Then she'd dash away to Surrey with her reputation and innocence intact. Unplucked, as it were.

His eyes narrowed. "I think you do."

She shrugged, as if she didn't care what he thought. "As you say, my reasons are my own."

But if she outwitted him . . . ah, if she emerged the victor! An insignificant nobody from some rustic village in God knew where, humbling the powerful and handsome Earl of Carlisle! A Somerset, no less. Then the *ton* would gossip about how history had repeated itself.

"I warn you, Miss Somerset—"

"I'm late for luncheon, my lord," she said in clipped tones. She didn't want to hear his warning. She might feel compelled to heed it, and it was far too late for that. "I find myself in need of refreshment. Good afternoon."

She gathered her skirts into her hands and turned to walk away, back straight and chin held high. She didn't turn back to look at him, but she felt his eyes following her every move until she disappeared inside the house.

Chapter Ten

"Never known you to be a liar before, Carlisle."

Archie took a long, leisurely draw on his cheroot, then blew a wreath of smoke into the air above his head. "You're an unpleasant fellow," he continued genially. "Ill-tempered. Arrogant. Always winning at billiards. But I've never known you to be a liar before."

Alec watched the tip of Archie's cheroot glow a hot red in the relative gloom of the study. He and Archie had retired here after what felt like the longest evening of Alec's life.

He sighed. No use fighting it. "What did I lie about, Archie?"

Archie leaned forward in his chair. "Miss Somerset, of course. You told me she was plain. Sharp-tongued and plain."

Alec rolled his eyes. "I never said—"

"Sharp-tongued and plain," Archie repeated. "A dreadful combination, you said."

"What's the matter, Archie?" Alec asked, grinning a

little, despite his annoyance. "Didn't you think she was sharp-tongued?"

Archie sat back in his chair and blew another plume of smoke into the air, considering. "No. She seemed quite sweet. Lovely, really, and she sure as hell isn't plain."

She *was* sweet. Ruin-a-man-for-other-sweets kind of sweet. Mouthwatering.

"No, she's not plain." That much was patently obvious.

"Neither is her sister," Archie said with a roguish grin. "Remarkable-looking girls, both of them."

"*Les yeux des feu bleu,*" Alec murmured, feeling foolish even as the words left his mouth.

Archie nodded. "Yes. Complicates things for you, doesn't it?"

"Indeed." Whatever else she may be, sweet or sharp-tongued, dreadful or lovely, one thing Delia Somerset most assuredly was, was *complicated.*

"Robyn didn't take his eyes off her all evening," Archie supplied helpfully. "Come to think of it, unless it was to gawk at her sister, neither did Shepherdson."

Alec's mouth tightened. Shepherdson was fortunate to-night's dinner had been a casual family affair, because he wouldn't have survived additional courses with his limbs intact. Watching Shepherdson ogle and drool like an animal over Delia Somerset made Alec unaccountably furious. Of course, he'd have the same concern for any young lady under his protection.

Of course he would.

Tomorrow he'd speak to his mother about changing the seating arrangements. No matter what kind of mischief she was up to, Miss Somerset didn't deserve to have a drunken fool like Shepherdson leering at her from across the dinner table.

"You looked at her a good deal, too, Carlisle," Archie observed. His tone was carefully neutral.

Alec leapt from his chair and paced to the fireplace, unable to sit still for one second longer. God, his muscles ached. He'd been as tight as a noose ever since this afternoon in the rose garden. And when had Archie become so bloody perceptive?

Archie startled at the sudden movement. "I'm not blaming you for looking." He held his hands up defensively. "Any man would."

"I have to watch her, Archie." Alec's voice sounded raw even to his own ears. "It's the only way to keep her apart from Robyn."

He had to watch her. He shouldn't want to watch her.

But he did.

"Not bad work, that," Archie murmured.

Alec leaned an arm against the mantel. "She's up to something."

"Up to something?" Archie stared at him, the forgotten cheroot dangling in his fingers. "What does that mean?"

Alec shrugged. "I'm not sure. She flirted with me."

At least she'd tried to. In spite of his foul mood, Alec grinned. She was hopeless at flirtation, probably because it required some level of deception. It had taken her all of five minutes this afternoon to drop her pretense and blurt out the truth.

Her version of the truth anyway.

"You don't seem too upset about it," Archie remarked. "You look rather pleased, in fact."

Alec's grin faded. "It doesn't make sense. Why would she want to flirt with me? What possible purpose could it serve?"

"Maybe she just finds you charming."

"She doesn't." That much was certain.

"No. Probably not." Archie frowned at his cheroot. "Maybe she's angling for a bigger fish."

Alec was staring into the fire, but at this, his head snapped toward Archie. "What do you mean?"

"Why settle for an earl's younger brother when you may have a chance to hook the earl himself?"

Alec froze. "Why should she think she has a chance to hook me?"

Aside from the fact that I can't take my eyes off her?

Archie gave him a disgusted look, as if Alec were a slow-witted child. "Let's see, Carlisle." He started ticking points off on his fingers. "Her eyes. Her hair. Her skin. Her figure. Why, her figure alone . . ."

But Alec had stopped listening.

Her mouth. He closed his eyes. *Good God, her mouth.*

"What's the matter with you, Carlisle? Do you have a pain? You look like you're in agony."

I am in agony. "I'm fine."

"Well? Do you think she's fishing for an earl?"

"It's possible. I wouldn't entirely dismiss the idea."

It did make perfect sense. If that was her object, this game would be over before it began. Whatever she was playing at, it didn't come naturally to her. That put her at a disadvantage, because he was born to play games.

To play them, and to win them.

Miss Somerset was intriguing and desirable, but in the end it didn't make any difference. It complicated matters, yes, but what satisfaction was to be had in a game too easily won? He did like a challenging game of chess, and it would be much more diverting with a living, breathing queen. Or a pawn? Yes. She was a tempting little pawn. He closed his eyes and imagined smooth ivory under his fingertips, except this ivory was warm, soft, translucent skin.

He could never have her, of course. There *were* limits. But fortunately there was a vast uncharted territory between a few harmless kisses and raising the skirts of a chaste young virgin.

Alec excelled at gray areas. He spent a good deal of time there.

He'd teach Miss Somerset a much-needed lesson about playing games with a man like him—that was, a man ruthless in pursuit of his desires, who enjoyed all of the advantages of wealth and social position. But he'd send her back to Surrey with her virginity intact.

Technically intact.

But she'd know he hadn't taken her because he chose not to, not because he couldn't have had her. It would humble her, and perhaps next time she'd know better.

"Maybe she's trying to make Robyn jealous," Archie said unexpectedly. "Or maybe she's just practicing on you. For when she's alone with Robyn."

A cold knot of fury settled in Alec's chest. "She's not going to be alone with him. Ever. Robyn can't control himself."

He didn't mention he'd nearly lost control of himself in the garden with her today. One more breathless sigh or shy smile and he'd have touched her. If he'd touched her, he'd have kissed her, and he wouldn't have been able to stop kissing her.

"You know, Alec," Archie began, but then paused, as if not sure how to continue.

That caught Alec's attention. Archie very rarely called him by his given name.

"Your father used to say the same thing about you. You resented it bitterly, if you remember."

Alec's body went rigid. "What the hell does that mean, Archie?" His voice was dangerously quiet.

Archie looked him right in the eye. "Stay out of Robyn's affairs. That's what it means."

Alec didn't move or speak for several minutes, but then he slowly shook his head. "I can't do that, Archie. I'm responsible for him. For all of them."

Archie looked hard at him, as if he wanted to say more, but then something like sympathy appeared in his eyes, and he merely nodded.

A tense silence settled over the room while Archie finished his cheroot and Alec stared into the fire. Finally, Archie stirred. "Where is Robyn?"

Alec jerked his chin in the direction of the door. "Playing billiards with Shepherdson."

"Have the ladies retired for the evening?"

"My sisters and Lily Somerset are strolling in the garden. Miss Somerset retired soon after dinner." Alec wouldn't be here if she hadn't. No, he'd be trailing after her, like an infant on leading strings. He didn't enjoy the image.

Alec turned from the fire and paced over to the tall glass doors that looked out onto the formal gardens. The cold, wet winter had given way to a glorious spring. The evening was warm for April, and the moon was nearly full. It cast its cool, unearthly light over the rose garden.

How romantic. It was a perfect setting for Miss Somerset to cast her lures, especially now he'd taught her just how to do it. Robyn would be dazzled, helpless, at the mercy of those brilliant blue eyes and lush pink lips. Alec's hands clenched. Tempting glances, smiles, teasing touches . . .

He'd been staring into the garden, unseeing, when his eye was caught by a flash of deep blue. Blue, in the rose garden? Unless he was mistaken, there were no blue roses.

But Miss Somerset had been wearing a violet blue gown this evening at dinner.

Without a word to Archie, Alec opened the door and slipped out onto the terrace. He searched the muted light of the garden, straining for another flash of what he was certain was a blue silk gown.

She was standing near the center of the garden, facing away from him, partially obscured by a towering rose arbor. Her deep blue gown fluttered and shimmered in the light breeze, and the moon drew gentle fingers of pale light over her smooth white shoulders and neck.

"I thought you'd retired for the evening, Miss Somerset."

Her slim body stiffened, and a slight tremor shivered down her back. She turned toward him. "I left my sketch book here this afternoon when we . . ." Her voice trailed off. "I came back down to fetch it." She was holding the book tightly against her bosom, as if for protection.

"You never told me which rose is your favorite." His voice was at once both soft and rough.

She turned away again to look at the roses. "May I guess yours instead?"

Alec drew a deep breath and held it. She never said what he expected her to say, and he seemed to be always holding his breath when he spoke with her, waiting to hear what she'd say next. Anticipating it.

He moved closer to her, because all at once the distance between them felt unbearable. He was close enough so the edges of his coat brushed against her gown. Alec closed his eyes and breathed in the delicate scent of her hair, so much more tempting than the scent of the roses surrounding them. Jasmine? The faintest hint of honey.

"Please," he murmured near her ear, not sure anymore what he asked for.

She paused for a moment, and for one delirious instant Alec thought she was savoring his nearness. Then she walked a few steps closer to the center of the garden and came to a halt next to a tall rose with a large, luxuriant red bloom. "This one, my lord." She turned to face him. "The red. So extravagant." She ran the tips of her fingers over the lush scarlet petals.

Alec understood immediately. The rose, spectacularly red, with its heavy sweet scent, was the showpiece of the rose garden. All of the other roses were just a prelude to it. Every path in the formal garden ended at this one elaborate bloom.

But Alec didn't spare the ornate red rose a glance. He fixed his eyes on hers, then reached out and wrapped his long fingers around her delicate wrist. He turned and walked deeper into the garden, past the arbor and into the dark shadows even this bright moon had failed to illuminate.

"Here." He tightened his fingers around her wrist and drew her forward, close beside him. "This is my favorite."

This rose hadn't yet fully opened. The outermost petals were still gathered around the center of the bloom, but the barest hint of deep gold was visible inside, peeking shyly out from the protective embrace of the velvety cream-colored petals.

"So delicate," Alec murmured. "Like honey in a bowl of cream."

He reached out and stroked a finger against one of the milky white petals. When he drew his hand away, a drop of dew clung to his fingertip. Still clasping her wrist, Alec turned her hand up and slowly drew his damp finger across the center of her palm.

Miss Somerset gasped softly. Desire shot through Alec, so powerful it nearly sent him to his knees. If he ran his tongue over her soft palm, what would she do? Would she cry out? What would she taste like?

Honey and cream.

Alec looked into her face. Her lips had parted and her breathing was shallow and quick. His own breathing had gone ragged.

But her eyes . . . they were enormous in her pale face, and though they were soft with desire, he also saw uncertainty there. It cleared his head just enough for him to be able to look closely at her.

She seemed very young, standing in the moonlight, gazing at him with wide eyes. She *was* young, she'd recently lost both parents, and despite the dangerous game she was playing, she was an innocent. His jaw went tight and a surge of shame dampened the desire raging inside him.

She was brave. Exceptionally so. Surely you must see that, Alec?

His mother's voice echoed in his head. He'd scoffed at her words at the time. She'd been speaking of Millicent Chase, but the same could be said of the young woman trembling before him. Where did an inexperienced little chit from Surrey get the courage to challenge an *earl*? She had no family, no wealth, and no social standing. No protection, even, except what he was willing to afford her as a guest in his house. And she was toying with him. Engaging in a contest of wills, as if she believed she had a prayer of winning it.

It was almost laughable, except Alec didn't find it amusing. He found it fascinating, and painfully arousing. He was riveted by her.

But there was something else, too. He recognized, deep in his gut, that if he kissed her now, it was, somehow, like moving his king across the chessboard to take her queen. God help him, but he wasn't yet ready for the game to end, even if it meant winning it.

It was this more than anything that made him release her hand and step away from her, away from the temptation of her parted pink lips and sweetly curved body. "It grows late, Miss Somerset." He stepped to the side and inclined his head toward the house. "You should retire now."

She hesitated long enough for Alec to notice the amazement on her face, but then she passed by him without a word. It took all his control to keep from wrapping his arm around her waist to pull her back against him.

"Delia?" he murmured as soon as she was safely out of reach.

She froze. Waited.

"Sweet dreams."

Chapter Eleven

She did dream, of cream-colored roses and knowing black eyes. A long, damp finger dragging lightly across the center of her palm. A voice, whispering.

Don't you like roses? If I desire something, I have it. Sweet dreams, Delia.

She dreamed of exquisite torture.

"Delia?"

She half opened one eye.

"Delia! Why would you hide something so important from me?" The voice was close to her ear, and a determined hand shook her shoulder. Delia opened the eye all the way and groaned. Lily stood by the side of the bed, looking at her with an injured air.

"You never used to keep secrets from me," Lily accused, putting her hands on her hips.

"Wha—" Delia croaked. She forced the other eye open and rolled over onto her back. "What secret?"

Which secret?

Lily rolled her eyes. "That Robyn Sutherland is courting you!"

Delia stared at Lily, her mouth dropping open. "He is?" *Now* she was awake.

Lily let out a long-suffering sigh. "Well, perhaps he's not courting you yet, but he grows more besotted by the day. Look what he sent you this morning." Lily gestured triumphantly to the table by the door.

Delia shot up to a sitting position in the bed. The little table was dwarfed by a huge bouquet of cream-colored roses, their delicate golden centers aglow in the late-morning light coming through the window.

"I—I—" Delia stuttered. Was she still dreaming?

"Let's see what the card says." Lily riffled carefully through the delicate blooms.

It wasn't a dream. It was a nightmare. Delia closed her eyes and prayed desperately.

Please don't let there be a card. Please . . .

"There's no card," Lily said, disappointed.

Thank God. Delia cast her eyes heavenward. *I promise to be good for the rest of the house party.*

"My goodness, Delia. Here we are just arrived and already Robyn has sent you flowers!" Lily smiled with delight. "It's quite romantic."

Good God. What a mess. Delia resisted the urge to pull the covers over her head. "Lily, Robyn isn't courting me. What a ridiculous notion! He must have noticed me admiring the roses, and he sent them to be kind."

No need to clarify who *he* was, or explain that kindness had nothing to do with it.

"Oh, it's very kind indeed," Lily agreed with a smirk.

"Lily," Delia began in a warning tone. "Promise me you won't discuss this with anyone else, especially not Ellie and Charlotte. Promise me, Lily."

"Oh, all right. I promise. Now you'd better get dressed.

You've already missed breakfast and you'll miss luncheon if you don't hurry. It's not like you to sleep so late. Are you well?"

No. "Yes, very well. You look rested this morning," she added after a moment, noting the color in Lily's cheeks and her clear, bright eyes. "I think Kent agrees with you."

Lily smoothed her hands down her pristine skirts. "Yes. I feel well, and I have an enormous appetite this afternoon, so I won't wait for you to dress, but will see you at luncheon." She hurried toward the door that connected her room to Delia's. "Stop worrying, Delia," she said before she disappeared into her own room.

Stop worrying. If only it were that easy.

Delia crawled out from underneath the warm cocoon of blankets and lowered her feet to the floor, pausing when her bare toes brushed against the edge of her sketchbook. She'd thrown it on the floor last night in a fit of temper. Now she was tempted to kick it the rest of the way under the bed. Let a maid find it and turn it over to Lord Carlisle after she was safely returned to Surrey.

Blasted thing. Delia snatched it up and ripped the offensive page from the book. She stared at it. Nothing less than fear of its discovery could have tempted her from her room last night, not after the afternoon encounter with Lord Carlisle in the rose garden. But leave her room she had, and now Lord Carlisle haunted her dreams *and* her reality.

If he did intend to seduce her, he'd had ample opportunity to attempt it last night. She closed her eyes and remembered the trail of fire his finger had left against her palm. Her cheeks flooded with heat. Instead, he'd sent her back to her room as untouched and unkissed as she'd left it.

Which was just as it should be, of course. She wasn't in the least disappointed.

But if a wicked rake doesn't kiss a young lady when they're alone in a moonlit rose garden, mightn't it mean he doesn't intend to? She thought there were rules about such things. They might even be written down somewhere. If not, then they should be. *A Treatise on Rakes*, written for Susceptible Young Ladies, by a Lady of Distinction.

Not that *she* was susceptible to Lord Carlisle's charms, of course. Still, what was he playing at? She wouldn't put it past him to tease her to amuse himself. She doubted he'd abandoned his dastardly plot to seduce her, but one thing was certain. A caress with one finger and a few dozen roses did not add up to a wicked seduction.

She considered destroying the sketch, but at the last minute she slipped it under her pillow instead, then washed her face and dressed simply in a pale pink day gown. It was the perfect dress for fading into the background, and that was what she intended to do until Lord Carlisle moved another piece across the chessboard.

She made her way down the stairs and into the breakfast room. The doors that led onto the terrace had been left open to catch the afternoon light and the fresh breeze. Ah, that was better. Delia stepped outside and turned her face up to the sun, relaxing a bit for the first time since she'd woken up to find Lily hovering over her.

"Good afternoon, Miss Somerset."

Delia froze. Lord Carlisle sat at the table, his long fingers wrapped around a cup and his legs stretched out in front of him, crossed at the ankles. He looked the picture of relaxed ease, but he pinned her with his dark eyes and tracked her every move as she hesitantly approached the table.

He was alone. Worse, he looked devastating this afternoon. He wore an exquisitely tailored dark green morning coat that emphasized his wide shoulders, and snug buff-colored breeches that seemed to cling for dear life to his muscular thighs. His hair was damp, as if he'd just bathed. Delia had to shake her head to dislodge the tantalizing image of that long, lean body reclined in a warm bath.

Oh, why did he have to be so handsome? Drat it. And where in the world was Lily?

"Tell me," he said, his tone pleasant. "Did you have sweet dreams? I know I did."

"I didn't—" She cleared her throat. "I didn't dream of anything." Her denial sounded a bit too emphatic.

"Ah. Pity." A sensual smile drifted across his lips. "I had very vivid dreams myself, and when I awoke, I found I had a powerful desire for honey."

Delia gaped at him, her face heating again at his suggestive tone. He may have let her escape untouched last night, but this morning he looked very much like a man bent on seduction. "Honey?" She slipped into a seat several spaces away from his. Perhaps it would help if she put the table between them.

But he abandoned his place at the table in favor of the chair across from hers. "Yes. I dreamed of something smooth and sweet on my tongue." He leaned back in his chair and grinned cockily, obviously gratified by her deepening blush.

Delia would have preferred not to hear him say the word *tongue* just then. "I'm not sure why you'd bother to tell *me*, my lord," she said, trying to gather her wits. "I suggest you have a word with your cook."

He chuckled. "Perhaps I will." There was a brief pause while he studied her face and she avoided looking at his. "The roses I sent you this morning are from the hothouse. I thought you might enjoy the chance to see them in full bloom. Do you like them?"

Yes, because they're your favorite, and I wouldn't have expected them to be.

"Don't all young ladies like roses?" Much to her dismay, her voice emerged as a breathy whisper.

"We've established you're not like most young ladies." He frowned a bit, as if that puzzled him, then searched her face, as if he could find the answer to the mystery there. "Surprising, like the honey in the center of the petals."

Delia felt her heart begin to pound in her chest, but she was excused from having to answer by Robyn, who stumbled onto the terrace at that moment, looking as if he wasn't sure how he'd gotten there.

"Good morning." Robyn dropped into a chair across the table from his brother. "My, Alec, don't you look smug this morning. I suppose that's no different from every other morning, though."

"Good *afternoon*, Robyn. It's always a pleasure to see you before teatime."

Robyn glowered at this, but his face altered completely when he turned his attention to Delia. "How sweet you look today, Delia." He gave her a slow smile and raised her hand to his lips.

"Good afternoon, Robyn." She looked up to return his smile but faltered in confusion when she caught the murderous look on Lord Carlisle's face. His entire body had gone rigid and his long fingers were wrapped so tightly around the delicate porcelain cup, Delia was afraid it would shatter in his hand.

What in God's name was the matter?

Lily and Charlotte followed Robyn onto the terrace just then, however, and Lord Carlisle's expression went blank, as if he'd pulled the shutters closed on a window.

"Where have you been, Lily?" Delia hissed when Lily settled into the chair next to hers.

Lily looked at her in surprise. "I ran to fetch Charlotte. She didn't care for her hat, so we went back to change it, and then I remembered I wanted to bring my hat . . ." She trailed off with a shrug.

"You don't need your sister's escort at Bellwood, Miss Somerset," Lord Carlisle drawled. "I hope you feel free to wander the house alone anytime you wish. And the gardens."

His eyes drifted slowly from her flushed face to where her hand rested on the table next to her plate. He didn't touch her, but his dark gaze scorched her skin, as surely as if he'd run a finger across her palm. Her eyes darted to his face, and her breath caught in her throat at the heat smoldering there. She knew he was thinking of how he'd touched her last night. "Especially the gardens," he murmured.

Delia stared at him, helpless against the stark desire she saw in his eyes. His fingers flexed, and for one awful, wonderful moment, she thought he'd touch her.

But the spell was broken by Eleanor, who approached the table and dropped into the chair next to Lily's. "Another fine day." She gazed up at the sky and sighed. "What a shame. One does feel compelled to do something active when the weather is fine, and I feel quite lazy today."

"We could sit on the terrace and laugh at the guests as they arrive," Charlotte suggested. "That would require very little effort, and it could be quite entertaining."

"I'm for that." Robyn slouched farther down in his chair. "I'm destroyed this morning." He ran a careful hand through his hair. "Good God—I think even my hair hurts. Where did you run off to last night, Delia? I looked for you after dinner, but you'd disappeared."

Lord Carlisle grinned at her, one eyebrow raised as if he dared her to tell Robyn how she'd ended her evening. "I thought I saw Miss Somerset admiring the roses last night."

Delia scowled at him, then turned back to Robyn. "Well, I—that is, I decided to retire early."

"But not *too* early," Lord Carlisle interrupted. "Isn't that right, Miss Somerset?"

"Not early enough," Delia snapped, but she regretted her sharp tone when Lily turned to stare at her, shocked at her rudeness. Now it was Delia's turn to sink down in her chair. She lowered her eyes to her cup of coffee, determined not to notice Lord Carlisle's teasing.

"Then it's your fault I feel so awful this morning, Delia," Robyn said, missing the exchange entirely. "I spent the evening with Shepherdson and he was on a tear last night. If you'd been there," he said with a wink, "I'm sure I would have behaved myself."

Ellie snorted. "Doubtful."

"Yes, Robyn," Alec said, shaking his head. "I think Miss Somerset's presence could tempt a man to all kinds of mischief."

He grinned widely at her. Delia raised an eyebrow at him but refrained from blurting out the first thought that came to mind—her presence last night hadn't tempted *him* to mischief.

Which was just as it should be, of course. She wasn't in the *least* disappointed.

He did seem bent on mischief this morning. Delia frowned, suddenly thankful she hadn't destroyed her sketch. He must have some fiendish reason to single her out for such torment. The sketch was a handy reminder that Lord Carlisle wasn't to be trusted. No matter how ludicrously handsome he was.

"You should have come with us last night, Delia." Charlotte gestured to include Lily and Eleanor. "Mother has transformed the wilderness into a kind of pleasure garden for the house party. We found the loveliest little pavilion tucked away behind a thick clump of bushes. I'm sure Mother put it there in case the young ladies wished to hide from overly persistent gentlemen." She looked pointedly at Robyn.

"Why are you looking at me?" Robyn protested. "After Delia went to bed, I was off to the billiards room with Shepherdson."

"And likely in no condition to be persistent with anyone, on any subject," Alec said.

"Well, it was really Archie we were avoiding," Charlotte admitted. "He appeared late in the evening and followed Lily about all night, pestering her with his ardent admiration."

"Indeed?" Delia darted a look at Lily.

Lily stirred her tea. "Yes, but there is nothing to worry about, Delia. Ellie and Charlotte are very good at finding hiding places."

But Delia *was* worried. She'd been so busy dallying with the earl she'd failed to keep a watchful eye on Lily.

Eleanor noticed Delia's dismay. "It's an excellent hiding place. Secluded, and only for the ladies. You should come with us tonight, Delia."

"I'll come, of course."

Robyn perked up. "A secluded pavilion full of young ladies and gentlemen not permitted? Ellie, Charlotte . . ." he began in a wheedling tone.

Eleanor shook her head. "No, Robyn. You're as bad as Lord Shepherdson, and he goes everywhere with you. You'll ruin everything if we let you come."

"But I promise to behave, Ellie," Robyn coaxed. "You'll never even know I'm there, and I promise to send Shepherdson away. Not just for tonight, but for the rest of the house party."

"Oh, very well. I suppose you can join us, but we'll banish you at the first sign of improper behavior."

"Does that rule apply to everyone?" Alec asked. "Will the ladies also be banished if they behave improperly? For instance, what if Miss Somerset were to try and flirt with me? Would she be banished from the party?"

Eleanor turned her attention to her other brother. "You are a dreadful tease, Alec. Anyway, I never saw *you* after dinner last night at all. Who knows what sort of deviltry you were engaged in? Will you be mysteriously disappearing again this evening?"

"No. It seems I'll be at the pavilion with your party, Eleanor, protecting Miss Lily from Archie and Miss Somerset from Robyn. Or Robyn from Miss Somerset, if necessary." His teasing dark eyes lingered on Delia.

"You're hardly a saint, Alec," Charlotte said tartly.

Too right! Delia couldn't resist shooting him a little smirk.

He smirked right back at her, and even had the effrontery to look delighted. "Oh, I think I can behave at least as well as Robyn does." He leaned back in his chair and stretched out his legs so his booted feet brushed against Delia's skirts.

She jerked her legs away from him, glaring.

"Oh, we can be assured Alec will behave, Charlotte," Robyn said. "He'll be at his saintliest for the remainder of the house party if he intends to be engaged by the end of it. Though why you'd want to get leg-shackled, Alec, I couldn't say—"

Robyn was interrupted by the sound of voices in the breakfast room. It was the countess, speaking in low, soothing tones. Delia did not recognize the other voice, but it was high and fretful. "You cannot imagine the dust and dirt, my lady! Intolerable. Mother retired to her chambers in a nervous fit."

Lady Carlisle came out onto the terrace looking rather hunted. "Ah, here we are." She stepped forward with a relieved expression when she spied her four children.

A dark-haired young lady swept along after her hostess, prattling away and daintily carrying the hem of a green gown in figured silk trimmed with matching wide green ribbon at the waist and hem.

Of course. The earl's future betrothed was arriving today. Had arrived, in fact, in all her aristocratic perfection. Delia took one look at Lady Lisette's mouthwatering gown and glanced down at her own plain pink gown with a sigh. She looked as if she'd just emerged from Hannah's scrap pile.

Lord Carlisle and Robyn rose at Lady Lisette's entrance. Robyn bowed and then flopped back into his chair, but Lord Carlisle took her hand, smiled down at her, and murmured something Delia couldn't hear.

It was easy to see why she was the belle of the season. She had straight, inky black hair gathered into a thick knot at the back of her long neck, smooth creamy skin, and melting dark brown eyes, thickly lashed and sparkling. Her gown fit her slim, petite figure to perfection. She flashed a pretty smile up at Lord Carlisle, who hovered over her as if she were in danger of collapsing at any moment into an extraordinarily graceful swoon.

Delia just resisted the urge to roll her eyes. Dainty, delicate ladies did seem to bring out a man's protective instincts. Judging from Lord Carlisle's ridiculous fawning, he wasn't an exception to that rule.

Well, it appeared Lord Carlisle preferred the gaudy, extravagant, showy red rose after all.

All of his formidable attention was now focused on Lady Lisette. He seemed to have forgotten Delia was even there. Which was just as it should be, of course. She *wasn't* disappointed. Not in the least. She was simply shocked at how effortlessly he drifted between ladies, as if he were wandering from rose to rose in the garden. Today he was every inch the aristocratic gentleman of the *ton*. A few days ago he'd been the rake who debauched village women on public roads.

And last night, for one brief moment with her, he'd been a gentleman. But who would he be tomorrow? The man who seduced an innocent young lady for sport and then sent her back to Surrey in disgrace?

Lord Carlisle drew Lady Lisette forward as if she were a prize to be presented to the rest of the gathering. "Lady

Lisette, you know my brother, Robyn, and my sisters, Eleanor and Charlotte. This is Miss Delia Somerset and her
sister, Miss Lily Somerset. This is Lady Lisette Cecil."

Delia and Lily nodded politely. Lady Lisette's wide
brown eyes narrowed. She measured Delia and Lily, noting
every detail. "These must be the two young ladies your
mother spoke of," she finally said dismissively. "She said
you have guests from the country."

There was a patronizing emphasis on the last words, as
though "the country" were equivalent in Lady Lisette's opinion to Dante's seventh circle of hell. Delia glanced at Lily,
who continued to sip her tea calmly. She gave Delia a tiny
shrug and a bland smile as if to say, *Who cares what she
thinks?*

Eleanor must have caught the subtle glance between
them. She sat up in her chair. "Yes, Delia and Lily were kind
enough to come from Surrey to be our guests for the house
party. They're our *particular friends*, you see."

It sounded like a warning, and Lady Lisette seemed to
consider it one, for her eyes went as cold and hard as stones.
"How lovely they were able to accommodate you, Eleanor.
It's kind of you to invite them. I imagine you don't have the
opportunity to spend much time in society, Miss Somerset."

This last comment was directed at Delia. Before she had
a chance to answer, however, Charlotte spoke up. "Eleanor
and I just returned from a visit to Surrey ourselves, Lady
Lisette. I think you'd be pleasantly surprised at the society
there. We found the company quite entertaining."

Lily held her napkin delicately to her lips at this blatant
lie, but Lady Lisette didn't seem to notice. Her eyes were
still fixed on Delia. "I would be surprised indeed," she said
in a bored tone; then she turned to Lord Carlisle with a
little toss of her head. "Alec," she cooed, laying her hand
flirtatiously on his arm. "I find myself in need of some ex-
ercise after such a long ride in the carriage. Isn't there an

archery course set up on the west lawn? I thought I saw it as we passed."

Alec gave her an indulgent smile. "There's an archery course, and cricket and bowls and a variety of other games. I think you'll find my mother has gone to great lengths to ensure our guests are well entertained over the next few weeks."

Lady Lisette inclined her head, as if the entertainments had been set up for her own exclusive enjoyment. "Splendid! You will escort me?" She turned away, clearly intending to exit the terrace on Alec's arm and leave the rest of the party behind.

Alec turned back to the group at the table. "Does anyone else fancy a game before luncheon?"

The last thing Delia wished to see at the moment was Lady Lisette deploying her arrows, but Ellie, who seemed to have shaken off her laziness, shot at once to her feet. "Archery sounds like just the thing. Come along, everyone! We don't wish to keep Lady Lisette waiting."

Robyn uttered a defeated groan, but he dragged himself to his feet and offered his arm to Delia. "Shall we go shoot some arrows at some targets?"

Delia glanced at Lord Carlisle as he walked away with Lady Lisette on his arm.

Don't tempt me.

Chapter Twelve

The sun continued to shine with cheerful insolence, despite Eleanor's wishes to the contrary. Guests began to arrive in earnest, and they crowded onto the lawn, drawn outdoors by the warm rays. The ladies, dressed in light muslin gowns of every color, strolled across the green expanse, peeking at the gentlemen from underneath the cover of their parasols. The gentlemen flapped and paraded around the lawn bowl court or the cricket pitch like a disorganized flock of birds, flaunting their skills for the ladies. It was all very romantic and picturesque. Delia would have enjoyed it immensely were it not for the blot on the landscape that ruined the effect.

The blot—Lady Lisette, hanging on the earl's arm, his dark head inclined toward hers. He seemed to be fascinated with whatever it was she was saying. Perhaps she was regaling him with tales of the dirt and dust on the roads? Describing her mother's recent nervous fit? Asking if he could help her locate Surrey on a map of England? Whatever it was, Delia hoped with all her heart he found it tedious.

"May I ask, Eleanor," Charlotte began peevishly, "why you were suddenly taken with a fit in favor of archery? I thought we were going to sit on the terrace and mock our guests as they arrived?"

"Too right," Robyn echoed. "Laze on the terrace all day and mock the guests. I'm destroyed this morning, you know, Eleanor."

Delia believed him. She thought he'd offered her his arm to be gallant, but gallantry seemed to be too taxing for Robyn this morning. The farther they walked, the more she began to suspect she was the only thing holding him upright.

"You're destroyed *every* morning, Robyn," Eleanor snapped.

Delia glanced at her curiously and noticed her mouth was a thin, tight line.

"Whatever is the matter, Eleanor?" Charlotte quickened her steps to catch up to her elder sister, and laid her hand lightly on Ellie's arm.

Eleanor thawed a little at the affectionate gesture. "I'm anticipating a game of archery with about as much enthusiasm as the rest of you. It's the dullest sport imaginable. But I refuse to leave Alec alone with that, that . . ."

She stopped, as if words failed her.

"That scheming snob?" Charlotte asked.

"Precisely," Eleanor said in grim tones. "I'm willing to spend a tedious afternoon at archery if it means delaying Lady Lisette's transformation from scheming snob into the Countess of Carlisle."

Lily looked surprised. "Oh, dear. You don't care for Lady Lisette?"

Delia said nothing. She trudged along, propping Robyn up and trying to hide the fact she was hanging on Eleanor's every word.

"No," Eleanor said shortly. "I don't relish the idea of

having her for a sister-in-law. Of course, my opinion would be nothing if I believed she'd make Alec happy."

Delia took a deep, quiet breath. Her heart jumped and thrashed in her chest until she was sure everyone could hear it. Alec and his lovely companion had disappeared around a corner, but Delia could still picture his dark head bent toward Lady Lisette, and the annoyingly enthralled expression on his face. Either he didn't find gallantry as taxing as Robyn did, or Eleanor was mistaken.

Robyn looked at his sister with a puzzled expression. "But Alec *asked* Mother to invite her. She's the toast of the *ton*, after all. If he wants to marry a scheming snob, I suppose that's his choice. Have you ever known Alec to do anything he didn't want to do, Eleanor?"

"Don't you see, Robyn?" Eleanor asked. "He *thinks* he wants to marry her, but the point is, Alec is most assuredly not in his right mind!"

"Not in his right mind!" Robyn repeated. "He seems remarkably sane for a man not in his right mind. I've known very few madmen with Alec's arrogance."

"At the risk of offending you, Robyn," Eleanor said, "I feel compelled to point out your brain is addled from an excess of whiskey, and has been for the better part of the past year. Otherwise you would have noticed a change in Alec's behavior since Father died."

There was a brief, charged moment of silence. Then Charlotte said, "He *is* the Earl of Carlisle. He has responsibilities now."

"Yes," Eleanor agreed. "And while it may be important for *the Earl of Carlisle* to marry the toast of the *ton*, I'm not sure Lady Lisette's much-vaunted charms would tempt *Alec*."

Was there a difference? Which of the two of them was toying with her? Whichever one it was, Delia felt sure it wasn't the same man who was courting Lady Lisette.

"Come, Eleanor," Charlotte said. She took Ellie's arm. "Do let's hurry and catch up with them."

The two of them hurried off, tugging Lily along with them. Robyn seemed disinclined to hurry, and Delia wasn't sure he could make it to the archery field without her, so they quickly fell behind. Robyn was silent, apparently lost in thought, but after a while he turned to Delia. "Do you think Alec is mad?"

"Must one be mad to consider marriage to Lady Lisette?" she asked, a bit ashamed of using such an obvious ploy.

Say yes say yes say yes.

He shrugged. "Not at all. She has her choice of suitors. Her father is a wealthy earl and she's a noted beauty."

Well. What a *very* long list of *very* fine qualities.

"I don't think Lord Carlisle is mad, no." A rake, yes. A tease, certainly. A base, conscienceless seducer? Possibly, though it was doubtful she'd ever find out now Lady Lisette had arrived.

Which was just as it should be. She wasn't in the least disappointed.

Delia doubted that young lady would allow her prey out of her sight for the remainder of the house party. She'd clutched at his arm as if she were starved, and he were a tender, delectable morsel of beef.

A frown settled between Robyn's brows and he was silent for some minutes. "If my father were alive, he'd insist his heir marry the toast of the *ton*. Perhaps that's what Ellie means—Alec is determined to make a spectacular marriage, as any proper earl would. I'm *damned* grateful I'm not the Earl of Carlisle."

"Perhaps," Delia replied. It was bad enough Lord Carlisle's hard body, teasing black eyes, and low, mocking laugh haunted her dreams, but it was becoming more and more difficult to see him only as a powerful, deceitful, arrogant earl. She'd fit the pieces of his character together so easily, only to have the puzzle knocked from her hands and spilled to the floor. Now it was as if she were missing pieces, or trying to force together pieces from a dozen different puzzles.

They had reached the west lawn by this time. Delia scanned the field and her heart sank. Most of the guests had gone off for luncheon. Ellie, Charlotte, and Lily had taken three targets lined up next to one another on the far side. The empty space next to them, the space for Delia and Robyn, was the one right beside Lord Carlisle and Lady Lisette.

There was no help for it. Delia stepped forward to take her place but stopped abruptly, her eyes widening.

Lord Carlisle stared at her, his eyes gone black with rage. "Where the devil have you been?" He kept his voice low, so only she could hear him.

Delia gaped at him, astonished. *Maybe he was going mad.*

"What do you mean? We were walking from the terrace."

"It took you long enough!" Lord Carlisle ground out. A muscle twitched in his tightly clenched jaw.

Robyn joined them and laid a hand on his brother's shoulder. "No need to get worked up, brother," he soothed, eyeing Alec as if he were a rabid dog who'd begun to foam at the mouth. "No need to unsettle yourself. We're here now. I apologize for keeping the party waiting."

Robyn turned to Delia then. "Are you an accomplished archer?" He motioned to the servant who held the bows and a quiver of arrows. The man stepped forward and Robyn selected a bow for her.

"I'm afraid not." She smiled at Robyn, determined to ignore Lord Carlisle's murderous expression.

But Lord Carlisle wasn't about to be ignored. "Perhaps you shouldn't play the game if you're not sure of winning, Miss Somerset." He glowered at her over Lady Lisette's shoulder. Lady Lisette turned and looked at Delia as if she were trying to remember who she was.

"Do you only play games you can win, my lord?" Delia asked, trying to keep her tone mild to hide the fact she was becoming nettled. *What in the world was the matter with him?*

"I do tend to win those I play." His dark eyes never left her face.

"Oh, I'm sure that's true," Lady Lisette gushed, trying to catch Lord Carlisle's attention.

His gaze remained fixed on Delia.

"I find that difficult to believe, my lord." Delia held up the bow Robyn had selected for her and adopted a shooting stance. "Overconfidence more often leads to failure than success, and no one wins every time."

"That one is too large for you, Delia," Robyn interrupted. He selected another bow from the servant. "Here." He stepped behind her, so her back was pressed against his chest, and his arms went around her. He placed her hand on the belly of the bow, closed his own hand over the top of hers, and together they pulled the bowstring back. "That's better," he said huskily into her ear.

Delia held the bow motionless, staring down the sight line to the target so she could avoid looking at Lord Carlisle. She didn't need to look at him to know his eyes bored into her. She could feel the heat of his gaze on her face, her body. She suppressed a shiver.

"Games would be dull indeed if we always knew the winner beforehand," Robyn said, oblivious to the tension in the air. He stepped away from Delia. "No one would ever want to play."

"Oh, I don't know, Robyn." Lord Carlisle seemed to be making a great effort to keep his voice even, but Delia heard the fury underlying his casual tone. "There are certain games where engaging in the play is tremendously satisfying, regardless of whether one wins or not. Have you ever played a game like that, Miss Somerset?"

Delia lowered the bow and turned around to face Lord Carlisle, but she had to fight the urge take a step backward when she saw his expression. He was white-faced and furious, as if he held on to his control by the merest thread. She swallowed. Either Robyn was right and Lord Carlisle had indeed gone mad, or they were no longer discussing archery.

"Oh, I know just what you mean, my lord," Lady Lisette interrupted eagerly. "I find it quite satisfying to shoot arrows, regardless of whether I hit the target or not."

Charlotte made a noise that sounded like a muffled laugh. Alec ignored both Lady Lisette and his sister, however, and remained focused on Delia with such furious intensity she began to feel like a butterfly pinned by its wings.

"Miss Somerset?" Lord Carlisle barked.

He wasn't going to let it go. "Yes, I have, my lord," Delia said hotly, losing her temper. "But my pleasure in a game depends almost entirely upon my partner. Any game is enjoyable if one's partner is pleasant, whereas if one's partner is insulting and bad-tempered, that same game becomes a misery."

Lord Carlisle laughed at this. "I'm afraid I can't agree with you, Miss Somerset. I find my pleasure in a game to be much, much greater when I'm matched with a *worthy* partner. It's the challenge that stimulates."

Over Alec's shoulder Delia saw Lady Lisette's puzzled expression. Lily and Charlotte fiddled with their bows and pretended not to listen, but Eleanor was staring at Delia and Alec, openmouthed, clearly listening to every word. *And speculating.* Delia felt a hot flush start at her neck and surge into her cheeks.

Robyn cleared his throat. "Ah, yes. Of course, that is, it's important one's partner . . . Ladies? Are you ready to shoot?" He'd obviously decided a change of topic was in order.

The ladies murmured their assent. Delia gripped the belly of the bow and pulled the bowstring back tight enough so it dug painfully into her fingers. She held, noticing that the head of her arrow trembled slightly.

She shot. Her arrow hit the white petticoat of the target.

It was a bad shot, and no wonder. Her hands shook with a combination of embarrassment and rage. She glanced to her left at Lady Lisette, who looked smugly pleased with herself and annoyingly lovely, her countenance tinged a delicate pink with victory. Her arrow had hit dead in the center, the gold heart of the target.

The gentlemen clapped politely, but Lord Carlisle didn't look at the targets. He watched Delia, his eyes moving insolently over her, one eyebrow aloft and a grim half smile twisting his lips.

All at once she started to envision a new target.

Robyn handed her another arrow, then stepped back and smiled his encouragement. Delia nocked the arrow and was just about to release the bowstring when she saw out of the corner of her eye that Lord Carlisle was next to her. She stiffened, holding the string taut as he leaned in closely—so closely she felt the heat of his body behind her. "Does our game please you, Delia?" He was so close his whispered breath tickled her ear. "I hope so, for I ache to give you pleasure."

Delia gasped, and her fingers twitched on the string. She watched in despair as the arrow flew over the top of the target into a stand of trees behind it. It disappeared from view just as Lady Lisette's arrow hit the center of the target with a firm snap.

"Bravo, Lady Lisette!" Alec called heartily, walking over

to her side and leaving Delia blinking at the space in her
target where the arrow should have hit. "An excellent shot."
He gave Lady Lisette an admiring look.

All right, then. As far as Delia was concerned, that shot
was her last. She'd had quite enough of games for the afternoon.

"No matter, Delia," Robyn said. He held out another arrow for her. "As Eleanor said, it's a ridiculous game."

Delia eyed the arrow. "It will be less so if I leave the field."
She gave him a rueful smile. "I believe I'll take a walk.
Perhaps I'll go and search for my arrow in the trees."

"Wait here for a moment. I'll come with you." Robyn
took the bow from her hand and left her alone for a moment
to return it to the servant.

Delia had hoped they might be able to sneak away without anyone commenting, but Lord Carlisle dashed those
hopes as soon as he saw she'd relinquished her bow. "Leaving so soon, Miss Somerset?" He made a disappointed noise
in his throat. "So easily discouraged," he added, shaking
his head in mock dismay. "You'll never perfect your game
if you give up so easily."

Eleanor, Lily, and Charlotte turned to regard Delia, as
did Lady Lisette, who shot her a look so full of venom Delia flinched. Her cheeks burned with embarrassment.

"I find I don't enjoy your game, Lord Carlisle," she said
through clenched teeth. "I don't wish to pursue it." She let
her glance slide behind him to Lady Lisette. "It appears to
me you have another game to attend to. I believe I'll leave
you to it."

Lord Carlisle studied her raised chin and stubborn expression and his face went cold and hard. He didn't spare a
glance behind him but leaned toward Delia. "Oh, it's far too
late for that, Miss Somerset. The game is in play now, and
it has become so stimulating I find I can think of nothing
else."

Delia didn't answer for a moment, just gazed over his shoulder as if something of great interest unfolded there.

Don't goad him. Don't reply at all. Simply walk away.

But she was furious, both at Lord Carlisle and at herself, because she'd started this madness in the first place. She ignored the voice inside her head and instead gave a little shrug and met his fierce black eyes. "I wonder, my lord," she murmured, forcing a smile, "if that means I've already won?"

Robyn returned the arrows to the servant and hurried back to her side. "Shall we?" He offered her his arm.

"Yes." She took Robyn's arm, but she kept her eyes on Lord Carlisle's face.

He glanced down at the place where her hand rested lightly on Robyn's arm, and then back up at her face. His black eyes burned into hers. "The game has just begun, Miss Somerset," he said under his breath as she and Robyn turned to walk away. "May the worthiest player win."

Chapter Thirteen

Alec batted away the hanging basket of purple pansies tickling his forehead and squinted into the dark, picking his way down the smudged, irregular shape at his feet. He hoped it was the pathway that led to the pavilion Eleanor had mentioned at luncheon this afternoon.

Had that only been this afternoon? It felt as if days had passed since then.

He'd spent half the morning giving himself a stern lecture about the perils of seducing virgins, and when he'd come down for luncheon, he'd been in perfect control of himself. Then Miss Somerset had walked onto the terrace, her skin dewy and her golden brown hair waving in tempting little curls around her face, wearing a muslin gown that made her look like a sweet confection laid out especially for him, and just like that his tight control had been swept away by a surge of lust that left him dizzy. He'd wanted to devour her, but he'd settled for teasing and provoking her instead. He'd been marveling at the profound effect her glittering eyes and flushed cheeks had on certain parts of his anatomy when Lisette arrived.

It went rapidly downhill after that. *The damn archery.* It had seemed like such a good idea—the perfect way to keep Lisette distracted without having to devote much of his attention to her, leaving him free to watch Miss Somerset.

Damn it. How had it all gone so terribly wrong?

He'd watched her, all right. Watched her leave the archery field and disappear, with Robyn panting after her. The rest of the day had been a complete waste of time. He'd been trapped with Lisette, pretending to be enthralled as she alternately shot arrows at the target and coy glances at him. Simper, shoot. Simper, shoot.

He didn't recall Lisette being this tiresome. He'd thought her pretty enough when they'd met, with her waterfall of dark hair and her melting brown eyes. He'd danced with her and found her pleasant. She danced beautifully. She laughed at all the right times. Her conversation was light and charming. Her family lines were impeccable, and her fortune was impressive. He'd have no trouble working up the enthusiasm to bed her. In short, she was the kind of young lady a wealthy, influential earl should choose as a wife.

He'd had a word with his mother, and Lisette had appeared at the house party as if she'd been conjured out of a magician's hat. All that was left now was for him to do his part—that was, smile, be pleasant, and court her until such a time when he could prostrate himself before her and beg her to become the Countess of Carlisle. Lady Lisette expected it. Her parents expected it. Alec's own mother, while perhaps not overjoyed by the prospect, expected it as well.

The trouble was, Alec was bored. Fickle, too, obviously, because he'd decided he preferred wavy golden brown hair to black, and he'd rather look into deep, thickly lashed eyes the color of bluebells than dark brown ones.

He'd been wild this afternoon, half-crazed with fury

when Robyn touched Delia. Robyn had stood so close to her Alec just knew he'd been enveloped in the scent of her hair. Robyn had wrapped his arms around her and pressed his body against hers, and Alec had thought he'd become violent. When Delia and Robyn left the archery field together, he'd been a hair's breadth away from charging after them.

He clenched his fists at the thought. He'd lost control of himself today. He didn't lose control. Ever. He certainly didn't lose control over some inconsequential chit from Surrey, no matter how tempting she might be.

It was a temporary madness, thankfully. It would end as soon the house party was over and Delia Somerset faded back into obscurity, where she belonged. Once she was returned to her proper place, he could return to his—courting Lady Lisette until such a time when she could conveniently become Lady Carlisle.

Then what?

An unwelcome image arose in Alec's mind of endless clipped green lawns and rows and rows of archery targets. Of him, holding quivers full of arrows and watching as Lisette fired one after another, hitting the dead center of the target perfectly, time after time.

Well, what of it? It was what he wanted. It was only this bloody game that made him behave like a tantrum-throwing child. How a sharp-tongued little rustic like Delia Somerset could offer him a serious challenge he couldn't explain, but since she'd arrived, it was as if Bellwood had been transformed into a massive chessboard, and he was locked in the most intriguing game he'd ever played.

He never could resist a challenge. That was why he was battling his way through hedges and darting down every half-lit twisting pathway in the garden. The challenge. It had nothing to do with the bluebell eyes, or fistfuls of shimmering golden brown hair. A stubborn little chin. Smooth, soft white skin and delicious deep pink lips. Arrows flying in unpredictable directions. Honey and cream.

Where was the damn pavilion? He paused, listening. He thought he heard low laughter and voices over to the left, behind a stand of shrubs trimmed to look like sea animals of some kind. And was that . . . Yes. He distinctly heard a high-pitched squeal.

Where females were squealing, Robyn couldn't be far behind.

Alec pushed his way through the layers of leafy marine animals and stepped into a small clearing. Soft light glowed in the branches of the trees above a small pavilion hung with baskets of lacy blue flowers and trailing green leaves. A small group of young ladies and gentlemen lazed on the divans, flirting and tousing one another.

Alec scanned the faces. His sisters were both there, and Lily Somerset. Robyn and Archie had also coaxed their way into the little Sapphic paradise, though judging from the giggles and squeals, both gentlemen had gone back on their promises to behave themselves.

Eleanor was right—it was a perfect little pavilion tucked into a perfectly intimate corner of a perfect miniature Vauxhall Gardens. Perfect, that was, but for one thing. Miss Somerset wasn't there. He should be pleased to see she was nowhere in Robyn's vicinity, but instead he felt an unexpected surge of disappointment.

"Alec!" Eleanor called, spotting him. She motioned for him to join them. He stepped farther into the clearing and Eleanor came down from the platform to meet him. "What are you doing lurking in the shadows?"

"Swimming?" Alec glanced at the seascape surrounding them. "Drowning, more accurately," he muttered under his breath.

Eleanor raised one inquiring eyebrow. "Lady Lisette is

looking for you." Her tone was so ominous it sounded more like *Run! Before Lady Lisette finds you!*

"You make that sound quite dire, Eleanor."

She shrugged. "Take it as you will. But swimming or drowning, beware of the little silver hook dangling in the water." Eleanor wiggled her fingers in his face. "You may just get reeled in when you least expect it."

Alec rolled his eyes. He wasn't in the mood for clever sisters.

"I told Lady Lisette I hadn't seen you yet this evening, which was true enough at the time. I believe she went back to the drawing room to search for you. Will you go find her?"

Alec had no intention of looking for Lady Lisette right now. He was going fishing for someone else entirely. "Eventually."

"Very well." Eleanor gave him a bland smile. "But before you do, will you do me a favor? Delia went off into the garden by herself a few moments ago. Would you mind fetching her for me?"

"Why would she go off by herself?" Alec asked, giving Robyn a sharp glance.

"To look for Lily. You see, Archie was teasing Lily again, so Lily slipped off in a bit of a huff to escape his attentions." Eleanor ticked each point off on her fingers. "Then Delia became concerned that Lily was wandering alone in the garden and went off to find her. But as you see," she added, as if this convoluted explanation made perfect sense, "Lily has returned. Archie has promised to behave, but Delia is still missing. Then Lady Lisette came looking for you."

Alec blinked. "It sounds like a twisted game of hide-and-seek."

"Indeed. But if you'd rather go straight to Lady Lisette, I can always send Robyn off to find Delia."

Send Robyn. To find Delia. Who was wandering alone

in a romantic, softly lit, flower-draped garden. A garden with hiding places around every corner and at the end of every pathway.

Just like that, there it was again—a wild, consuming fury. A red haze burned in front of Alec's eyes. "No! That is . . ." He lowered his voice with an effort. "That's not necessary. I'll go find her."

"Very well." Eleanor gave Alec a gentle push back in the direction from which he'd come. "She went in that direction. She can't have gone far."

Alec retraced his path through the shrubbery. Eleanor was wrong. Delia *had* gone too far. She'd gone much too far, and so had he. He should return to the drawing room at once. He should find Lisette, fetch her a glass of ratafia, and spend the rest of the evening congratulating her on her superb skills with an arrow. He should be—

Alec stopped in the middle of the pathway and peered through a thick cluster of branches. Was that a hanging basket of flowers? A swathe of rose-colored silk draped artfully from a tree? No. It was a silk gown. Delia had been wearing a silk gown that same color this evening at dinner. He should know. He'd spent enough time staring at it.

He just stopped himself from vaulting through the thicket of branches to the adjacent pathway, and if he dashed down the pathway and around the corner like a schoolboy trying to escape his math's tutor, who was there to see it?

She stood with her back to him, a slender, sweetly curved column of deep rose against the lush greenery. Her hair was gathered into a loose twist and tied with a dark pink ribbon. Soft, golden brown tendrils floated in waves about her neck.

Alec's heart thundered in his chest and the truth slammed into him with each frantic rush of blood through his body. It wasn't the game that maddened him. It was *her*.

He wanted her. Badly. He wanted to come up behind her and place his lips on that soft, white neck, and urge her slender body back against his so she could feel his heat, his desire. When his lips touched her neck, her throat, she'd moan his name. She would know it was *he* who held her.

His own dark possessiveness shocked him. Another truth surfaced, one that had whispered at the edges of his consciousness all afternoon. He hadn't been only furious today on the west lawn. He'd been jealous.

He moved forward as though in a trance, but before he could touch her, she turned. He saw the moment when it dawned on her she was in a secluded part of the garden alone with him. Her eyes widened. Panic, stubborn determination, anticipation—all of these expressions crossed her face in a split second.

Anticipation? Alec caught his breath.

But then it was gone. She wiped every emotion from her face as quickly as the incoming tide wiped the footprints from the sand. She'd become good at that. Her face had been an open canvas only days ago. Before long she'd resemble the rest of the *ton*, with a face as cold and unrevealing as a marble statue. The realization felt like a fist landing hard in his stomach.

Alec cleared his throat. "Eleanor is looking for you. She sent me into the garden to find you."

"Did she?" She reached up to pluck at some low-hanging leaves from a branch above her.

Alec watched her fingers close around the glossy green leaf. "She noticed you hadn't returned to the pavilion. Lily has returned and Archie is on his most gentlemanly behavior. Eleanor didn't like the idea of you wandering alone in the garden."

"For good reason, it seems." She twirled the leaf in her fingers.

Alec didn't deny it. He moved several steps closer to her, aware she couldn't leave the alcove pathway without touching him as she brushed by.

"Tell me, my lord," she said. "Is there a lascivious noble-man lurking around every corner of this garden?"

"Alec." He moved another step closer to her, so close he could see the way the rose-colored gown turned her eyes a deeper shade of blue. "All noblemen are lascivious, aren't they?"

A small frown appeared between her brows. "What does that mean?"

Alec reached behind her head and plucked a leaf of his own. He rolled it between his fingers, savoring the feel of the cool, slick skin. "Just that you seem to prefer it when people fall neatly into place. All ladies like roses. All noble-men are lascivious. I suppose it's easier that way."

She shook her head. "I didn't say all lords—"

"You didn't need to. Your scorn for the *ton* is obvious."

She didn't deny it, which perversely pleased him.

"I have every reason in the world to despise the *ton*, my lord," she said. "But even putting my mother's case aside, I don't trust people who place the expectations of society before every other consideration, even happiness."

Alec frowned. He thought of his prospective bride, who waited for him in the drawing room while he chased this infuriating, irresistible woman all over the garden. He thought of his own mother, who'd been sacrificed to a mis-erable marriage. He thought of all he'd done and all he'd continue to do to keep Robyn away from the woman who stood before him. Was he sacrificing Robyn's happiness?

No. She was wrong. She couldn't understand the obliga-tions he had to his family and the Sutherland name. For one moment Alec bitterly envied her the simplicity of her life. Her freedom.

He held her eyes and slowly shook his head. "It's not as simple as you make it sound. Aristocrats or not, we all act out of a desire to protect our family." His voice dropped to a husky drawl. "Here you are, wandering around the garden searching for Lily to protect her from the attentions of a lascivious lord." He tipped her face up to his with a finger under her chin. "This part of the garden is dark and remote, and you're alone. I can't decide if you're daring or merely foolish, for you must have known I would search until I found you."

He trailed the tip of his finger down her chin to her neck, stopping at the pulse that beat in the base of her throat. "I'll have a word with Archie about Lily," he murmured, riveted by the faint flush that rose in her cheeks at his touch. "Despite his ardor, Archie is harmless."

"What about you, Alec?" She took a deep breath, and when she spoke again, her voice was low and breathy, challenging. "Are you harmless?"

She'd never called him Alec before. "Not to you." He caught a loose tendril of her golden brown hair and rubbed the long, soft strands between his fingers.

They stood for what felt to Alec like an eternity. They might have been two motionless statues adorning this quiet corner of the garden, but for their breathing, which deepened and quickened as moment after moment slipped by and neither of them was able to look away.

Alec let the strands of her hair slip through his fingers and laid his palm against her face. His middle finger pressed behind her ear to test the wild fluttering of her pulse. He tensed when she gasped softly, the sound profoundly erotic in the otherwise silent garden.

"So soft, like warm silk." He lightly traced her jaw.

He took another step toward her, close enough to feel the silk skirts of her gown brush against his thighs. Her deep blue eyes grew huge in her face, but she didn't back away from him.

"Tell me to stop, Delia," he whispered urgently, his voice both a command and a plea. "No," he growled when she dropped her eyes. "Look at me." He captured her face in

both hands and tilted it up to his so she had no choice but
to *see* him. "You shouldn't play with a man like me," he
managed to whisper, just before his lips descended and
crushed hers beneath them.

God, she was sweet—so soft and sweet. *She's innocent.*
But the frantic words in his mind were no match for the wild
desire flooding through him, catching him in its relentless
undertow. He took her mouth roughly, starved for her. His
tongue traced the seam of her lips, seeking an opportunity
to surge inside.

She opened to him with a soft cry that went straight to
his groin. Alec groaned when her shy tongue met his urgent
thrusts, and then he was lost inside the hot honey of her
mouth. His lips slid over hers, teaching her, coaxing her
until her tongue stroked eagerly against his, wet and slick
and devastating.

He couldn't get enough of her mouth, her skin. He wanted
to bury himself inside her until he drowned in an ocean of
warmth and rose-colored silk. In some dim recess of his
mind Alec knew he was losing control. *It's just a kiss.* He'd
kissed many, many women.

But not like this—*never* like this. The soft strokes of her
tongue against his made him wild. My God, what was she
doing to him?

Be gentle.

Alec took a deep breath, pulled the night air into his
lungs, and forced himself to slow, to calm. His restraint was
rewarded when she melted against him with a breathy sigh.
She wound her arms around his neck and he felt her fingers
slide into his hair. Her palm brushed the back of his neck
and Alec was sure he'd go mad from the caress, because it
wasn't enough.

He trailed his fingers from her neck down to her throat
while he nipped lightly at her bottom lip and made teasing,
shallow forays into her mouth with his tongue. She made a

strangled, impatient sound and tightened her fingers in his hair to pull his head down, seeking a firmer contact with his lips.

"Hush," he whispered, soothing her.

His fingers lingered at the base of her neck to stroke the soft skin there. He smiled triumphantly against her lips when he felt the frantic beat of her pulse and heard her quickened breathing. He slid his other hand down to her waist, hot against the silk of her gown, and stroked her there, urging her body against his.

She was so warm. Everywhere he touched her she was warm and breathless and *alive*. Every stroke of his fingers against her skin, every touch of his tongue, made her sigh and gasp. She shivered with pleasure and he shivered with her, astonished at the depth of her passion.

He followed the path of his fingers with his lips, trailing hot kisses along her neck. He stopped briefly to lick the sensitive skin behind her ear, then moved down her throat to taste her fluttering pulse. He moved lower, then lower still. With one shaking finger he traced the narrow band of lace at her neckline, let his finger stroke just inside the fabric, against her hot skin.

"So beautiful," he murmured. "So lovely, sweet." He dragged his other hand up her rib cage, slippery against the silk. She strained toward him, and his hand was inches from cupping her breast.

She wore a low-cut gown—had she thought of him when she chose it? Had she known the swells of her perfect white breasts would make his mouth dry with want? Had that been her intention? A sliver of sanity stabbed into his passion-fogged brain. It would be a clever move, to render him helpless with desire. He couldn't play the game if he was on his knees.

Or had she chosen the gown for Robyn?

Christ—what was he doing?

Alec groaned in defeat and grasped Delia's shoulders to push her gently away from him. He ran one shaking hand through his hair. When he spoke, his voice was harsh from frustration. "Go back to the pavilion." Fury surged through him at sending her straight back to Robyn, but he had no choice. He had to get away from her *now*. If he looked into her eyes or at her kiss-swollen lips any longer, he'd take her back into his arms, and they would both be lost.

She didn't reply. It was as if she hadn't heard him. She raised shaking hands to her face as though they weren't a part of her body, and her cheeks flooded red with shame. Before he could utter another word, she brushed past him and fled down the garden path.

He gazed after her, watching the rose-colored silk disappear into an ocean of dark green.

Chapter Fourteen

"Hand me the brush, Delia. I'll do it myself." Lily held out her hand impatiently, frowning at Delia in the mirror.

Delia laid the brush in Lily's palm. "I told you, Lily. You need Hyacinth. I have no talent with hair." She collapsed on top of the bed, avoiding her sister's eyes. "I can brush it out for you, and then we can just tie it with the green ribbon. It will look very nice."

Lily tilted her head this way and that, examining the effect in the mirror. "Very well," she replied at length, sighing. "It's just that I rather hoped for a little more than *very nice* this evening. This isn't a country dance in Surrey, you know."

Delia rose and joined Lily at the vanity, and for a second they both gazed at their two similar reflections in the mirror. "I know, dear, but you always look beautiful, no matter how we dress your hair." Delia tried to smile.

"What shall we do with yours?" Lily ran the brush

through Delia's hair, which still hung in loose waves down her back.

"Oh, the same as always, I suppose," Delia replied, without interest. She turned to the wardrobe to sift halfheartedly through the slim selection of dinner gowns. The blue would do, but Lily was right. It *would* be wonderful to have a special gown to wear. She thought of the delicious green figured silk gown Lady Lisette had worn the day she'd arrived. She'd looked like a butterfly in it. A fretful, petulant butterfly, to be sure, but a butterfly nonetheless.

Alec hadn't been able to take his eyes off her.

Delia pulled the blue gown out of the wardrobe with a little more force than necessary and laid it on the bed, then stood back and regarded it with a small frown.

Lily pulled her long braid over one shoulder and ran the brush through the wavy ends, regarding her sister in the mirror with narrowed eyes. "You look pale, Delia. Have you been sleeping well?"

Oh, certainly. She'd been sleeping splendidly, like a veritable babe in arms. A kitten in a silk-lined basket. A fuzzy baby chick still nested in its egg. A bear during winter hibernation. Up until three days ago, that was, when Alec Sutherland had kissed her. Not just once, but over and over again. Now she wasn't sleeping. She was lying in her bed, remembering the way her lips opened helplessly under his, and how his hot tongue had slipped into her mouth. How her body had leapt to quivering, burning life under his touch. When she did sleep, it was fitfully, and she dreamed of his fingers brushing lightly across her bodice and the tops of her breasts. When she awoke, she was breathless and panting, aching for him.

Once again, if he meant to seduce her, he'd had ample opportunity. So then why had he stopped? He'd pushed her away almost desperately, as if he couldn't trust himself not to touch her again. She'd been afraid to look at him, afraid she'd see triumph or smug satisfaction on his face, but when she'd managed at last to raise her eyes to his, he'd looked . . . nearly *wild*. He'd wanted her. She knew it—her every instinct screamed it. Yet he'd touched her so gently, and murmured to her so tenderly. He hadn't seemed at all like a man in the midst of a calculated seduction.

But then, what did she know about such things? Perhaps this was what seducers did. Made you dream about them. Made you ache for them. It hadn't occurred to her when she began this madness that he could *make* her want him like this. But he had, and it had shaken her. She hadn't been toying with him that night in the garden. She wanted him as much as he wanted her, and it was this more than anything that haunted her when she awoke in the night.

Perhaps Alec had been shaken, too, for he hadn't approached her or spoken to her since those disastrous, exquisite moments in the garden. He hadn't left Lady Lisette's side over the past few days. He'd walked with her, their two dark heads close together as if they shared some delicious secret. He'd escorted her through the gardens and down to the lake. He'd taken her into dinner every night. His intentions toward her couldn't be any clearer. He was the model of an eager suitor. Delia could almost believe he'd forgotten the game entirely, forgotten the passionate kisses in the garden. But every moment of every day since, he watched her with such heated intensity she thought his eyes would singe holes in her clothes. Those hot, dark eyes followed her everywhere.

Lily laid the brush down on the dressing table and walked over to the bed. They stood together and stared down at the blue gown. "A dark blue satin trim would look nice with it, I think. Fashionable, too. If we stare long enough, do you think it will sprout Brussels lace?"

"No, I don't," Delia snapped, "so there's no point standing here waiting for a miracle."

Lily turned to look at her sister with wide, bewildered eyes. "Delia, I know something is bothering you—" she began, but she was interrupted by a brisk knock on the door. Lily hurried over and opened it, then stood back in amazement as a small troop of maids crossed the threshold. Ellie and Charlotte followed, issuing orders as they sailed into the room.

"I think Miss Somerset's hair first, Bridget." Eleanor moved forward to give Delia a quick kiss on the cheek. "Is this your gown for the evening?" she asked, spying the blue dress laid out on the bed. She ran a practiced eye over it. "Lovely color." She tapped her finger against her chin. "It will suit you nicely, Delia."

Eleanor turned to the waiting maid. "Some silk flowers and ribbons twisted in Miss Somerset's hair, Bridget, but first, can you fetch that dark blue satin ribbon I had? We can add some trim here." She pointed to the neckline of the gown. "Here, as well." She indicated the bodice. "Miss Somerset has such a lovely bosom," she added with a naughty grin. "Charlotte? What do you think about your ice pink silk for Lily?"

Delia and Lily stood openmouthed as the maids scurried into action. The pink gown was produced and gratefully accepted. Hair was curled and piled high. Ribbons, silk flowers, and satin trim flew from hand to hand. By the time Delia and Lily were laced into their gowns, flowers, ribbons, and scraps of fabric littered the floor.

"You spoke too soon, Delia." Lily studied her reflection in the mirror with satisfaction. "Never underestimate the possibility of a miracle."

It would be a bloody miracle if he survived this evening.

Alec surveyed the modest gathering. It was mostly neighbors from the surrounding estates and a few close friends who'd arrived early from London in anticipation of the ball. The evening seemed to be progressing much as he might expect. Archie was flirting with Mrs. Ashton. Lady Lisette and her mother were deeply engaged in a conversation with Lord and Lady Barrow, which suited Alec's purposes perfectly. He didn't want Lisette underfoot just now.

Alec was impeccably dressed in severe black evening attire. He stood next to the fireplace, a snifter of brandy in his hand, looking every inch the elegant lord of the manor.

He was ready to explode.

He hadn't spoken to Delia in three days, not since his disgraceful loss of control in the garden. He hadn't touched her again, either, but he could still feel her warm, silky skin under his fingertips and taste the sweet honey of her mouth on his lips. It was as if his body had sprouted nerve endings he never knew he had, for the sole purpose of remembering what it felt like to touch and taste *her*. He couldn't trust himself with her. He realized that now. But every moment he didn't spend with her was another moment Robyn would. The past few days had proved that.

Alec resisted the urge to tear at the tight cravat at his neck and glanced across the room. Robyn greeted a few friends and returned a few coquettish glances, but he was restless and distracted. His eyes kept darting toward the door. Alec watched Robyn's restless pacing and took a deep swallow of brandy. His brother looked about as relaxed as a stallion ready to be taken to stud. With every day that passed, Robyn grew more enamored of Delia.

She had to leave the house party. At once.

A ripple of subdued excitement passed through the room. Alec turned toward the door, and at once he forgot about Robyn, his brandy, and his tight cravat. Delia had entered, her arm linked with Eleanor's. Charlotte followed behind with Lily. The energy in the room changed subtly, the way it does when a captivating guest arrives. Heads turned. Alec saw more than one male gaze linger.

Delia's hair was piled high. Tiny dark blue silk flowers peeked out from among the thick wavy tendrils. Long curls escaped and brushed her smooth white shoulders. Her pale blue gown was not lavishly trimmed. It was not in the first stare of fashion, either, and compared to some of the other gowns in the room, the neckline was almost prudish. She wore no gems at all—only a small length of blue ribbon around her white throat. It was almost laughably quaint, but it made no difference. Alec drank her in greedily. He couldn't tear his gaze away from her.

"Delia!" Robyn crossed the room to Delia's side with an eagerness that drew the attention of the other guests. Alec stiffened as Robyn raised one of Delia's white-gloved hands to his lips.

He started across the room toward them. It had to be done, and it was best done quickly. "Good evening, Miss Somerset." Alec bowed. His formal tone sliced through the intimacy. "You look very well this evening," he said, perfunctorily enough.

Delia curtsied and touched one hand self-consciously to the ribbon at her neck. "Good evening, my lord. Thank you."

"Mother asked you to escort her into dinner this evening, Robyn," Alec said, turning to his brother. "I believe she hopes to avoid the attentions of Major Lytton." He gestured across the room to his mother, who was speaking to an elderly gray-haired gentleman in uniform.

"Of course." Robyn paused to raise Delia's hand slowly to his lips once more, then bowed and walked across the room to offer his arm to his mother.

"May I take you in, Miss Somerset?" Alec offered her his arm.

She looked up at him in surprise, but after a brief hesitation she accepted his arm, just as he'd known she would. She was far too gracious and well-bred to refuse his escort. They entered the dining room, where Alec seated her at the head of the table, then deliberately took his seat across from her. There was no seat to her right.

How would she react when she realized Major Lytton, who was seated to her left, was as deaf as a post?

Delia raised puzzled blue eyes to his and then glanced around. Lady Cecil and Lady Lisette were seated farther down the table near the countess, and both of them were glaring daggers at her. Delia's face flushed with embarrassment. She dropped her gaze to the napkin in her lap and kept it there as the soup course was served.

Alec did his best to ignore the way his chest tightened at her expression. He signaled to the footman, who stepped forward and filled their wineglasses. "Do any of your acquaintances in Surrey hunt, Miss Somerset? The major is an enthusiastic huntsman."

"I'm afraid not." She still wasn't looking at him. "I don't care for hunting, my lord."

Major Lytton sprang into life. "What, a hunt?" he shouted. "Capital, Carlisle. Capital! I predict excellent sport this winter!"

Delia jumped, startled; then her eyes narrowed on Alec. A tempest had begun to gather in those blue depths. Oddly, Alec was relieved. He could tolerate her anger, but not that look of hurt betrayal.

The footman placed soup tureens in front of them. "You *do* ride?" he asked her, managing to sound just a little dubious.

Delia had been about to sample the consommé, but she put down her soup spoon with a sharp metallic click. "Do you imagine I never learned to ride, my lord?" she asked. "Of course, in Surrey we have no Hyde Park, so perhaps you think there is no reason for ladies in the country to learn to ride at all? There is no Rotten Row. No parade of aristo-crats in shiny curricles and fashionable gowns. No fine horses. No opportunity to see and be seen. Oh!" she added, as if she'd just understood him. "Perhaps that's what you mean by *hunting*?"

"Hunting in Hyde Park?" the major yelled, going red in the face. "On Rotten Row? Oh no, my dear. Dangerous, that. Someone could get hurt." He looked at Delia reproachfully.

"Quite right, Major." Alec ignored Delia's outburst, as if he'd also gone deaf. "Quite right." He took a sip of his wine. "Did you bring your riding habit to Kent?" he asked, return-ing his attention to Delia, who looked as if she'd lost her appetite.

"Yes, of course." She sounded a bit deflated. "I'd hoped to ride through the grounds. They're too large to see on foot."

"Are you a competent rider, Miss Somerset?"

"Competent!" Major Lytton shouted indignantly before Delia could reply. "My dear Carlisle, every man in Her Maj-esty's service can ride."

"Of course, Major. Forgive me. Miss Somerset?"

She glanced at Major Lytton. "Perfectly competent, yes."

The major, absorbed by his consommé, had drifted back into obliviousness.

"I'm riding out tomorrow morning to see one of the es-tate's tenants," Alec said. "It means riding over a large section of the western grounds. I would be pleased to have your company."

She blinked at him in surprise, but then an unguarded look of longing crossed her face. That strange, hollow feel-ing surged in his chest again, but he ruthlessly shoved it back. She'd set this game in motion, and she'd proved herself a worthy opponent. Now he was going to oblige her to play it, even if watching her face light with anticipation nearly stopped his breath, and even if he was suddenly appalled at the thought of coldly manipulating her.

"Will Robyn accompany us? Or your sisters?"

Alec's face went rigid at the mention of Robyn's name, and his attack of conscience evaporated. "Certainly. The entire party is welcome, though I doubt any of our friends will be in a state to rise early tomorrow morning for a hard ride." He jerked his head toward the other end of the table.

She followed his glance. Eleanor was absorbed in a conversation with Archie and Robyn, helped along by liberal servings of wine. Charlotte and Lily had their heads together, giggling. It didn't look as if any of them intended to retire early.

"I must see my tenant tomorrow," Alec said, "but if you're afraid to go alone with me, then you can wait for another opportunity to see the grounds with the rest of the party." His tone insinuated it was unlikely another such opportunity would arise. Unless he missed his mark, he doubted Delia Somerset thought of herself as *afraid* of anything.

He shrugged as if her answer were of no consequence to him, but he watched her closely, surprised to find he was holding his breath.

"Afraid, my lord? Why would I be afraid of you?"

Alec's eyes dropped to her lips. He could think of any number of reasons, but a lie jumped easily out of his mouth. "No reason whatsoever, unless you're worried about propriety." He emphasized the last word slightly, as if such a worry were absurdly prim.

"There can be no impropriety in a ride around the grounds, surely."

Alec smiled grimly. She hadn't any idea how spiteful the *ton* could be. Before they even returned from their ride tomorrow, Delia would be at the center of a storm of malicious gossip. Lady Lisette and her mother, Lady Cecil, would be more than happy to stir up a scandal, especially after the seating arrangements at dinner this evening. Delia would be on her way back to Surrey as early as the day after tomorrow.

Alec clenched his fists and tried to ignore the sharp stab of anguish he felt every time he imagined her exposed to the derision of the *ton*. It was better this way. It would hurt her to be sneered at, but in the end it was better for her, too. She and Lily didn't belong here.

"I imagine you're knowledgeable about the estate and the countryside, and I should be glad to learn something about them. You are a *competent* guide, my lord?"

"More than competent, I assure you, Miss Somerset."

"Competent!" Major Lytton bellowed, catching only the last word of the conversation. "Oh yes, miss. Very competent. Carlisle knows his way about. You could not be in better hands, miss. No better hands than Carlisle's."

"Thank you, Major." Alec raised his glass to Miss Somerset. "Thank you very much indeed."

Chapter Fifteen

At last the countess rose from the table and signaled the other ladies to retire. The endless dinner was over. Delia felt like an inmate at Newgate who'd been released into the sunshine after a prolonged incarceration. Odd, but as interminable as the dinner was, she didn't think she'd eaten much of anything.

There had been soup. Had she tasted it?

Alec must be mad to seat her at the head of the table. And Major Lytton! The poor major was likely even now wondering about the date of the fictional fox hunt this winter.

"Delia!" Lily caught up to her at the entrance to the drawing room, Ellie and Charlotte right behind her, and caught Delia's arm. "My goodness, Delia, however did you end up at the head of the table?"

"Next to Major Lytton, no less." Charlotte gave Delia a sympathetic look. "The last time I was seated next to him, I was dyspeptic for a week. The shouting, you know."

"It does quite put one off their appetite," Eleanor said. "It's very tiresome of Alec to seat you so far away. What could he be thinking?"

Delia surveyed the four curious faces surrounding her and shrugged helplessly. She was as mystified as they were, but she was sure it hadn't been an accident. Perhaps it was the next step in a complicated seduction that involved kissing her in a garden, and then ignoring her for three days. For all she knew, that was how rakes seduced young ladies.

"Tiresome, to say the least," Charlotte said. "At worst, it's a serious breach in etiquette. I overheard Lady Lisette . . ." She stopped speaking and darted a quick glance around them. "I overheard Lady Lisette and her mother talking," she continued breathlessly, her voice lowered. The four heads surrounding her leaned closer. "They were quite angry to see Delia seated *alone* at the head of the table with Alec."

"We weren't alone," Delia protested. "Major Lytton—"

"Is as deaf as a teapot," Eleanor interrupted. "You can't have failed to notice he hears only two words out of ten, Delia."

"Well, no. I did notice. I was so startled at one point I nearly jumped out of my chair and into my soup."

Charlotte tittered. "Yes, well, it would have been quieter in your soup dish. But now Lady Lisette and her mother are frothing and spitting like two wet cats."

"Why should they be?" Lily asked. "Did one of them wish to sit next to Major Lytton and swim in their soup and become dyspeptic?" For the sake of economy, Lily threw it all together in one breath.

"Because Alec escorted Delia into dinner and then seated her at the head of the table when her rank demands she be seated further down," Charlotte whispered. "He should have escorted Lady Lisette."

Lily gave a dainty sniff. "Yes, of course that's so, but this is a casual dinner with friends, is it not? It seems an awful fuss over nothing."

"Lady Cecil and Lady Lisette are very concerned with propriety, especially when it comes to rank. Even more so when the young lady moved to the head of the table looks like Delia." Charlotte snickered. "Well, that, and because they enjoy being enraged. They're both very good at righteous indignation."

"They are," Eleanor said. "It makes the prospect of their joining the family pleasant indeed."

Charlotte shrugged. "In some ways it's a good match. In terms of fortune and social connection."

Eleanor frowned. "But not in terms of temperament."

Charlotte's face looked grim. "Do you think Alec cares about that?"

"He used to care about a great many things," Eleanor said. "But I suppose if he's foolish enough to care only for fortune and the opinion of the *ton*, then he *deserves* to marry Lady Lisette and spend the rest of his life being driven mad by her, for that's what will happen."

"Shhh! Mother is coming," Charlotte hissed. "And, oh Lord, look what she's dragging in her wake." Lady Carlisle had started across the room. Lady Cecil and her daughter followed, looking like two enraged ships battling choppy water in the channel.

"This is all very provoking!" Eleanor whispered. "I can't imagine what came over Alec tonight."

There was no time to discuss it, because the countess and her two seething vessels had arrived in port. "Good evening, girls," Lady Carlisle said with a smile. "Miss Somerset, Miss Lily, Lady Cecil wishes to have a word. She tells me she remembers your mother."

Not with fondness, if one could judge by the sour expression on Lady Cecil's face. At one time Lady Cecil must have been quite pretty, but her face had long since settled into lines of petulant dissatisfaction.

Delia dipped into a polite curtsy, and Lily did the same. Lady Cecil squinted at Delia for longer than was polite. She had small brown eyes set closely together, which unfortunately exaggerated the squint. She peered at Delia, and she peered at Lily, and then she peered at Delia again.

Finally, Lady Cecil returned the curtsy with a very brief one. Lady Lisette followed her mother's lead with a shallow curtsy of her own.

"Miss Somerset," Lady Cecil said with icy politeness. "I do remember your mother, Lady Millicent Chase. Quite well, in fact. Indeed, I think everyone remembers *her*, though she hasn't shown her face in London for years."

Delia stiffened. Beside her, Lily gasped. For one horrible moment Delia felt numb, her mind a blank, but then a cleansing anger flooded through her. "My mother found London tedious, my lady. She chose to spend as little time as possible among the *ton*. I believe she found the endless round of trivial social engagements tedious, as well."

She found people like you tedious, Lady Cecil.

Lady Lisette tossed her head. "You don't seem to share your mother's opinion on that subject. My impression is you were quite captivated by the *ton* at dinner." Underneath her saccharine tone her voice throbbed with venom.

"Yes, Delia," Ellie drawled with mock censure. "You must stop monopolizing Major Lytton in that selfish way."

Charlotte made a strangled sound, which she rapidly turned into a cough. She cleared her throat. "You can't blame Delia, Eleanor. Many young ladies become distracted when they dine with Major Lytton."

Ellie turned away, as if to rearrange the skirts of her gown, but Delia saw her bite her lip, and her shoulders were shaking.

Lady Lisette scowled at Delia. "It was *not* Major Lytton who distracted Miss Somerset."

Delia opened her mouth to reply when Lily spoke up. "Lady Carlisle," she asked, ignoring Lady Lisette, "will there be any dancing this evening?"

"Perhaps there will be." The countess smiled. "Most of the party here tonight hasn't yet seen the pleasure gardens, and I find I'm eager to show them off."

"The gardens are lovely, Mama." Eleanor squeezed her mother's hand.

Charlotte stepped forward and kissed Lady Carlisle's cheek. "They're beautiful, Mama. Thank you for them."

The countess glowed with pleasure. "Rylands, please have the footmen remove the screens." She laughed and clapped her hands together with anticipation as the servants began to move the screens to the side of the room.

Delia forgot all about Lady Lisette and her enraged mother and stared at Lady Carlisle. Her throat closed with emotion as she watched Lady Carlisle's face transform with pleasure.

She looks years younger when she smiles.

The ladies all gathered into an excited, chattering knot in the middle of the drawing room as the small army of footmen slid the screens aside. Every head was turned toward the glass doors, and a collective gasp went up as the last screen was removed.

There was a brief astonished silence, then a mighty rustle of silk as all the ladies moved *en masse* toward the terrace doors, jostling one another out of the way in their eagerness.

"Lovely!" one young lady exclaimed, looking as if she were about to swoon with excitement. "It looks like a miniature Vauxhall Gardens!"

"Come, ladies," Charlotte said, observing the crush. She linked her arm with Lily's on one side and Ellie's on the other. "We may be able to overpower the stampede if we all stay together."

Eleanor took Delia's arm. "My goodness. Look at young Miss Entwistle! She seems to have forgotten herself entirely. Why, she almost trampled poor Mrs. Pennyworth under her heels. Perhaps she's anticipating a romantic interlude in the gardens. Though that seems rather unlikely, given the gentlemen are still at their brandy."

"Shall we visit our pavilion, ladies?" Eleanor caught Lily's arm and headed toward the terrace doors.

Delia floated through the doors, drawn forward by Ellie and the gentle glow of light from the garden. Flickering lanterns glimmered overhead in the leaves and lined the pathways at her feet. She'd never seen fireflies, but she'd read about the tiny little insects that carried miniature lights on their bodies. This was what it must look like when thousands of them gathered together and their combined light set everything around them aglow.

She drifted along, not minding her direction. She made turn after turn, stopping here and there to admire an elegant arch or a display of flowers. At the end of the path in front of her she could see a pavilion decorated with lanterns and long swathes of white silk, caught at the corners with extravagant bunches of white flowers. She moved toward it until she found herself standing alone at the farthest end of the garden.

"Delia!" Lily called, but her voice was drowned out by the soft music that seemed to come from nowhere and everywhere at once, as if it rose from the air of the garden itself. The musicians were hidden among the shrubberies and behind pavilions and graceful groupings of statuary.

"You must see the Chinese pavilion at the end of this walk . . ." Lily's voice became fainter and fainter and then faded away as Delia melted into the light surrounding her.

Eleanor no longer held her arm. Lily and Charlotte had disappeared.

It was almost as if she'd never seen the garden before. It appeared more beautiful than ever tonight, perhaps because seeing Lady Carlisle's joy in it made it so. Her face—when the footmen drew the screens aside, and again when her daughters kissed her—Lady Carlisle's face had glowed as brightly as any light in the garden.

To Delia's dismay, tears blurred her eyes. They hadn't yet started to fall when she heard footsteps behind her. All of the fine hairs on the back of her neck rose in reaction, as if someone had laid a warm hand there.

She knew without turning it was Alec.

"Your mother . . ." she began, but her throat closed before she could continue. How could she explain to him how it felt to watch the years being erased from Lady Carlisle's face, or how affected she'd been at the depth of feeling between the countess and her daughters? "She's . . . Your sisters are attached to her. She seems very happy tonight," she finished lamely.

"She hasn't always been so happy. She's an entirely different person, it seems, since . . ." Alec's voice trailed off.

He didn't mention his father. He didn't need to.

Delia's throat worked for a moment. "It must be wonderful to see her enjoy the happiness she deserves," she said, her voice choked.

There was a pause. "Your mother," he began, surprising her with the uncertainty in his voice. "You and your sisters were attached to her?"

She stiffened, as she always did at any mention of her parents. She was never sure she'd be able to speak of them, and her voice caught a little. "Yes. Very attached. To both our parents. We miss them terribly."

"I envy you that." There was a trace of bitterness in his voice. "I don't miss my father at all."

She looked away from him, down toward the river. "To struggle to love someone, or to watch a beloved parent suffer for years in an unhappy marriage, would be as painful as losing them too soon, I think. My parents were so happy together. All our memories of them are joyful ones."

Delia was horrified as soon as she heard her words hanging in the air between them. Her own mother could have been in Lady Carlisle's place, trapped in a loveless marriage with Hart Sutherland. "I didn't mean—"

"We haven't known each other long," Alec said, his dark eyes softer than she'd ever seen them before. "But I know you're not cruel."

He bowed then and began to turn away. She thought he'd leave her, but at the last moment he hesitated, took her hand, and raised it to his lips. "I'll see you in the foyer at six o'clock tomorrow morning."

The kiss was utterly proper. Brief. His mouth merely grazed her glove. His hand did not touch her skin. But she felt the kiss in her chest, her stomach, and all the way down to her toes.

Chapter Sixteen

Alec paced across the black-and-white marble floor of the foyer, snapping his riding crop against his polished black boots and grumbling to himself.

I said six o'clock. Where the devil was she?

"Good morning, my lord."

Alec swung around to face the stairs. Delia was descending, wearing a tight-fitting midnight blue riding habit trimmed in black cord around the neckline and bodice. Two very bright blue eyes peeked out from under a jaunty black hat with dangling dark blue satin ribbons.

Alec swallowed. "You appear to have slept well. You look . . ."

Captivating. Delicious. Tempting.

". . . refreshed."

At least one of them had slept. He'd been on the verge of escaping to his chambers last night after a tedious evening admiring Lady Lisette when Eleanor had cornered him in the hallway. Eleanor's lectures usually had about as much impact on him as being pelted with a ball of yarn, but this one had the force of a cricket bat. His ears were still ringing. She'd demanded an explanation for the sudden change in seating arrangements at dinner, and then she'd rung a peal over his head about his unforgiveable carelessness in exposing Delia to the notice of the other guests.

He'd be deaf by now if Eleanor knew the whole truth.

He offered Delia his arm. "It's a fine day for a ride." He led her through the foyer toward the stables. "Thomas will accompany us with provisions." He gestured to a footman who stood next to the door holding a small hamper.

His highly strung black stallion, Ceres, danced impatiently in the stable yard. Next to Ceres was a sedate dappled gray mare, the horse he'd chosen for Delia. Alec looked at the horse and then glanced down at her in her smart blue habit and saw at once he'd made the wrong choice. She didn't say so, but she quietly vibrated with disappointment. Even the ribbons on her hat quivered with it.

"Dawkins!" Alec called. A stooped, gray-haired man appeared at the stable door. "Please saddle Athena. I believe Miss Somerset prefers a livelier mount."

"Oh," Delia breathed as Dawkins led out a sleek golden-brown horse. Athena was several hands higher than most mares, with a lovely arched neck and surprisingly dainty feet. "She's lovely!"

"She is, isn't she?" Alec rubbed the horse's neck. "She was sickly when she was born, but to see her now, one would never guess it."

Delia reached up to stroke the horse's soft black nose. "Eleanor and Charlotte told me about Athena. They said she was a weak foal, and you nursed her for a year until she started to show promise. To hear them tell it, your actions were nothing short of heroic."

She looked up at him with a smile that started at her lush lips and ended with her eyes.

Alec was startled into smiling back at her as the memory of that summer rushed back to him. His triumph with Athena had also been a triumph over his father, who'd wanted to have the foal shot.

But then reality intruded like a stinging slap to the face. He doubted either his sisters or Robyn would describe him as heroic now. He hardly even saw them anymore. And he had no right to enjoy Delia's smiles, not when he was doing everything in his power to make sure Robyn didn't. "That was a very long time ago. Will Athena do?" His voice was clipped.

She blinked at his dour tone, but nodded. "I would love to ride her."

"She's a lively horse. Are you sure you can manage her?" His tone implied he had his doubts, because it would be easier to get through the day without touching her if she didn't smile at him.

It worked. Her smile faded and her jaw set with determination. "Of course." She marched coolly over to the block and turned and looked back at him, waiting. Alec had the distinct impression only impeccable manners kept her from stamping her foot.

"If you would, Dawkins." Alec gestured to the groom to bring Athena over to the block, and Delia swung up onto the horse with easy grace. Alec allowed himself one tormenting moment to admire her straight, slender back and the way the riding habit tightened around the long slim line of her leg; then he forced his eyes away. He'd seen enough. She sat Athena beautifully.

He set off at a brisk trot, then eased into a gallop as they cleared the stable yard. He liked a hard ride, so he gave Ceres his head. Delia matched his pace easily. The horses' hooves pounded the ground and sent up great splashes of mud and turf. The countryside was completely open here.

He'd been riding across the same endless rolling green hills since he was old enough to mount a horse. As a child he'd spent hours exploring the marshes, a wonderland of wild birds and fascinating plants, and lingering in the bluebell wood when it was in full bloom.

It was too early in the year for the May bluebells. By the time the flowers spread like a deep blue blanket in the dappled sunlight under the trees, Delia would be long gone from Kent. Alec jerked on Ceres's reins and the horse whinnied a little in protest. It was absurd he should feel a sting of regret when he was going to such lengths to hasten her departure. By the time they returned to Bellwood late this evening, her name would be on the lips of every guest at the house party. He was still considered a rake by most of society. Worse, as far as the *ton* was concerned, he was a rake who was as good as engaged to Lady Lisette. They would all claim to be shocked that Delia would ride off alone with him, but they would excuse him for luring her away. Even Lady Lisette would excuse him.

It wasn't fair, but it was the way it was.

It was done, and he didn't want to think about it anymore. Not while they were miles from Bellwood and Robyn and the *ton*. Delia would be gone tomorrow. It was selfish, but for today he wanted to pretend there wasn't any of this ugliness between them. Just for today, they were simply out for a ride on a sunny spring morning.

They had been out for several hours when Alec reined Ceres to a stop at the crest of a grassy knoll. He swung down from the horse's back and walked over to Delia. He held out his hand to assist her to dismount, but before she could accept it, he impulsively wrapped his hands lightly around her waist and lifted her down.

Shouldn't touch her, but it's just for today. She'll be out of reach tomorrow.

"My lord!" She gave a little squeal of surprise that weakened his knees. "I'm perfectly capable of dismounting by myself."

"Undoubtedly." Alec resisted the urge to hold her against his body as she slid to the ground. "You'd do Rotten Row credit," he added honestly, surprising himself.

Thomas handed the hamper to Alec and disappeared to water the horses. Alec spread the picnic blanket out on the grass, shrugged off his coat, and plopped to the ground. He looked up at Delia and patted the spot next to him on the blanket.

"I won't bite you, Delia." He gave her an intentionally wolfish grin. "Make yourself comfortable." He took a large bite out of a shiny apple he'd unpacked from the basket, holding her eyes as he did.

It wouldn't do to have her *too* comfortable.

She gave him a suspicious look, but perched on the edge of the blanket, as far away from him as she could get.

"I find it difficult to picture Rotten Row," she said. "Vauxhall, as well. One of the ladies last night said your mother's pleasure garden resembles Vauxhall, and I wondered whether it did."

Alec stretched his legs out in front of him. "Does it matter?"

Delia hesitated. "It never did before."

Alec took another bite of his apple. "Then why should it now?"

"If London has such a garden, then it must be more than the dirty, crowded city I always imagined it to be. I never wished to see London before, but now I wonder if to miss it is to miss something indeed."

"London *is* dirty and crowded," Alec said, "and teeming with crime, poverty, and disease. But you do miss something if you never see it. It's a fascinating city, both appalling and magnificent at once."

Delia glanced at him with raised eyebrows, as if she'd

expected condescending amusement, and was surprised at his sincerity. "Yes. I suppose places are just like people that way. Appalling and magnificent."

"You sound as if you have someone in particular in mind."

Delia laughed a little. "No one who is both at once. But you did warn me those of the *ton* who remember my mother will remark on our presence here, and they have done. Many of them more kindly than I expected, come to think on it, and the censure of a woman like the Countess of Cecil can be of no consequence to me."

Alec choked down the bit of apple he'd been chewing. He should feel nothing but triumph to find his plan was already working, but instead an unexpected, savage fury swept through him. His expression must have turned menacing, for Delia looked as if she wished she hadn't spoken at all. "What does Lady Cecil find to disapprove of?"

"Me. Lily. My mother. It's not surprising, is it? Lady Cecil isn't the type of woman who hides her disapproval."

"Your presence at Bellwood should be sufficient reason for Lady Cecil to treat you with politeness." Alec's body was rigid with barely leashed fury. "You are my sisters' friends, and my mother's guest."

"Oh, Lady Cecil is no match for your sisters. Your mother, either. If only more members of the *ton* were like Lady Carlisle," she said with a sigh. "*She* is rather magnificent."

"But alas," he said, making an effort to calm himself, "most resemble Lady Cecil—appalling."

Delia laughed and seemed to relax then. She peeked into the picnic basket and took out an apple.

"Tell me," Alec said, trying to tear his gaze away from the sight of her even white teeth nibbling at the juicy flesh. "I know you draw, and you're a superb horsewoman. Do you sing and play the pianoforte? Speak French and Italian?"

She nodded. "Yes. Some German, as well. What of it?"

He shrugged. "Only that you have all the graces that distinguish a young lady of the *ton*. That's the real reason Lady Cecil disapproves of you."

She looked at him in surprise. "Whatever do you mean? Why would Lady Cecil disapprove of me if I'm just like the rest of the *ton*?"

That wasn't what he'd said, and she *wasn't* just like the rest of the *ton*. She wasn't like anyone he'd ever known, but there didn't seem to be any point in saying so. She'd be gone tomorrow. "It's simple. Every reasonably attractive young lady with decent manners and even mild accomplishments is a potential rival for Lady Lisette."

"Reasonably attractive . . . decent manners . . . mild accomplishments. You'll turn my head with your extravagant compliments, my lord."

"I only hope you're not a gifted dancer," he replied with mock seriousness. "I begin to fear for your very safety if you are."

"Oh, dear. Then I'm frightened indeed, for I dance divinely."

She was teasing, but Alec could easily imagine her lithe body floating across a dance floor. He cleared his throat. "If you were clumsy and awkward, with bad skin and a lisp, Lady Cecil would welcome you with wide-open arms."

Delia cocked her head to one side, as if considering this. "I find that prospect even more terrifying than her disapproval," she said with a mischievous little smile.

Alec gazed into her thickly lashed eyes and thought of thousands of bluebells carpeting the forest floor. He could take her in his arms. He could kiss her and keep kissing her until he forgot all about Robyn, and the scandal between their families, and the shameful reason he'd brought her here today. He could plunder her hot, sweet mouth until everything else faded into oblivion.

"Anyway," she said, "Lady Cecil hasn't anything to worry about. Accomplishments won't make the *ton* forget my name."

No. The *ton* would never forget she was a Somerset, or forgive her for it. He couldn't, either, and he'd do well to remember that instead of fantasizing about the taste of apples on her lips.

But not now. Not today. Just for today, he didn't want to remember it. "What, you mean Delphinium?" He gave her a teasing smile. "Named so because of your eyes. Delphinium, Lily . . ."

He looked at her expectantly.

"Iris, Hyacinth, and Violet." She colored slightly. "We're all named after blue flowers. My parents were a bit, well, whimsical."

"A bit," he agreed, abandoning his efforts not to watch her lips. "What would your parents have done if one of you had been born with brown eyes?" His smile widened.

She frowned thoughtfully. "Named her Poppy probably. Or Milkweed. Those are brown flowers, aren't they? I suppose we should all be grateful to have blue eyes."

Alec laughed. He couldn't help himself. He liked talking with her. It wasn't just that she was clever and amusing—it was more that he was never sure what she'd say next, or what expression would cross her face. "Are you whimsical, too? Did you inherit that from your mother, along with her blue eyes?"

"No," she answered after a brief pause. "I suppose I was once, before . . ." She stopped speaking for a moment, and her smile faded. "Now I try to be practical, though Lily would tell you I mostly fail miserably at it."

Alec didn't like to see her smile disappear. "I think you must be whimsical still. With a name like Delphinium and blue eyes to match, you can't help it. For that reason alone, you always will be."

For once he'd said just the right thing. She glanced up at him a little shyly, her face pink with pleasure. "What a lovely thought. You could even reconcile me to the name *Milkweed*, I think."

Alec looked at her glowing face and the same dull ache from last night lodged in his chest. He thought of her stricken expression when she'd fled from the garden three nights ago, the way the blood had rushed into her face and then as quickly receded, leaving her pale and unsteady. And again last night, in the garden, when he'd realized she was close to tears, and a pain so acute it was nearly agony ripped through his chest.

If the gossips in London could be believed, he was a ruthless adversary—a cold, calculating man who'd stop at nothing to win. Who'd crush anyone who got in his way. Maybe he was that, and worse. More so since he'd become the earl. It had been a long time since he'd felt like the hero his sisters once thought him. But did that mean he was the kind of man who would crush Delia like a flower under his boot heel, because her name was Somerset? The kind of coldly manipulative man his father had been?

What he was doing was despicable. No matter what kind of threat Delia was, it didn't justify his low and dishonorable behavior. This was beneath him. Every time he thought about what he planned to do, his chest felt hollow and his gut clenched, because deep down he knew he was a better man than this. A better man than his father had been.

And Delia—*Christ*, she didn't deserve this. She was better than all of them. Better than Lady Cecil and the rest of the *ton*, and better than him, too. Not because she was a rare beauty, but because of everything else about her—the way she held her head high when the *ton* gossiped about her mother, and the way she challenged him with her every breath, when all the rules of society demanded she charm and flatter him.

He was punishing her because she was too tempting. Because he was afraid he couldn't resist her. When she smiled, he couldn't help but grin back at her. Watching her eat an apple became exquisite torture because her lips aroused him to distraction. He'd ride miles out of his way for the chance to see her blush.

He couldn't do this to her. He couldn't do this to himself, because if he hurt her like this, he'd be just like his father, and he couldn't live with that.

It was all an awful mistake. *But maybe it wasn't too late to set it right.*

Alec looked at the sky—it was still only about nine in the morning. If they rushed, they could be back at Bellwood by eleven, likely before anyone even realized they'd been gone.

With sudden, jerky movements he gathered up the remains of their meal and shoved it haphazardly into the hamper. "I'm afraid we'll need to return to Bellwood at once. I've just recalled some urgent business."

Delia stared at him, astonished. "What about your tenant? Didn't you say you needed to see him today?"

Alec knew he sounded as though he'd gone mad, but there was no help for it. They had to leave *now*. "I'll send my steward out when we return. He can conclude the business." He paused. "I'm sorry to cut our ride short. I promised you a tour of the western grounds."

"Another day perhaps." She rose to her feet.

Within minutes they had retrieved Thomas and were mounted on their horses. Alec squeezed Ceres's ribs with his knees and the horse shot forward and tore across the ground like a bird in flight, back to Bellwood.

Chapter Seventeen

It was a quick ride home. Alec spurred Ceres to ungodly speeds, riding as if the hounds of hell chased him. Delia didn't mind. She loved the way the wind whipped her hair and coaxed color into her cheeks. Athena surged beneath her, and she could almost imagine she'd sprouted wings as the horse's long, smooth strides sent her soaring across the grounds. Alec rode just ahead of her, expertly controlling the gigantic black horse with his powerful thighs, his back straight, with the wind tossing his wavy dark hair.

It had been a glorious ride. A glorious morning.

She looked up when they reached Bellwood, surprised at how short the ride home had seemed. Rylands, with the uncanny prescience of all perfectly trained butlers, had already opened the door and stood stoically waiting for them.

"Hello, Rylands." She waved gaily.

Rylands bowed. "Miss Somerset. Lord Carlisle. Luncheon will be served at noon."

Alec drew Ceres to an abrupt halt. "Has my mother come down yet this morning, Rylands? The other guests?"

Rylands shook his head. "It's been a quiet morning, my lord. Lady Carlisle took her breakfast in her room." The butler hesitated, then added blandly, his face impassive, "As did Lady Cecil and her daughter."

Alec merely nodded, but his body relaxed and the tightness in his jaw eased. "Very good." He turned to Delia. "Thank you for your company this morning, Miss Somerset."

Delia supposed this was her cue to dismount. She did so reluctantly, taking a moment to stroke Athena's neck and murmur to her. She glanced shyly up at Alec, about to thank him for the wonderful ride, but before she could say a word, he gathered Athena's reins, gave her a cursory nod, and trotted off to the stables.

Delia watched him go. She felt vaguely dissatisfied, though she couldn't have said why.

She hurried up the stairs to her bedchamber to dress, and found Lily sitting in front of the mirror, puzzling over which ribbon best matched her gown. Delia gazed at her sister's reflection and smiled. Lily's cheeks were pink and the dark circles under her eyes had faded.

"The white one." Delia hurried into the room and discarded her hat on the bed.

"Goodness, Delia. Where have you been? Off on a ride? You'd best hurry; it's nearly time for luncheon." Lily turned away from the mirror and eyed Delia with curiosity.

"Blast! I left my hat ribbons in Thomas's saddlebag."

The wind had loosened the silk ribbons on her riding hat. Fortunately she'd noticed it and she'd given the ribbons to Thomas, who'd tucked them into his saddlebag for safe-keeping.

"You look as if you rode home without a hat alto-gether. It would explain your hair." Lily turned back to the glass and gave her own perfectly arranged hair a complacent pat.

Delia reached up to touch her hair and groaned. She didn't need to look in the glass to know it was a mass of tangles. "It'll take me ages to brush it out. Do you suppose I could retrieve the ribbons after luncheon?" Her stomach gave a hopeful growl.

"If you forget and the ribbons are lost, Hyacinth and Violet will go mad." Lily turned away from the mirror and eyed Delia sternly. "I wouldn't blame them, for you'll never match the color, and the hat is the best part of the costume."

"Blast," Delia repeated, this time with resignation. "I'm going." She was already halfway out the door.

"If you hurry back, I'll help you with your hair!" Lily called out, just as Delia closed the door behind her.

"Help me indeed," she muttered, taking the stairs at a near run. "If you really wanted to help, you'd go down to the stables with your perfect hair and fetch the ribbons for me."

Rylands saw her bolting down the stairs and opened the front door. "Luncheon is served at noon," he repeated as Delia flew out the door and ran in the direction of the stables.

"I know, Rylands. I know!" she called over her shoulder. She couldn't be sure, but she thought she heard the butler sigh heavily.

She arrived at the stable doors and was about to hurry in when she heard raised male voices coming from inside. She paused, not sure what to do. She didn't want to interrupt, but—

". . . don't know what the hell you think you're doing, Alec, sneaking around last night and then disappearing for the entire morning today!"

It was Robyn Sutherland's voice, and he sounded furious. Delia let out a long, quiet breath. The ribbons would have to wait. She couldn't barge into the stables in the middle of an argument.

"You don't need to know, Robyn." Alec's voice was cold.

"It's only necessary I *do*. And I hardly disappeared with Miss Somerset."

Delia froze. Were they arguing about *her*? She instinctively drew closer to the stables, into the deeper shadows at the side of the building.

"Oh, I'm sure you do know just what you're doing, Alec—you always do. But I find myself wondering what you could have to gain by spending the morning alone with her, without a chaperone."

"Thomas was with us the entire time." Alec's voice sounded strained.

"A servant! Not quite the same as a proper escort, is it, Alec? Rather like Major Lytton at dinner last night. You were careful to make sure no one overheard that conversation."

"Have you taken your eyes off her even once since she arrived, Robyn? You seem to be watching her very closely."

"Not as closely as you are," Robyn snapped. "And now everyone else is watching her, too, brother, since you've exposed her to their notice with your pointed attentions."

"If she didn't want to be noticed, she should have stayed in Surrey. Would to God she had," Alec added in a dark voice, as if to himself.

Delia wrapped her arms around herself and squeezed. The wind had picked up, hadn't it? She shivered and pressed her back against the stable wall. If she pressed hard enough, maybe she'd disappear.

Robyn gave an angry snort. "What are you talking about? Why shouldn't she be here?"

"She doesn't belong here. You know it's true, Robyn. Even Miss Somerset knows it, naïve as she is."

Delia's throat went tight when she thought of the rush of pleasure she'd felt just this morning when Alec said she was as accomplished as any young lady of the *ton*. He hadn't meant it, then. Her heart throbbed with misery. God, she was such a fool to believe she could ever belong here.

Robyn's voice had gone very low. Delia didn't want to hear anymore, but still she found herself straining to make out his words.

"I see." But Robyn sounded as if he didn't see. Not at all. "Perhaps we should clarify your objection, Alec. Is it her behavior you find offensive? Her manners? Her conversation? In what way does she fall short of your lofty expectations?"

"There's nothing wrong with the girl's behavior."

Delia had never heard the word *girl* sound like such an insult before. Alec's tone was utterly dismissive.

Robyn must have thought so, too, for his voice had gone as cold as the wind that clamped its icy hand on Delia's neck. "What's this all about, Alec? You can't mean you object to her simply because of her birth?"

There was a pause. Delia clenched her hands so tightly her nails dug into her palms, but she didn't notice the sting. Her whole body had gone numb.

"Simple? If only it were." It sounded as if Alec's calm demeanor was crumbling. "But it goes way beyond that. Delia Somerset's father was a nobody, and her mother was at the center of a scandal that humiliated our family. Their own grandmother, Lady Chase, doesn't even acknowledge them. Do you think the *ton* will welcome her into society when her own grandmother has rejected her?"

"I didn't think of the *ton* at all when I urged Charlotte and Eleanor to invite her here," Robyn said. "I thought only that she's charming, and our sisters' friend. I didn't realize you expect me to take the *ton*'s opinion into consideration every time I issue an invitation."

"I don't expect anything of you anymore, Robyn. So it falls to me to point out the *ton* will be tittering over the Sutherland name in every drawing room in London if the scandal is revived. Do you wish to see our mother and sisters exposed to society's derision again? Have you no family loyalty, Robyn?"

"Family loyalty?" Robyn echoed faintly, as if he couldn't believe what he'd heard. "That scandal is decades old, Alec! You can't seriously accuse me of lacking family loyalty on the grounds of a house party invitation."

"Christ, Robyn!" Alec's voice cracked off the high rafters and echoed through the stables. "Do you really expect me to believe that's all it is? Anyone can see you're besotted with her! You can't take your eyes off her. You can't stop thinking—"

Alec broke off abruptly and there was a moment of tense, stunned silence, like the hush after a gun discharges unexpectedly. When he spoke again, his voice was tight. "I accuse you on the grounds you're seriously pursuing her when a match between you is impossible. It's out of the question, Robyn."

"It seems to me as though *you're* pursuing her," Robyn shot back. "I've hardly seen her since her arrival because you're always alone in some dark corner of the garden with her, or off on some mysterious ride."

"Don't be ridiculous," Alec replied very quickly. "I've been trying to keep her out of your way!"

The sound of the flies buzzing around the stable door was deafening. Delia waited, motionless, nausea roiling in her stomach. Alec hadn't been trying to seduce her, then. She knew she should be relieved. Thankful, even. So why did it hurt her so much? Because he'd gone to such great lengths to keep her out of his family?

It must have been so odious to him to pretend interest in a *nobody* like her. But like the rest of the *ton*, he was a skilled dissembler. She'd actually believed he enjoyed spending time with her. What had he felt when he'd kissed her? Touched her? Tears stung the corners of her eyes. Had he imagined he was kissing and touching Lady Lisette instead?

Finally Robyn spoke. "What if I said I was in love with

her, Alec? What then? Would you encourage my suit? Or would the potential scandal be more important to you than my happiness?"

There was a long silence. Alec's voice when it came was flat, toneless. "Are you trying to tell me you're in love with her, Robyn?"

"I'm asking you if it would make any difference to you if I was. What if my happiness depended on her?"

"There are other ways to get what you want. Perhaps if you took her as your mistress . . ."

Delia pressed her hand to her stomach, directly over the chasm that opened there at Alec's words. Oh God, she was going to be sick. She'd be sick and they would find her here, and they would know she'd overheard every awful, painful word . . .

There was a furious snarl and then she heard what sounded like an angry scuffle. One of the horses whinnied nervously, but it ended almost as quickly as it had begun.

"God *damn* you, Alec." Robyn's voice shook, and he'd abandoned any pretense at restraint. "Do you think Delia Somerset would consent to be any man's *mistress*? Or that I would ruin a gently bred young lady?" Robyn was nearly spitting with rage. "You don't know her at all, Alec. What's worse, you don't know *me*."

The nervous horse stirred for a few moments, then settled down into the stall with a snort. Delia watched the dust motes dance in the one remaining shaft of weak sunlight. Alec was silent.

At last Robyn took a deep breath. "I wish I could say I don't recognize you anymore, Alec, but I do. You're just like Father. Just as cold and manipulative. Oh, you're far more charming than Father was. You put a better face on it. But no matter how polished the surface, it's still the same underneath." His voice was quiet and final. "If carrying the title means being like Father, then I'm damned thankful I'm not the Earl of Carlisle."

Delia heard footsteps and shrank back against the wall, in a near frenzy at the thought of being discovered. When no one appeared, she realized Robyn must have exited from the opposite side of the stables. At least she thought it was Robyn. It had sounded as if he had nothing else to say.

She needed to get away from there as quickly and as quietly as possible, but she was trembling from head to toe and she didn't trust herself to move. It would be a disaster if Alec found her there—

She went still as a realization swept through her. It would be a disaster for *him* to find out she'd overheard his hateful words, but it wasn't one for her. She'd done nothing wrong, except to choose a deucedly bad time to search for her ribbons.

A pure, cleansing anger took hold of her at that moment, a glittering, frozen anger unlike any she'd ever felt before. She'd be *damned* if she'd skulk away like a common criminal. Before she could talk herself out of it, Delia stepped away from the side of the building and through the stable door.

As soon as she saw Alec's face, she almost regretted her bravery. His sensuous mouth was a thin, grim line. His fists were clenched so tightly on his riding crop, his knuckles had gone white, and he was deathly pale under his sun-bronzed skin.

When he looked up and saw her, his face went even paler. For one fleeting moment her heart seized with pain for him. But then she remembered.

Her own grandmother rejected her . . . Her father was a nobody . . . She doesn't belong here . . . Perhaps if you took her as your mistress.

Delia wanted to put her hands over her ears to shut out

the words, but she knew it would do no good. Those hateful words would echo in her head for as long as she lived.

Good. They would remind her never to be so foolish again.

"All this time I've wondered why an insignificant, naïve girl like me should be fortunate enough to enjoy the attentions of the great Lord Carlisle," she said in a dead voice. "At one point I even believed you were trying to seduce me." She laughed a little, but the sound was hard and cold. "You're certainly determined to keep my family's disgraceful scandal from polluting the pure Sutherland name, aren't you, Alec? How ironic," she added with another near-hysterical laugh, "since I never remotely considered Robyn a marriage prospect."

She was furious to hear her voice quaver at the end of her little speech. Alec took a step toward her. "Delia, don't—"

She held up a shaking hand. "No." A thread of panic entered her voice. "Don't come near me. I don't want you near me, and I don't want to hear any explanations."

He came to a halt, his eyes searching hers. "I won't come near you. I only want to say I regret you overheard such an ugly argument."

"Do you regret you said those things, or that I overheard them?"

She already knew the answer.

He took one step closer, despite his promise. "I regret you overheard them, but I meant it when I said there will *never* be anything between you and Robyn." His voice was low and fierce, and his black eyes glinted dangerously.

To Delia's fury, his words cut through her like a thousand shards of glass. "Yes, I deduced that, my lord." She caught her breath painfully. "Of course, there is one consolation. It seems I would make an admirable mistress, so perhaps the journey to Kent wasn't wasted after all."

She tried to keep the misery out of her voice, but as soon

as the words fell into the heavy, dusty air of the stables, she knew she'd failed. The words hung there, a noose choking the life out of their fragile intimacy of that morning.

Alec flinched when she said "mistress," but otherwise he was silent. He simply watched her, an odd expression in his eyes. Was it regret? Or, so help her God, was it *pity*? Suddenly Delia's every limb was trembling again. Her throat closed. Tears of rage and humiliation pressed behind her eyes. He *dared* to pity her?

"As I said, my lord, I didn't come here to trap Robyn into marriage. It never even occurred to me." Delia wanted to stop talking, but the words tumbled from her lips. "But it has now."

Before she could move, Alec leapt toward her, closing the distance between them. He grabbed her upper arms. "What do you mean by that, Delia?" His voice was a whisper, lethal and dark.

Delia shivered but didn't answer. His hands tightened on her shoulders and he pulled her toward him until their bodies were touching. His heat overwhelmed her, and she found herself swaying into him. "What did you mean, Delia?"

She didn't know what she'd meant. She'd said it to wipe the pity from his eyes. To make him angry. To hurt him. She hadn't thought beyond that.

His breath was fast and harsh, and his dark eyes had gone black. He towered over her, his lean, hard-muscled body far too close to hers, seething with fury and frustration and, she knew instinctively, passion and desire. As if this experience hadn't been humiliating enough, she realized every cell in her body ached in response to his nearness.

"Let go of me, *my lord.*" She twisted in an attempt to free her shoulders from his grip. His hands tightened for a moment and his eyes dropped to her lips, but then he released her so suddenly she stumbled backward.

He took a step forward again as if to help steady her, but

froze when she backed away from him. "I should thank you for your honesty, *my lord*—your honesty to your brother, that is, as opposed to the lies you told me during our ride today. I would much rather know the truth, even if it's spoken behind my back."

"I don't know what the truth is, damn it. All of it is true. Or none of it. Since you came here, I can't tell the difference anymore."

His voice throbbed with some emotion Delia couldn't name, but she was past caring. "I have a very hard time believing that, Lord Carlisle." She turned her back on him and walked toward the stable doors.

"This isn't a game anymore, Delia." His voice was soft, deadly. "You'll never belong to Robyn. Stay away from him. Don't do anything unworthy of you."

Delia kept her back to him so he couldn't see the tears wetting her cheeks. "From what I overheard today, my lord, I think there is very little you'd consider unworthy of me."

She paused, but he didn't correct her or deny her words. Delia's back stiffened. "I may not be a suitable match for Robyn, but *he* is an excellent match for *me*. Do you imagine I'll overlook my own best interests?" She tried to laugh, but the sound that emerged sounded more like a sob. "You expect a great deal from a social outcast with *a nobody for a father.*"

After that, there seemed to be nothing left for either of them to say, so she walked away.

Chapter Eighteen

He'd have to demand more whiskey. Alec frowned at the bottom of his empty glass. He gave it a little shake and the ice rattled merrily. He shook it again. Maybe if he kept shaking it, someone would come fill it with whiskey.

He wasn't drunk—not at all. He knew he wasn't drunk, because he never lazed about in his study like some degenerate and drank alone. That would be pathetic. Still, if he *were* going to get drunk, this would be a good time to do it.

Christ, what a dismal evening.

She'd seemed to enjoy herself. He thought after the scene at the stables Delia would find an excuse to skip dinner, but as usual she'd surprised him. Wearing a pink gown that turned her skin the color of rich cream, her countenance smooth and unruffled if slightly pale, she'd taken her seat at table with meticulous punctuality, as though she hadn't a care in the world.

She hadn't looked at him once the entire evening.

She looked at Robyn, though. As far as Alec could tell,

she'd done little else besides look at Robyn. She drank wine and ate next to nothing, and all the while she smiled at Robyn and laughed at Robyn's conversation until Alec was ready to throw his wineglass over the heads of his unsuspecting guests directly into Robyn's dinner plate.

Alec raised his glass to his lips and cursed when he remembered it was empty. He pulled the bell, rattled the ice in his glass, and pulled the bell again.

Where the bloody hell were the servants?

Robyn was delighted, of course. Any man would be delighted to have her full attention. How did she get her lips such a deep pink color? It must be paint. No woman's lips were such a color naturally.

But it didn't look like paint. It looked real. It had been days since Alec had kissed her, but he remembered with painful clarity how her lips tasted. They were delicious: hot, eager, wet. Real. Alec knew well enough one taste of them wasn't enough. Robyn might be tasting them right now. Her deep blue eyes might be closed, her lips parted, and Robyn might be leaning down toward her . . .

Alec hurled his glass across the room. It slammed into the heavy oak mantelpiece with a sharp crack and shards of shattered glass and ice hit the floor.

She hadn't turned away quickly enough this afternoon. He'd seen the tears in her eyes and he'd known, down to the deepest recesses of his black soul, he'd done something unforgivable, like trampling a carpet of bluebells under his heavy, muddy boots.

Maybe Robyn was right. Maybe he was just like his father. His father used to drink alone in this very study. It was a coincidence worth noting.

Someone knocked at the door. "Finally," Alec mumbled. "Come!"

Rylands himself entered the room. "My lord—" Rylands

began, but he stopped at the sight of the broken glass and melting ice by the fireplace. The butler looked from Alec to the mess and his perfect impassivity faltered. Alec kept his temper under tight control most of the time, so such a display was rather shocking.

"Ah, Rylands. Another bottle of whiskey, if you please." Alec glanced toward the fireplace. "And another glass. Mine appears to be broken."

Archie peered around the half-open door. "All right there, Carlisle? I thought I heard a gunshot." He stepped into the room.

"I dropped my glass." Alec gestured vaguely toward the fireplace.

Archie strolled through the door. He looked at Alec's morose expression, the smashed glass on the floor at the other end of the room, and raised an eyebrow. "I see that. How unfortunate."

"I'll send a maid in right away to clean up the mess, my lord." Rylands bowed and turned to leave the room.

Alec sighed with irritation. "If you must. But don't forget my whiskey."

"Yes, of course, my lord. Right away." Rylands scurried out the door and closed it quietly behind him.

Archie sat down in the seat across from Alec. He looked around and took in the coat tossed over the back of a leather chair, a crumpled cravat on top of it. Alec's long legs were stretched out before him and his boots rested on the mahogany table.

"So. Carlisle. How are you this evening?"

Alec scowled.

A maid hurried into the room and began to clean up the broken glass on the floor. Rylands followed, carrying a bottle of whiskey and three glasses on a silver tray.

Alec eyed the glasses. "Are you going to join us, Rylands?"

"No, my lord." Rylands gave an offended sniff. "The second glass is for Lord Archibald. The third glass is an extra one, in case there is another, ah, mishap."

Alec's scowl deepened. "How cautious of you."

"Yes, my lord." Rylands placed the tray on the edge of the mahogany table, as far away from Alec's boots as possible. "Thank you, my lord."

"Damn impertinent," Alec muttered as the door closed behind the servants. Still, it was by no means certain he wouldn't hurl another glass across the room, so perhaps it was just as well.

"What are you hiding in here for?" Archie asked.

Alec gave Archie a sullen look and slumped down farther in his seat. "I had an argument with Robyn today."

"Ah. Curious, that. A fight with Robyn, I mean. Surprising. Explains why you'd be holed up in here like a hermit, of course, soused and tossing glasses about."

Alec slammed the heel of his boot into the table. "Robyn wasn't at all pleased when I attempted to take away his favorite new toy."

Archie frowned, and Alec felt a rush of savage satisfaction. Even in his whiskey-addled state, it occurred to him that maybe he *wanted* Archie to be disgusted with him.

"And by 'new toy,' I suppose you mean Miss Somerset?"

"Who else? Robyn demanded to know why I was sneaking around with her, or disappearing into dark corners with her, or spiriting her down mysterious pathways, or some similar nonsense. The discussion deteriorated quickly after that."

"No doubt it did. What did you tell him?"

Alec drained the whiskey from his glass and poured another. "Told him he couldn't have her, that's what. Reminded him of his duty to his family."

Archie leaned back in his chair, considering. "So Robyn really is courting her, then? Did he say as much?"

"Course not. Robyn never admits to anything. You know that, Archie. He did ask if—" Alec broke off. He didn't want to remember this part of the conversation, much less repeat it, but he didn't see any way around it. "He asked if I would approve the match if he were in love with Delia."

Love. Robyn. With Delia. A sick emptiness started in Alec's chest and began to claw its way up his throat. He took a deep swallow of whiskey to force it back down.

"Did he?" Archie's tone was deceptively casual. "What did you say to that?"

Alec winced. He wasn't proud of what he'd said next. "I might have mentioned something about Robyn taking Delia as his mistress."

There was a charged silence, and then Archie leaned forward in his chair, his face grim. "Christ, Carlisle," he began, but then his eyes narrowed on Alec. "But that doesn't sound like you. You didn't mean it."

It wasn't a question.

"No. I didn't mean it. I may be a bastard, Archie, but even I draw the line at despoiling virgins."

"Why say it at all, then?" Archie asked in a maddeningly reasonable tone.

"To hear him deny it, of course!" Alec took another swallow of whiskey and made an effort to lower his voice. "I feel as if I don't know Robyn anymore, and I wanted to be sure *he* still draws the line at despoiling virgins."

Archie ignored Alec's outburst. "Does he? What did he say?"

"He was furious. Thank God for that. He told me I didn't know him or Delia at all if I believed either one of them would consent to such an arrangement."

Archie let out a long breath. "Thank God indeed," he murmured, as if he hadn't been at all sure of the answer. "Damned unpleasant scene. Glad that *wasn't* a gunshot I heard earlier, come to think of it."

But Alec shrugged off Archie's concern. He didn't know the worst of it yet. "Delia overheard every word of it."

Archie's eyes nearly popped out of his head and fell into his whiskey glass. "Jesus." All trace of levity vanished. "She heard everything?" He sounded truly aghast.

"Yes. I don't know what she was doing there, but she was standing outside the stable doors the entire time. She heard *every bloody word.*"

"You're an unlucky one, Carlisle." Archie shook his head. "What a disaster."

"It was. Even more so than you can imagine. I've never seen anyone more hurt or angry in my life." The pain and disbelief in her expressive blue eyes flashed in his mind. The same image had tormented him all evening.

Bluebells smashed under his boot heels.

"The worst of it is Robyn will find Delia Somerset more irresistible than ever now." Alec kept the fact that he also found her irresistible to himself, however. What difference did it make now? She despised him.

"*That's* the worst of it?"

"Of course. You remember Robyn as a boy, Archie. Always angling after whatever bauble was forbidden to him. Delia seems far more interested in Robyn now, too, after she overheard him defend her so valiantly."

Something in Alec's voice caught Archie's attention. "Robyn's not a boy now, Carlisle." His expression was unreadable. "He's a grown man, and for all her shining beauty, Delia Somerset isn't a bauble."

Alec shrugged. "It amounts to the same thing."

Archie shook his head. "No. It doesn't. Not a bit of it, Carlisle."

"Then she said she hadn't come here intending to marry Robyn, but after today, perhaps she'd reconsider." He'd flown into a fit of savage, jealous rage then, and had stopped just shy of showing her who she truly belonged to—

Alec took a deep, unsteady breath and drained the rest of the whiskey from his glass. Even now, remembering her words, he felt fury rise like bile in his throat.

Alec had forgotten Archie was even in the room with him and was taken aback when he heard him chuckle. "She actually said that?"

"Not in so many words, but yes—that's what she meant."

"Ah." Archie nodded. "And now you're embracing your whiskey as if you believe it will squeeze you back because you think she's going to encourage Robyn's attentions?"

Alec exploded again. "She's already encouraging his attentions! Didn't you see her at dinner? She may as well have been sitting in Robyn's lap."

Archie blinked at him. "No, Carlisle, I confess I didn't see Miss Somerset enthroned on Robyn's lap at dinner this evening. I can't think how I missed it."

Alec shrugged. Then he picked up Archie's whiskey glass and drank the contents in one swallow. "Me either." He wiped a hand across his mouth. "S'matter with you, Archie?"

Archie sighed. "What do you intend to do now? Perhaps it would be best if you stepped aside."

Alec stared at him. Now. He was going to throw the glass *now.* "The devil I will." He sloshed more whiskey into his glass.

"Very well, Carlisle." Archie got to his feet. "I'll leave it to you, then." He placed his whiskey glass on the table, then picked up the bottle and handed it to Alec. "I believe you're going to need this. Good evening."

Alec didn't notice Archie leave. He sat in front of the fire drinking whiskey and trying to remember why he'd objected to Delia as a match for Robyn in the first place. Didn't it have something to do with the *beau monde* tittering about the Sutherlands in every drawing room in London?

Was that it? Odd. He couldn't quite remember anymore.

He frowned, concentrating. He thought it had something

to do with Robyn. He didn't want Robyn to kiss Delia. That much he was damn sure of. Or touch her.

Or look at her or talk to her or walk with her or make her laugh or smell her hair or taste her or anything else her.

Ah, yes. He smiled happily at his glass. *That* was it.

Delia felt weary down to her bones. She looked at the stairs in front of her and wondered if she had the energy to climb them.

Dinner had been interminable. The food had undoubtedly been delicious, but every bite felt as if it would choke her. She'd conversed with Robyn and smiled and laughed until her face ached from the effort. It took every ounce of her control not to look at Alec, but still she felt him, the heat from his intense dark eyes as palpable as a hand sliding down her back.

"Off to bed at last, Delia?"

Delia nearly jumped out of her skin. The low drawling voice seemed to come out of the darkness itself, but when she turned from the stairs, there he was, arms crossed over his broad chest, leaning against the wall next to his study door.

He'd removed his coat, waistcoat, and cravat, and the neck of his fine white cambric shirt gaped open. He'd shoved his sleeves up past his elbows, exposing an endless length of muscular forearm. He must have been running his hands through his thick dark hair, too—he had a habit of doing that. Too-long locks fell across his forehead and the start of a dark beard shadowed his face.

He looks like a pirate. Delia's eyes drifted to the tanned skin of his chest left exposed by the open shirt, and an unwelcome shiver of awareness tickled down her spine. A pirate who was a bit worse off from drink, that was.

What a perfect end to a perfect day—alone in a dark hallway with a drunken pirate who was about to fall out of his shirt.

"You're drunk." She hoped her abruptness would disguise her sudden breathlessness. She turned to start up the stairs, but before she could take a step, he wrapped a hand around her arm and turned her back around to face him.

She looked down at the long fingers grasping her arm, then pointedly back into his face, but he ignored the hint and drew her closer. "Just drunk enough," he said, in a low, amused voice.

Don't ask. Don't ask. Don't ask.

"Just drunk enough for what?" *Blast.*

But he was the only one permitted to ask questions, it seemed. "Did you enjoy your evening, Delia? You appeared to be pleased with your dinner companion."

Well, that settled it. If she'd appeared to enjoy herself tonight, then it was time for her to tread the boards at Drury Lane. "Oh, yes." She made a futile attempt to tug her arm free from his grasp. "I do prefer to *participate* in a conversation rather than overhear it."

She raised her chin with a defiant jerk. *There.* That should serve to remind him of what an awful, terrible man he was. Hopefully it would remind her, as well.

But if she was expecting him to look ashamed, she was disappointed. He took in her raised chin and a slow, wicked smile drifted across his lips. "You mean you prefer to participate rather than eavesdrop?"

"Eavesdrop! How *dare*—"

"But then, eavesdropping has advantages, too," he went on, as if she hadn't spoken. "For example, I'd have been very interested to overhear any part of your conversation with Robyn tonight."

Delia bristled. "My conversations with Robyn or anyone else are none of your business, Lord Carlisle."

His face darkened and his fingers tightened on her arm. "Ah, but I think it is my business, given the circumstances."

Delia felt an angry flush rise in her cheeks. "Oh, yes. How could I forget the circumstances? You must be referring to my devious plot to trap your brother into marrying me." She cocked her head to one side, as if considering this. "Well, you will be glad to know I'm off to a promising start. Robyn and I"—she paused dramatically—"*walked in the garden together this evening.*"

Alec stiffened and his mocking smile vanished. Suddenly there was tension in every line of his hard body.

Perhaps she shouldn't have goaded him—

But it was too late. He was already reaching for her. Delia backed away from him, but he pursued her until the stair banister pressed into her spine. He slipped one long finger under her chin and raised her face to his. His other hand was still wrapped around her arm.

"Indeed? How romantic." That lazy smile started at the corner of his mouth again, but his dark eyes were hot with fury. He gazed at her for a moment, then slowly teased that long finger across her cheek. "What other intimacies did you permit?"

She couldn't look away from him. Delia tried to gather her wits, but all of her attention was focused on that warm, seeking finger. "What do you mean?"

Her heart hammered as he moved his hand so his palm cupped her face. He brushed his fingertips lightly across the shell of her ear and the sensitive skin behind it, and leaned forward so his breath stirred the tendrils of hair at her temple. He pressed his lips softly against her ear. "I think you know. Did he touch you?"

Delia closed her eyes at the sensation of his hot breath teasing her skin. He smelled faintly of woodsmoke and fine whiskey. "Yes." She tried for a firm tone, but her voice emerged faint and breathless. "Of—of course he did. He took my arm."

Some strong emotion surged through his body. He was so close to her now Delia felt an echo of it low in her own belly. The tip of his tongue grazed her earlobe. Delia jumped in shock and then shuddered with pleasure. "Oh, don't," she pleaded in a sudden panic.

He let out a ragged breath. "Don't what?" His voice had gone husky, but it still vibrated with anger. "Don't touch you?" His hand drifted down until it reached the small of her back. He held her body tightly against his own as one hard thigh moved between her legs to press against her through her skirts. "Don't put my mouth on you?" His lips roamed deliberately from her ear across her cheek and then down to her throat. "Or don't ask any more questions?" His mouth stopped at the soft skin between her neck and her shoulder and nipped lightly. "Did you let my brother kiss you?"

Delia couldn't speak. She was drowning. She cursed both him and herself even as she wrapped her arms around his neck, desperate to stay afloat. He groaned low in his chest. "Answer me, Delia." He nipped gently at her neck with his teeth, then licked at the bite with his darting tongue.

"N-no." Delia bit back a moan, not sure if she was answering his question or begging him to stop. Or was she begging him not to stop? "No."

Some of the tightly leashed anger drained from his body then. Her frantic grip on his shoulders eased as she felt him draw a deep breath. "Damned good thing," he whispered, right before his mouth came down on hers, not gently but voraciously, crushing her lips. He tasted her, then pulled her plump bottom lip into his mouth and sucked.

Delia moaned, and he took ruthless advantage of her desire. He plunged his tongue roughly into her open mouth, invading her. She hesitated, shocked but also unbearably excited. Her tongue crept forward and hesitantly touched his. He groaned and his hands moved from the small of her back to her hips, drawing her tight against his hardening cock.

With every delicate stroke of her tongue, his control seemed to slip another notch. His powerful body shook with pleasure. Emboldened by his reaction, Delia sank her fingers into the deep waves of his crisp black hair and tugged, pulling his head down to hers. He growled against her mouth, then captured her tugging fingers in his and pressed her hands inside the open neck of his shirt, against the bare skin of his chest.

His skin was hot, so hot. She moved her hands to the opening at his neck so she could feel more of it.

He lifted his mouth from hers. "You will *never* let him kiss you," he commanded fiercely in a low, savage voice, his mouth still hovering over hers.

His words penetrated the dense fog of her desire. She'd been lost in his kiss, one breath away from tearing his shirt off, and he'd been thinking—what? That she'd allow Robyn to kiss her this way, too? That she was some grand seductress who practiced on one brother so she could seduce the other?

Alec's hateful words from this afternoon flooded over her, each syllable like a hard slap across her face. Yes. He did think that of her, and worse, too. She'd sworn to herself she'd remember his vile words and never be such a fool again, but here she was with her arms around his neck, kissing him as if nectar flowed from his mouth and she was starved for nourishment.

Her cheeks burned with shame.

She placed her hands flat against his chest and pushed— hard. She caught him off guard and he released her at once, his arms falling away. He stared at her, his expression stunned, his hands clenched at his sides.

"Why shouldn't I let Robyn kiss me?" Her voice was strong and clear in spite of her breathlessness. "Isn't that what mistresses do?"

Alec's face went so pale his dark eyes seemed to burn. "Delia, I didn't—" He broke off, and when he spoke again, he seemed to be pleading with her. "I know you would never . . ."

He stopped and ran an unsteady hand down his face. He seemed to be struggling to find the right words.

Delia stared at him, shocked at his anguished expression. She gasped as her heart clenched painfully in her chest. When had it happened? When had his pain become hers?

"Don't say that," he whispered fiercely. "You will *never* be his mistress."

Delia shook her head as a wave of unbearable sadness swept through her. "But I didn't say it, Alec. *You* did. Now it can never be unsaid."

He stared at her for a moment longer, his face ashen. "So I did," he murmured at last. "And so it can't."

He turned, walked back into his study, and closed the door quietly behind him.

Chapter Nineteen

"*No, no, Lily! You cannot wear a fichu with that ball* gown! It isn't at all the thing, you know." Charlotte sounded as if she were about to collapse with laughter.

The door connecting the two rooms stood open, and another shriek of glee made Delia clutch her head in pain. Charlotte and Lily had been closeted in Lily's room all morning, deep in consultations over their gowns for the ball the following evening.

Delia had retreated to her own room after breakfast and spent the rest of the morning hiding there under the pretense of writing a letter home. She picked up her latest attempt and slowly crumpled it in her hands. The sheet was so crossed and blotted it was unreadable.

Her eyes felt swollen and dry, and her head ached terribly.

There was another screech of laughter from Lily's room. "Hide it? Nonsense, my dear. We'll do all we can to call attention to it!"

"But, Charlotte." Poor Lily sounded a little desperate. "It's cut *so* low. I'm not accustomed to . . . That is, it exposes so much of my . . ." Her voice trailed off into a forlorn squeak.

"Exactly. That's the very point. You may count yourself fortunate you have a bosom worth displaying. I know at least one gentleman who will be exceedingly grateful indeed."

"Lord Archibald?" Lily sounded resigned. "But he's such an awful rogue, Charlotte."

"Oh my, yes," Charlotte replied blithely. "But a rich, handsome, and titled one!"

Delia rose from the desk, crossed the room, and closed the door that connected her room to Lily's. The last thing she wished to hear about this morning was rich, handsome, and titled rogues. She lay down on the bed, pulled a fluffy pillow over her face, and immediately commenced thinking about rich, handsome, and titled rogues.

Well, one specific one anyway. She didn't *want* to think about him or the scene in the stables, but the effort to keep from doing so was exhausting her. She was sure it was the reason she had such a dreadful headache. She pulled the pillow off her face and shoved it under her head. So she was going to lie here and think about it, and when she'd done so, she was never, ever going to think about it again.

Alec wished she'd never come here. Well, that made two of them, so that wasn't what was making her feel as though her heart had been cut to ribbons.

So her father had been "a nobody" and her mother a scandal, so much so even their own grandmother pretended she and her sisters didn't exist. Very well. Delia could bear that. The part about her father hurt a bit, but the truth was Henry Somerset had been *somebody*, somebody very special indeed, and nothing anyone said about him could change that.

What else? Oh, yes. A marriage to Delia would disgrace the entire Sutherland family, so Alec had only been pretending he desired her, in order to keep her out of Robyn's way.

She was fit to be Robyn's mistress, but men like the Sutherlands only married wealthy aristocrats like Lady Lisette.
As far as Alec was concerned, Delia was no more significant
than the young woman he'd been debauching on the day she
arrived in Kent.

Oh, God. That did hurt. It hurt terribly. She rolled onto
her back, threw an arm over her eyes, and let the misery
wash over her.

But even this wasn't the worst of it. She'd tried to deny
it, and she'd tried to pretend it wasn't true, but there was no
help for it. The truth, the very worst part of the whole awful
affair, was she knew how much it must have hurt Alec when
Robyn said he was just like their father, the late earl. Every
time she closed her eyes, she saw Alec's face when she'd
walked into the stables after Robyn stormed out. He'd looked
so pale, so lost. Of all the ugly, hurtful words said that day,
it was these words that left Delia gasping with the pain that
flooded her heart.

The more fool she, but there it was.

It was time for her to go back to Surrey. Back home. She'd
thought she could come here and prove something to these
people. To Alec. To herself, really. But she wasn't as strong
as her mother, after all. Millicent hadn't been exiled by
society. She'd chosen not to be a part of this world, and she'd
orchestrated her own exit on her own terms, and never
looked back.

Running away back to Surrey with a broken heart wasn't
the same thing at all, was it?

Delia rolled over onto her side, drew her knees up against
her chest, and closed her eyes. A few tears leaked out to
dampen her pillow, but she tamped them down before they
could become a deluge. What good would it do to lie there
and snivel and whimper about it? It was over and done with,
and she wasn't going to waste any more time thinking about
it. Crying about it. Wishing things were different . . .

"Delia? Delia!"

Delia woke a little while later to find Lily standing over her bed, shaking her shoulder gently. "You missed luncheon." Lily sat down at the foot of the bed and looked at Delia with concern. "I almost woke you, but you looked so tired."

"It's all right." Delia sat up. "I wasn't hungry anyway." She felt a little better now. Her heart was still bleeding, but at least her headache had eased somewhat. "Where's Charlotte?"

"She went for a walk with Lord Archibald."

"You didn't want to walk with them?"

"No." Lily avoided her sister's eyes. "I want to talk to you about something, actually."

Delia groaned to herself. Oh, for pity's sake! What now? She wasn't sure she could handle any more surprises.

"Charlotte has invited us to accompany the family to London for the season," Lily began carefully. "Lady Carlisle extended a formal invitation yesterday afternoon. You are invited, as well, of course."

Delia felt her heart plummet into her stomach. It was lovely of Lady Carlisle to invite them, but there was no way she could go, given the circumstances. The only place she was going was back to Surrey. Soon. And now it looked like she was going alone.

She bit her lip to keep from loudly enumerating all the reasons why Lily shouldn't go, either. London was wicked. The *ton* was wicked, especially the gentlemen. It wasn't proper for Lily to go without Delia. Lily didn't have the right clothes. The right slippers. The right jewelry. Or, indeed, any jewelry at all. And finally, grasping at straws: the journey was too long and wet. Lily could catch cold.

It was all nonsense, of course. London might be wicked, but one could get up to wickedness anywhere, like a house party in Kent, for example. Delia couldn't argue that *she* was a more appropriate chaperone than Lady Carlisle, either, who had not, as far as Delia knew, been locked in a passionate embrace with an almost-engaged rake of an earl at the bottom of the staircase last night. As to clothes, well— Charlotte had mountains of them. Enough for a dozen young ladies to attend every party of the season without ever appearing twice in the same gown.

"That is so kind of Lady Carlisle," Delia said, "but I can't go, dear."

"No, I didn't suppose you would. I don't think this visit has agreed with you, Delia. You've been rather out of sorts since we arrived." There was a pause, then, "Do you suppose I may go, just the same?"

Lily looked at her with pleading eyes.

Delia sighed. Oh, how she'd miss her pristine, fastidious little sister! But she couldn't think of a single person who deserved a chance to see some of the world beyond Surrey more than Lily did, and this was likely Lily's best chance to do so. They had one other connection in London—Lady Anne Chase, their maternal grandmother. But Alec was right about her. There was only resounding silence from that quarter. She would never acknowledge them.

"Of course you must go." Delia was thankful her voice wasn't shaking. "I would like to have a word with Lady Carlisle first to settle the details, but that's simple enough."

Lily clapped her hands with delight. "Oh, thank you, Delia! Oh, how wonderful." Lily's face glowed with excitement. "I'll miss you terribly, though." She looked at Delia, her bright expression fading a little. "I wish we could both—"

"You won't even notice I'm not there after a week, because you'll be so engaged with parties and balls." Delia tried to ignore the sharp pang in her chest. "Besides, one of us must go back to Surrey and make sure our sisters haven't locked Hannah in a cupboard."

Lily laughed. "I hadn't thought of that. Poor Hannah. When will you go?"

"Soon, I think," Delia replied vaguely. *Very soon.*

"I must go tell Charlotte." Lily jumped up from the bed and rushed to the door. "Oh, Delia, before I forget. Eleanor is looking for you. She'd like you to come to her bedchamber when you wake. She said she wants to show you something."

Delia threw her legs over the side of the bed. She enjoyed Eleanor's company very much, and a visit with her friend sounded like just the thing. "Have you seen Lady Carlisle this afternoon?"

"Charlotte said she's in her private sitting room, finalizing details for the ball tomorrow night. Will you go and see her now?"

Delia nodded. "Yes, I think so. I'll go to Eleanor afterwards."

"I'll go find Charlotte. Lord Archibald awaits, after all." She gave Delia an impish smile. "Delia?"

Delia stood at the looking glass, repinning her hair. "Yes?"

"I know you've been unhappy since we arrived here. No," she continued quickly, when Delia started to speak. "I'm not going to ask why, because you'll tell me yourself if you want to. I know you didn't want to come to Kent, and that you came for my sake. Thank you. You're a wonderful sister. I just wanted to say that."

"Oh, Lily." Delia's throat went tight.

"Now fix your hair," Lily said with a grin before Delia could say another word. "It's a disaster."

"One of many, I'm afraid," Delia murmured to herself after the door had closed behind Lily.

Within the quarter hour she'd tidied her appearance and was standing in the hallway outside Lady Carlisle's private sitting room, her hand poised in front of the handsomely carved door like a pale bird arrested in mid-flight. It was silly to be nervous. Lady Carlisle had been nothing but kind since they'd arrived at Bellwood, but Delia wasn't looking forward to discussing the one little nasty of piece of business that brought her here.

She sighed and willed her knuckles to make contact with the polished wood.

"Yes?" Lady Carlisle's voice carried clearly into the hallway.

Delia opened the door and peeked around it. "Good afternoon, my lady."

"Oh, Miss Somerset. Please come in. Won't you sit down?" Lady Carlisle gestured to the tea service on a small table next to a sumptuous blue velvet chair. "Will you take tea?"

"No, thank you, my lady." Delia took a seat on a tufted yellow satin settee.

Lady Carlisle settled herself on the chair across from Delia and folded her hands serenely in her lap. "What a surprise to see you here." She regarded Delia with her kind dark eyes.

But Lady Carlisle didn't look surprised. Delia had the oddest sense the older woman knew precisely why she was there. *Oh, good God.* Surely Alec hadn't confided the details of their sordid little game to his mother? Just the thought made Delia squirm nervously in her seat.

She twisted her hands in her lap. "I'm sorry to disturb you. Lily tells me she's been invited to accompany your family to London for the season."

Lady Carlisle nodded. "Yes. I do know you have responsibilities at home, however. Three younger sisters, I believe? I hope we don't presume too much in extending the invitation."

"Presume? Oh, no, my lady. Not at all. It's just . . ." She stopped, not sure how to get the next words out gracefully. "That is, our grandmother . . . I did want to make it clear our maternal grandmother does not . . ." Delia trailed off hopelessly, realizing too late there was no graceful way to explain their wretched grandmother would likely cut Lily directly if she were to see her at a party or ball in London.

"Ah, yes. Lady Chase." Lady Carlisle set her porcelain teacup carefully in the saucer. "I'm acquainted with her. She's very grand, is she not? I believe you wish to tell me she doesn't receive you?"

"Yes." Delia released the breath she was holding. She was grateful to Lady Carlisle for so generously excusing her from having to say it. "Doubtless you will encounter her at various social functions, and I'm afraid there may be some awkwardness. Lily and I have no wish to embarrass the Sutherlands—"

"My dear Miss Somerset," Lady Carlisle interrupted gently. "Please don't concern yourself with this. I don't think any of us need concern ourselves with Lady Chase at all."

Delia gazed at her companion with admiration. Lady Carlisle was saying, in her refined way, that the Sutherlands had more than enough social clout to withstand being cut by Lady Chase. Delia's own mother had had the same gift of saying a great deal with a few well-placed words.

"Then I have no hesitation at all in encouraging Lily to accompany you to London," Delia replied with a smile. "It's a wonderful adventure for her. Lily will make the most of this opportunity without ever causing you a moment's concern."

Lady Carlisle raised one fine, dark eyebrow. "The invitation was extended to you, as well, Miss Somerset. My daughters have such pleasure in your company."

Delia's face fell.

The trouble isn't your daughters, my lady. It's your son. The elder has rather too much pleasure in my company, and for all the wrong reasons.

But it would never do to say so, no matter that Delia was almost irresistibly tempted to confide everything to the countess. She pressed her lips together to keep from blurting out the truth. "You are very kind, my lady. But under the circumstances—"

Oops. That wasn't quite what she'd intended to say, for she'd much rather believe Lady Carlisle didn't have any inkling of the circumstances she referred to. Delia bit her lip and tried again. "What I mean is, it would be better for everyone if . . ."

Blast. It was impossible to lie with Lady Carlisle's benevolent dark eyes upon her. Fortunately there was outright lying, and then there was simply withholding the entire truth. Delia clenched her hands in her lap. "As you said, my lady, I have responsibilities at home. Our younger sisters need a steady influence."

Not that I'm qualified to provide one. Look at what a mess she'd made of things during her short visit to Bellwood.

But Lady Carlisle nodded in understanding. "Yes, of course. We'll feel your loss most keenly, though."

"Thank you, my lady." Delia rose from her seat and dipped into a curtsy.

She was at the door when Lady Carlisle stopped her. "Miss Somerset? I hope you will not judge my son too harshly."

Delia froze. Her heart rushed up from her chest and lodged in her throat.

Lady Carlisle watched her steadily. "His father was a . . . difficult man. Alec, as the eldest, suffered the worst of it, I'm afraid, and since he became the earl, he's had to muddle through as best he can. He's made many mistakes, but most of them arise from his wish to protect this family. Indeed, he tries rather too hard sometimes." She paused and looked calmly up at Delia, who still hovered by the door. "I'm sure you can understand that kind of concern for one's family. Can't you, Miss Somerset?"

Delia looked into Lady Carlisle's intelligent dark eyes.

She understood it perfectly. It had never occurred to her before, but perhaps in some ways she and Alec were quite a lot alike. "Yes, I believe I can."

Lady Carlisle smiled. "I thought so." With that cryptic reply, she retrieved her tea from the table and nodded politely.

Delia considered herself dismissed. She closed the door behind her and walked down the hallway in the direction of Eleanor's room, lost in thought. When she reached the family wing of the house, however, she stopped and looked around blankly.

Drat. She was staring down a long hallway of identical closed doors. She retraced her steps back to the staircase and then walked forward again, counting doors this time, but it was no use.

She couldn't remember which room was Eleanor's.

Chapter Twenty

Alec threw a handful of cold water on his face and watched in the glass as it dripped off his chin. He'd been disgustingly cup-shot last night. If there were any justice in the world, he'd be unable to move this morning.

Fortunately for him, justice was fickle, at best. Then again, he hadn't drunk so much he couldn't remember what he'd done. Or what he'd said. Or the look on Delia's face when he'd done and said it. So maybe there was justice, after all.

He'd been a complete bastard yesterday, but he'd outdone himself last night when he'd turned an already dismal situation into a disaster by acting like an utter ass. By his tally, he should beg the pardon of every person in this house for one thing or another.

He dried his face and pulled on his coat. He'd find Delia today and he'd beg her pardon. Period. There would be no touching. No angry fits or jealous rages. No kissing.

Certainly no kissing. He was an *earl*, damn it. It was time he started to act like one.

Resolutions firmly in hand, Alec opened his chamber door and stepped out into the hallway.

And instantly tossed every single one of them aside.

Delia stood there alone, about to knock on a door across the hall.

Robyn's door.

Without any hesitation or conscious thought, Alec strode toward her, grasped her by the wrist, tugged her with him straight back to his room, and slammed the door behind them.

For a moment they stared at each other warily, neither saying a word. Then, almost as if he weren't aware he was doing it, Alec began a rhythmic stroking against her wrist with his thumb. "What are you doing, Delia?" His voice was ominously quiet. He eased her back against the door and pinned her there with his body. "Is this checkmate?"

She ignored both questions. "I can't be in your bedchamber with you, Lord Carlisle." Her hand began to go limp in his grip. "You know that."

He turned her hand over and ran his finger lightly across the center of her palm. "But you can be in Robyn's bedchamber? I confess I don't see the distinction."

"Robyn?" Her brow wrinkled in confusion. "I was looking for Eleanor." She made a halfhearted attempt to withdraw her hand from his grasp.

"Were you?" He began to draw slow, lazy circles in the center of her palm with his fingertip. "I'm not sure I believe you, Delia. I think you're pursuing Robyn, just as you threatened to."

She shook her head, looking him straight in the eyes. "No more threats, Alec, and no more lies. The game is over."

He pressed a hot, openmouthed kiss into the center of

her hand, the tip of his tongue just grazing her palm. A flush started in her cheeks, washed across her neck in a flood of pink, and then disappeared into her bodice.

Alec watched it, fascinated, and far too aware his bed was mere steps away. He raised her hand to his mouth and slipped the tip of one of her fingers between his lips. "It doesn't *feel* over," he crooned wickedly.

A little sigh escaped her, as if she was overcome by the sensation of the hot, rough velvet of his tongue against her fingertip. She was trembling. "I'm leaving Bellwood, Alec."

That got his attention. He released her hand abruptly and pulled away from her so he could look into her face. "What do you mean, you're leaving? You and Lily will accompany the family to London the day after the ball."

She dropped her eyes to the ground, as if she were afraid to look at him. Did she think she'd see relief on his face? Triumph? "I promised Lily I'd stay for the ball, but—"

"You're not going anywhere," Alec growled, cutting her off. "You will not walk away from me that easily."

Alec knew he *should* be relieved. He should let her go and do everything in his power to forget about her. But he wasn't relieved. He was unaccountably furious. He caught her wrist again in a hard grip.

Delia stared up at him, shocked. "Walk away from you? But, but . . . I thought you'd be—"

Let her go. It's the only thing that makes sense. It's for the best.

But his reaction was immediate and from the deepest part of his gut.

One word. *No.*

"You thought I'd be what?" He was shocked to hear the fury in his voice. "Pleased to see you go? I don't even know why you started the game to begin with! This isn't over yet, Delia."

She didn't say anything for a moment, just looked at him with an expression Alec knew he'd never forget. She looked so terribly sad.

"It doesn't matter why, and it *is* over." Her voice caught a little on the last word and Alec felt his heart plummet. "It should never have begun. You know it as well as I do, Alec."

He wanted to rail at her. Shake her. Shout at her it *wasn't* over. Not for him. But it was madness, this game. It had to end before anyone else got hurt. His fingers fell numbly away from her wrist.

But he had to know one last thing before he could let her go, because this would never be over for him until he knew whether or not she was in love with his brother. "What about Robyn?" He held his breath, waiting for her answer.

"I never sought to engage his affections. I'm fond of Robyn, and I consider him my friend. But that's all. I—" She stopped, as if the next words were difficult for her to say. "I only said otherwise to hurt you. I beg your pardon for that, Alec."

She was apologizing to him? She was saying she was sorry. *To him.* Her apology felt like a fist slammed into his stomach.

She turned away from him and opened the door, but then she looked back again. "What a reckless game it was. I don't feel like I've won. Do you?"

Alec watched, stunned, as she slipped out the door. Without thinking, he started after her. "Delia, wait—"

He came to a sudden halt as soon as he reached the hallway. Eleanor stood at the door of her room. She opened her door wider so Delia could pass through. "There you are, Delia. I've waited for you this age."

Delia disappeared into Eleanor's room without sparing Alec another word or glance, but Eleanor lingered in the doorway, her eyes narrowed on him. "I'll see *you* later, Alec." Then she closed the door in his face.

Alec walked blindly down the hallway, not sure where he was going.

He didn't feel like he'd won. He should have told Delia that. He'd see her again, at meals and at the ball tomorrow night, but he wouldn't tell her then, either. It was over, just as she'd said it was. There wasn't any reason to say anything anymore.

He should have kissed her one more time. He hadn't known last night would be the last time. If he had, he'd have made sure to memorize the taste and feel of her lips against his mouth.

The crushed rock of the pathway crunched under his boots as he walked. He looked around and realized vaguely that he'd entered the rose garden. He must have walked outside at some point. He didn't remember.

"What the devil—" He stopped and kicked at the ground, digging a little with his boot. His heel had come down on something hard, half-buried in the dirt next to an outside corner of the rose arbor. He leaned down to pull the thing loose, then turned it over in his hands and brushed some of the soil away.

He stared at it. It was a small statue of Bacchus. He turned it over and over in his hands and traced with one finger the rough edge where Bacchus's chalice used to be. It was missing now, a victim of a trampling by another pair of boots, a long time ago.

He'd never forget that day. He and Robyn had been home on a holiday. Robyn had been involved in some minor prank at school and their father, disgusted as usual by any sign of boyish high spirits, had taken Robyn into his study for a severe dressing-down. Alec lingered in the hallway outside the door, waiting as he always did for Robyn to emerge. But this time when Robyn came out at last, he'd been ashen, his dark eyes hunted.

Alec remembered it because it was the day he decided

he'd had enough. Enough of his father. Enough of seeing that expression on his brother's face.

The study door hadn't closed behind their father before Alec was leading Robyn through the house. They'd both grabbed small bits of statuary off mantels and tables and sneaked them outdoors under their coats. They'd built an intricate obstacle course on the far side of the garden, behind the rose arbor, so their father couldn't see them from his study. By the middle of the morning, Charlotte and Eleanor had caught on to the game, and the four of them had spent the entire afternoon running races until they were streaked with dirt and mud and their sides ached from laughter.

Bacchus had been a casualty of the events of that day. But Robyn hadn't.

He and Robyn had somehow lost their way since then. They were so lost, in fact, Alec hadn't spared a thought for his brother at all since Delia had arrived. Was Robyn in love with her? Would he be devastated when he found out she was leaving? Alec didn't know. He hadn't given any thought at all to how Robyn might feel. He'd been too focused on controlling the chessboard to spare any thought for the pieces.

What if I was in love with her? What if my happiness depended on her?

Robyn had tried to tell him yesterday, but Alec hadn't listened.

He looked down at Bacchus cradled in his hands and ran his palm again and again over the smooth stone. It was cold under his fingers. Alec had sworn all those years ago he wouldn't let his father or anyone else crush Robyn's spirit. It never occurred to him he'd need to protect Robyn from him.

"Alec?"

Alec's head came up. Eleanor stood there, an odd expression on her face. She took a deep breath and let it out. "What was Delia doing in your bedchamber?"

Alec stiffened. Eleanor had seen them, then. He wasn't sure how he could explain it to her when he didn't understand it himself, but if she'd witnessed him drag Delia into his bedchamber and close the door behind them, he supposed she did deserve an explanation.

Eleanor was waiting, watching him so intently Alec began to feel like an insect trapped under glass. "It isn't what it looks like." It was a hardly an explanation, but it was the best he could do right now.

"Shall I tell you what it looks like?" Eleanor asked. "It *looks* like an incorrigible, wicked, and unrepentant rake dragged an innocent young lady into his bedchamber to ruin her. But that's not what it *is*, is it, Alec? That's not why she was there."

Alec stared at his sister in disbelief. "Since you know so much, Eleanor, why don't you tell me why she was there?"

"Don't you *know*, Alec?" Eleanor arched an eyebrow. "Very well. You've been infatuated with Delia almost since the moment she arrived here. But this isn't one of your typical *amours*. Far from it, in fact. You dragged Delia into your chamber because you simply couldn't help yourself."

Alec gaped at her, his jaw hanging open. He was damned if he could see how Eleanor knew so much about his affairs, but he couldn't help but be impressed at how perceptive she was. Still, she didn't know everything. "I've made a mess of it. I hurt her. I treated her like—"

"Like you couldn't keep your hands off her? Like she's the most beautiful and desirable woman you've ever known? I think she'll forgive you, Alec."

He shook his head. "No. She's just told me she's leaving for Surrey after the ball. Nothing is going to come of it, Eleanor."

Delia was leaving, and everything was going to go back to the way it should be. She'd go back to Surrey, where she belonged, and he'd marry Lady Lisette, just as he'd planned.

Robyn would go back to London and carry on as usual, and over time he'd forget about Delia. He'd fall in love with someone else.

"But *why*, Alec? Please tell me this isn't that foolishness about the scandal over her mother. It was ages ago! It hardly matters now, does it?"

Alec didn't answer right away, but looked down at the statue in his hands for a moment. "I thought it did, at first. But no. You're right. It doesn't matter."

"I wondered why you made such an effort to keep Robyn and Delia apart when she first arrived," Eleanor said. "You were trying to discourage a romance between them, weren't you?"

Eleanor hadn't missed a thing, it seemed. "That was how it started, yes, and now I've been caught in my own trap." For one moment he felt an absurd urge to laugh. What perfect irony! Justice wasn't so fickle, after all, was she? She was a cruel, lying shrew, but she wasn't fickle. She'd dealt out an appropriate punishment.

"I can think of far worse fates than being caught in the parson's mousetrap with Delia," Eleanor said, "especially since you're hopelessly in love with her."

Was that it? Was he in love with Delia? Is this what love felt like? Christ. It was awful. Hopeless seemed a good word for it.

"I'm not the only one who fell into the trap, Eleanor." He ran a weary hand across his eyes. God, he was tired. He couldn't recall ever being this tired before. "Robyn did, too."

Eleanor considered that for a moment. "I'm not sure that's true," she said at last. "Robyn is difficult to read. But even if it's true, Delia doesn't love Robyn. She's in love with you, Alec."

For one joyful moment Alec thought his heart would soar out his chest, but in the next it was as if a cold hand had reached inside him, grabbed his heart in a fist, and squeezed it until it dropped like a lead ball into his stomach. "It doesn't matter." He struggled to force the words past his numb lips. "It doesn't matter if she loves me or not."

Eleanor stared at him. "How can it not matter? Alec—"

"What if Robyn is in love with her, Eleanor? Do you think I would rival my own brother?"

"Alec," Eleanor began gently. "I know you and Robyn have had a difficult time of it since Father died, but he wouldn't want to see you unhappy. You haven't done anything wrong. You fell in love. That's all. He would never try and stand between you and the woman you love."

"But I would. I *did*. I tried to stand between them." He refused to allow Eleanor to excuse his behavior. "I objected to Delia from the first and I made no secret of it to Robyn. I did everything I could think of to keep them apart, and all the while I pursued her myself. I didn't *know* I was pursuing her at first, but that hardly matters. I've spent the last few weeks trying to take for myself what I did my damndest to keep Robyn from having."

"Delia isn't some child's toy you and Robyn are squabbling over, Alec. This is about your future happiness." Eleanor stopped when she saw Alec was unmoved by her speech. "I have no wish to see Robyn suffer, but he'll get over it," Eleanor whispered. She'd begun to look a little desperate when Alec still appeared unconvinced. "Eventually he'll forgive you."

"But I would never forgive myself. So there's an end to it."

Chapter Twenty-one

*Alec stood at the top of the line and waited for Lady Li-*sette to call the dance.

He glanced out across the ballroom. The guests whirled around the floor, their faces aglow with pleasure. In another half hour the party would adjourn to supper, where a sumptuous feast awaited them.

In short, the ball was a great success.

All was as it should be. Everything was back in its proper place, just the way Alec wanted it. The musicians raised their instruments and began to play.

Another country dance. Christ. He was about to go mad.

He'd told himself he wouldn't look for Delia tonight, but he saw her the second she stepped into the ballroom, her arm linked with Eleanor's. After that it was as if she were the only person in the room he *could* see, and she was everywhere at once, dazzling in her pale blue gown. She danced and she laughed and Alec's heart lurched in his chest each time her honey-colored hair caught the candlelight or she smiled at one of her many partners.

He glanced down at the woman in his arms. Lisette looked lovely tonight. She wore a very pale green silk gown. The color suited her. Small diamond pins were scattered throughout her sleek dark hair and more diamonds encircled her neck. She glittered.

He looked at her and felt nothing.

He must be disguising it well, however, because he could tell by the arrogant tilt of her head that Lisette was enjoying herself. So, she was satisfied with his assiduous attention this evening. He supposed it was her due. No doubt she'd expected a greater degree of devotion from him than he'd shown her since she arrived. She'd be far less satisfied if she knew the truth. Even as he bowed and smiled and fetched glasses of lemonade for her, he was exhaustively, obsessively aware of Delia Somerset.

". . . attending the Ashtons' ball next week?" Lady Lisette asked. "I had thought to decline, but if the Sutherlands will be in town by then, perhaps I will . . ."

Would she never cease prattling? Alec settled his gaze on her endlessly moving lips. It was odd her lips didn't move him to any emotion other than irritation. He'd once thought them rather pretty. Now his only thought was they weren't the full, indescribably soft lips of such a rosy, perfect pink just thinking of them was enough to send him to his knees in the middle of the ballroom.

"The Ashtons are not quite the thing, of course, but . . ."

He nodded at Lady Lisette, as if he were listening to her prattle.

But it wasn't their softness or even their delicious pink color that made Delia's lips so tantalizing. No, it was her shy but eager response, her soft sighs as his tongue swept against the warm curves of her mouth. Her lips opened so sweetly under his, shattering his fragile control into a thousand tiny shards at his feet.

". . . settled, then. You will call on me in London and our families will attend the ball together."

Alec looked at Lisette blankly. What was she nattering on about? What ball? An image rose in his mind of himself partnering Lady Lisette through the figures of one country dance after another.

He just managed to suppress a shudder. "I'm afraid that won't be possible. I have another engagement that evening . . ." He looked over Lisette's shoulder, searching for the pale blue gown. His eyes wandered over the ballroom, but he didn't see Delia.

"Miss Somerset has made herself conspicuous tonight," Lady Lisette said suddenly, her tone waspish. Alec glanced down at her to find her regarding him with narrowed eyes. An angry flush stained her cheeks.

"Has she?" Envy had an unattractive effect on Lisette's complexion.

"Yes," she snapped, gratified to have caught his full attention at last. "Mamma says it's unconscionable, the fuss that's made over her."

"Does she really?" Alec drawled. He was a gentleman, so he resisted the urge to tell Lisette when she quoted her mamma, she also began to *look* like her. But he couldn't quite escape the irony of it. How unpleasant to find he'd ever shared the same sentiments as an old dragon like Lady Cecil.

Lisette's mouth was a tight, petulant line. "Mamma says Miss Somerset's mother was a disgrace."

"Was she, now?" Alec asked idly, masking the hot rage that surged through him at her words. Was this what he wanted? A lifetime of listening to Lisette repeat every foolish word her mamma uttered while he silently, endlessly obsessed over the taste of Delia Somerset's lips?

Lisette, encouraged by his responses, began to warm to her subject. "Robyn seems to be utterly taken in by her. I do hope he isn't fool enough to marry her. I don't desire her as a sister-in-law." Too late she realized what she'd said. Her face turned a mottled shade of red. "That is, I mean—"

"You look quite flushed, Lisette." Alec's voice was cold. "Perhaps you've danced too much this evening. I'll escort you back to your mother."

"No, indeed, I'm not fatigued—"

But Alec was. He was fatigued down to his soul. He was sick to death of Lady Lisette and her mother, with their cruelty and petty jealousy. It was all a farce. There was no way he could marry this woman.

The dance had not yet ended, but Alec took Lisette's arm and escorted her to the side of the ballroom. Before she could utter another word, he'd deposited her with her mother, who looked none too pleased to receive her.

Alec was pleased, however—as pleased as any man who has successfully dodged a bullet aimed at his heart.

As soon as she'd entered the ballroom earlier, she'd caught herself searching for a familiar dark head that towered over the rest of the party. She'd found him at once, by the massive oak fireplace at one end of the room, standing a little apart from the milling crowd.

He stood with Lady Lisette, who looked ravishing in an extravagantly trimmed ice green silk gown with a diamond choker around her slender neck. She smiled coquettishly up into his face, one possessive hand on his arm. His dark head was bent toward her, and an amused smile tugged at one corner of his sensuous mouth.

Delia's breath caught painfully in her throat, and she turned away. God help her, but she couldn't stand to watch them together.

She'd spent most of the day trying not to think about Alec, but he hovered always on the edge of her mind, ready to creep into her thoughts when she least expected it. One minute she was brushing her hair and the next he was there, his hands threading through the long locks, his tongue making teasing forays into her mouth, and his firm lips nipping at the sensitive skin of her neck. And again, as she walked down the hallway, he'd appear as if he'd materialized from the shadows themselves, laughing softly and pressing his hard, warm body into hers, whispering that her lips tasted like honey and cream.

"Delia?"

For one second Delia thought she'd conjured Alec with her heated imaginings, but when she opened her eyes, Robyn was there, staring at her curiously. How many times had he said her name?

"You look lovely tonight." His eyes moved over her with warm appreciation.

"And you are very dashing, Robyn." Delia smoothed her hands nervously down the floating skirts of the exquisite sky blue silk gown. Eleanor had insisted she borrow it. She'd said the gown wanted fair skin and blue eyes.

It was simply cut with a fine, sheer white overskirt that drifted like a cloud over the sky blue silk. The deep neckline was trimmed with tiny flowers and birds embroidered in silver thread. The same thread trimmed the elegant puffed sleeves, and the dainty little birds were scattered across the floating skirt of the gown and flew gracefully around the hem. It was exquisite. Delia had accepted it from Eleanor with tears in her eyes. Maybe tonight, just for one night, she'd feel like she belonged here.

"Are you too warm?" Robyn asked. "You look flushed."

Delia raised her hands to her heated cheeks. "Too much dancing, I suppose. But I'm so happy to see you, Robyn. Indeed, I've wanted to speak with you all day."

"Have you really? How gratifying." Robyn gave her a teasing, open grin, not quite able to hide the touch of masculine satisfaction in his voice. "Then you'll allow me to take you for a turn in the garden?"

"Of course." She laid a hand on his arm, in part to hide her shaking fingers. She wasn't looking forward to this conversation, but she owed Robyn an explanation.

"Did you want to talk about London? I can't wait to escort you to the theater, and the parks alone will keep us busy for—"

Delia interrupted him. "I do want to talk about London, but not about the theater or the parks. Robyn, I . . ." Delia started to trail off, but she cleared her throat and began again, determined to get the words out. "I'm not going to accompany the family to London. I'm traveling back to Surrey tomorrow."

Robyn looked at her without speaking for a long moment, baffled. "But why?"

Delia sighed. "My younger sisters need me. You can have no idea how much mischief three young ladies can get into." She attempted a smile.

"Perhaps Lily . . ." Robyn began, though to his credit he looked half-ashamed of himself even as the words left his mouth.

"No. No. Lily will get much more pleasure out of seeing London than I ever could."

"But I'm sure you *would* get pleasure from it." Robyn stopped walking, turned to face her, and took both of her hands in his. "I'll see to it personally." He looked meaningfully into her eyes.

It was an effort for Delia to keep from closing them against his hopeful expression. This conversation was proving to be much harder than she'd thought it would be, especially with his expressive dark eyes fixed on her. "I know you would, Robyn and that's one reason I can't come with you, I have . . ." She hesitated awkwardly. "I've taken up too much of your time already." She looked down at her slippers and prayed he'd understand what she meant without her having to say anything more.

But her hopes were immediately dashed. He bent toward her and tried to catch her eyes with his own. "But I enjoy spending time with you, Delia. I enjoy it more than I've enjoyed anything in quite some time."

A sob threatened and Delia bit her lip to push it back. "You've been kind to me." She forced herself to look into his eyes. "That's why I treasure your friendship so. I consider you a dear *friend*, Robyn."

There was a short pause, and then all at once Robyn seemed to understand her. "Ah." That was all he said, for quite a long time.

Delia followed him silently through the garden. Funny, she'd never noticed the way the lanterns drew the moths. They hovered around the glowing light, but they were silent, as well, with none of the fluttering and flapping one often heard with moths. The only sound was the soft crunch of her slippers and Robyn's boots against the crushed rock of the pathway.

"That's it, then," Robyn said at last. "I suppose there's nothing more to say, is there?" He turned to look at her and his face softened at what she imagined was her stricken expression. "My heart is not yet engaged, Delia, but it may soon have been. Would have been, I think, had you accompanied us to London. So it's best this way."

Delia felt a sob rise again at his gentleness. "Oh, Robyn. I'm so terribly sorry."

He shrugged, but Delia could see the effort it took for him to appear nonchalant. "But I'm not, because I consider you my friend, too. As to the other." He smiled at her with some of his old playfulness. "Well, I'm notoriously inconstant. Perhaps I'll fall in love and marry this season. My brother would certainly be delighted to see me safely leg-shackled."

The last thing Delia wanted to discuss at this particular moment was Alec, so she said only, "Perhaps you will. Would it be such an awful thing to fall truly in love?" She held her breath as she waited for his answer. Maybe Robyn could offer some priceless masculine insights into the confusing topic of love.

But he only chuckled. "Honestly? I haven't the slightest idea."

"Neither have I." She felt an absurd urge to laugh, though it wasn't at all funny, for she *should* know, as madly in love with Alec as she was. Instead she knew less about love now than she ever had, despite falling headlong into it.

"It's a question for the ages," Robyn said with mock seriousness. He turned to walk back toward the ballroom. "Certainly not one to be attempted at a ball, especially before supper."

They had nearly reached the terrace when Delia saw him. *Alec.* Her heart lurched in her chest. He stood on the terrace, his eyes locked on her face, his expression inscrutable.

"Miss Somerset." Alec grasped her firmly by the elbow. "A word, if you would."

"I don't think so—" she began. She tried to tug her elbow from his grasp.

Alec refused to release her. "Please, Delia," he said in a low tone. "I leave for London tomorrow. I must speak with you before I go."

Robyn looked from one to the other of them, his eyes narrowed. "Delia?"

She glanced at Robyn and nodded briefly. He gave Alec a long, searching look, but then he bowed to Delia and disappeared into the ballroom.

"Very well." She allowed Alec to escort her back into the

garden. "For a moment only," she added when he didn't stop on the terrace, but tugged her along with him into a darker, more private part of the garden.

Once they were shielded from the guests on the terrace, he released her arm abruptly, as if her skin burned him. He gazed at her for a moment, but then turned away without a word, running a hand roughly through his hair. Delia waited for him to speak, but when at last he faced her, he looked so tormented she felt her calm desert her.

A shocked little cry escaped her lips. "Alec?"

Alec stepped toward her and grasped her shoulders in his strong hands. "Delia, the conversation you overheard the other day," he began in a rush. "I have to explain—"

But she was already trying to squirm out of his grasp. "No, Alec! I don't want to hear an explanation."

Alec's hands tightened. "But you *will*. I know you would never agree to be any man's mistress. I never thought it of you. I never *could* think it."

"You must have done, Alec. Why else would you suggest such a thing to Robyn?"

"I suggested it to Robyn to hear him deny it. I hoped he'd deeply resent the suggestion." He dropped his hands from her shoulders and dragged them down his face. "Robyn has spent most of this year carousing through London with a wild group of young noblemen. I had heard rumors he . . ." He stopped. "Well, it doesn't matter what I heard. It doesn't bear repeating."

"Why not simply ask him?" Delia said, puzzled.

"He doesn't confide in me, and I had to know the truth, for the family's sake. It never occurred to me you would overhear us, but that doesn't excuse my behavior. It was unforgivable. Cruel. It's driven me mad, thinking of the look on your face that day."

Delia took a deep, shuddering breath. She couldn't identify the strong emotion that passed through her then. She knew only the hard, cold, bitter thing lodged in her heart since yesterday suddenly gave way.

Alec wasn't finished. His hand shot out to grab her wrist and he pulled her roughly against him. "Do you know why I hate to see you with Robyn? Do you, Delia?"

"Y-yes," she gasped, her hands flying to his chest. "To protect him. To protect your family from a shameful connection—"

"No." Alec's voice had gone low and ragged and his breath came in harsh pants. "It's because I can't bear to see you with him. Because you're *mine*."

Delia's heart stopped and then surged to life again on a tremendous, aching shudder. She opened her mouth to speak, but only a quiet sob emerged. Hot tears pressed behind her eyes. Alec's hands came up to cradle her face almost desperately. He brushed his thumbs gently under her eyes to catch her tears, his face a mask of anguish. "Don't." And then he was kissing her, his warm mouth moving tenderly across her eyes and her cheeks, tasting her tears. The garden, the ball, it all faded away as her entire being focused only on the feel of his mouth as it glided across her skin. "Say it, Delia," he commanded softly, the whisper like a brush of silk against her ear. "You're mine. *Say it*."

But she couldn't speak. She couldn't breathe or even think. She could only feel. She snaked her arms around Alec's neck and her mouth sought his, her tongue stroking inside to tell him what he demanded to know, without words.

"No." Alec's quick, labored breaths sawed in and out of his chest. "We can't." He tried to pull away from her. "Come back to the ballroom."

No. She wouldn't let him go.

She tugged boldly at the knot in his cravat, making a frustrated noise in her throat when it didn't yield. Desperate to feel more of him, she reached her hands inside his coat to caress his lean waist, pulling on his shirt until at last it came loose from his breeches. She plunged her hands inside, glorying in his sharp gasp and the way the hot velvet of his skin moved over his taut muscles under her questing fingers.

"My God. *Delia*." With a defeated groan he at last surged urgently into her mouth. He dragged her hard against his body as he took masterful possession, stroking and caressing her tongue with his own until her head fell helplessly backward against his invasion.

She unclasped her arms from around his neck so she could move her hands over his broad chest. She paused to stroke her fingers shyly against his masculine nipples, at first curious, then fascinated when she heard his low growl and felt his entire body go rigid with need. She brushed her hand wonderingly against his hard belly then, excitement pooling low in her own belly when his head fell back on a deep groan at the caress.

"Yes," he hissed softly.

His hands felt hot and heavy against the silk at the back of her gown, but his fingers were deft as he coaxed the top buttons open. The neck of the gown relaxed around her and then his lips were there, his demanding tongue like rough silk against the tops of her breasts.

Delia knew she should be shocked, that she should stop him, but instead she felt only a heated flood of desire as his fingers and mouth moved against the skin revealed by the sagging gown. She strained closer, desperate to feel his hands on every part of her body.

"Alec," she gasped. "Please, I want . . ."

But he already knew what she wanted, even if she didn't. He murmured soothingly to her and ran his fingers lightly under the swells of her breasts. "Hush. I know, love." He pressed hot kisses against her skin as his hands inched up slowly, slowly, torturously. They both moaned when he brushed his thumbs at last across the hard, straining peaks of her breasts. She jerked in his arms, overcome by the shocking pleasure of his touch.

Alec's head descended then and Delia felt the rough scrape of an emerging beard against the tender skin of her breast. She triumphed in it. She tilted her head back and invited him in, gasping when she felt his tongue dart out to lick the pink tip of one breast. Her fingers closed in his hair, holding him to her as his mouth lingered over the place where her heart jumped madly in her chest before he closed his lips over her other nipple and drew it into the heat of his mouth, suckling her.

Delia's head fell back and she pressed the back of her hand against her mouth to keep from crying aloud as he drew on her nipple, his tongue circling lazily. "*Alec, please . . .*" She clung to him, trembling, shivering in his arms, and her sweet arousal inflamed him to madness. His control slipped farther away with each of her breathless sighs. His hands drifted from her waist to cup her bottom and draw her harder against his body, groaning at the intense pleasure. He urged her against his hard arousal, thrusting slowly, letting her feel his desire through the gathered fabric of her skirts. His restless hands roamed across her back until they settled at her hips, caressing her there and drawing her even tighter against his hard length.

She made a small sound—a sigh of protest? Surrender? It didn't matter. *It didn't matter.* Because he was gathering fistfuls of her silk skirts in his hands and raising them . . .

His tongue invaded her mouth, his fingers stroking the smooth warm skin above her garter. Just as Alec's fingers skimmed across the sensitive skin of her upper thigh, he felt her tense in his arms. He felt her hands on his chest, trying to push him away.

He ached for her. He'd gone nearly mindless with need, but he wrestled to subdue his body, to come to the surface. "Delia? What is it, love?"

Then he heard it. A gasp, and a woman's strangled exclamation. Alec turned and instantly stepped in front of Delia to shield her.

But it was too late. Lily stood there, stricken, her hand over her mouth and her face drained of color. "Delia?" Her voice was incoherent with shock. "Oh, Delia," she whispered, her voice low and despairing. "You're ruined."

Chapter Twenty-two

Lily was pacing. The door to the bed to the window. Door, bed, window.

Delia watched Lily retrace her steps over and over again. Door, bed, window. The carpet was thick, but even so she began to watch for a tear to appear under Lily's daintily slippered feet.

The room throbbed with silence. Lily hadn't said one word since she and Delia had fled the garden. They might all still be standing down there gaping at one another had Lily not gathered her wits and swept into action like a general marshaling the troops.

"Come with me, Delia," she ordered. Then she turned to Alec, averting her eyes from his disheveled clothing. "Lord Carlisle, please make our apologies to your mother. You may tell her Delia has the headache and I've taken her upstairs. No one need be the wiser about this."

Like proper marionettes, they'd all done as Lily ordered, and it seemed no one *was* the wiser, though for all Delia knew, the *ton* could even now be whispering gleefully behind their fans about poor, ruined Delia Somerset.

Now she had to face Lily, who was still pacing. *Door, bed, window.*

Delia waited. Lily wasn't one to speak until she was sure of her words. She wasn't given to impulsive exclamations or wild assumptions. Delia had always admired that about her sister. They did say, didn't they, that one tended to admire in others the qualities one lacked themselves?

Whoever *they* were.

"Are you terribly ashamed of me, Lily?" Delia finally blurted out miserably, unable to bear the silence another second.

Lily turned to face her at last. "Ashamed? Astonished is more like it, Delia. What can you have been thinking? In the garden! Why, anyone could have stumbled upon you. It could have been Lady Cecil." The horror of that possibility made her face go white again. "You'd have to flee much farther than Surrey to escape the effects of her vicious tongue."

"But it wasn't Lady Cecil, Lily." Delia made her voice as reasonable as she could, given the circumstances. "It was you."

"By the merest stroke of luck only." Lily crossed the room and threw herself into the chair opposite Delia's. "I blame Lord Carlisle. I wouldn't have believed he could behave so disgracefully, but it's clear he has no honor—"

"Indeed, Lily, you are very wrong!" Delia cried, leaping to Alec's defense. "He is honorable, and a gentleman. It wasn't his idea . . . That is"—she swallowed nervously—"I'm to blame."

Alec had tried to draw away from her. He'd tried to escort her back to the ballroom. Her response had been to tug his shirt from his breeches. A flush of heat raced through her at the memory, not all of it from embarrassment. Surely tearing off Alec's clothing meant she bore some responsibility for this debacle?

But Lily didn't seem to think so. She shook her head. "No, Delia. Everyone knows the *ton* is wicked, especially the gentlemen. You're an innocent young lady. What can you possibly know of seduction?"

How could she explain to Lily it had nothing to do with *knowing*? Or seduction, even, which was far too cold and bloodless a word for what had happened with Alec in the garden tonight. How could she tell Lily that Alec's gentle kiss had led to a devouring, hungry possession of her mouth, a stroke of fingertips on fevered skin, until there was nothing else to do but to surrender to it? The press of his body against hers had led to a maelstrom of desire so sweet there was no thinking and no knowing. There was only *feeling*.

Some of what she felt must have shown on her face, because Lily frowned. "How long have you and Lord Carlisle been . . ." She trailed off primly.

"Sneaking away to the garden?" It had been difficult, hiding the truth from Lily. Delia didn't want to lie anymore. "There has been an attraction almost from the moment we arrived at Bellwood."

Lily's mouth dropped open. "What about Robyn, Delia? Have you not been encouraging his attentions? It appeared to me as though you were, and I think Robyn believes so, as well."

Delia hadn't thought she was, but Alec had been so convinced by her threat to pursue Robyn she was forced to be honest with herself. The truth was she *had* used Robyn. She'd maneuvered him as coolly as if he were nothing more than a pawn in her reckless game with Alec. "I spoke with him tonight. He knows I leave for Surrey tomorrow. I told him . . ." Delia swallowed, thinking of the moment when Robyn's hopeful eyes had darkened with disappointment. "I told him how sorry I was."

Lily relented a little at Delia's obvious distress. "Well, it's not entirely your fault, I suppose. It would take very little encouragement for Robyn to think your affections were engaged. It would be a triumphant match for you, but you were never very practical, Delia."

"No, I suppose not." Delia's voice was faint. "The practical thing would have been to fall in love with Robyn, not Alec."

Lily stared at her sister, her eyes wide. "*Love!* My goodness, Delia. Are you *in love* with Lord Carlisle?"

"I'm afraid I am." Delia tried to smile even as she felt the hot press of tears in her throat. "Quite hopelessly so."

Lily's face softened and she took Delia's hands in her own. "Does he . . . That is, do you think he has a regard for you?"

You are mine. Say it, Delia.

In the dark of the garden, with her arms wrapped around his neck and his lips on her skin, Alec's words had sounded like a passionate declaration. But now, in the cold reality of her bedchamber, with Lily's anxious eyes on her, Delia wondered *what* Alec had been declaring. Not love, at any rate. She felt her heart squeeze with painful doubts. Alec felt something for her, but was it any more than he'd felt last week for the young woman he'd been dallying with? Even if it was more, what difference did it make? The same ugly scandal still cast its shadow over them both. It was a long shadow. Far longer, she suspected, than any fleeting desire Alec might feel for her.

Delia took a deep, shuddering breath. It was all rather hopeless. "I think whatever he may feel for me will not withstand the *ton*'s contempt."

Lily's hopeful face came crashing down at this. "But if you are not sure of his regard, then how could you—"

"Fall in love with him? Kiss him in the garden?" Delia smiled sadly. "As you say, Lily, I've never been very practical, for if I were, I would have chosen love with my head, not my heart."

"That sounds like something Mother would say. You're

very much like her, you know, Delia. Mother was a romantic, all the way down to her soul, just as you are."

"Oh, yes, I'm very romantic, and a great fool as well. At least Mother had the sense not to fall in love with an aristocrat. I think she'd be quite ashamed of me. Just think of the risk Mother took to escape Hart Sutherland, Lily, only to have me fall in love with his son."

Lily's brow wrinkled in confusion. "Well, Lord Carlisle is nothing like his father, is he?"

Delia shook her head. "No. I don't know much about the previous earl, but what little I have heard isn't to his credit. I believe he was quite cold and unfeeling. Still, Alec is one of the *ton*, and that's bad enough."

Lily still looked confused. "Are you suggesting Mother would have disapproved of a *tendre* between you simply because Lord Carlisle is an aristocrat? What nonsense, Delia! She'd have done no such thing."

Delia stared at her sister in astonishment. "Of course she would, Lily. Why, you just said yourself the *ton* is wicked."

Lily gave a little sniff. "You know better than to listen to me when I'm angry, and you just vigorously defended Lord Carlisle, if you remember. You said he's an honorable man. Your word is good enough for me, and it would have been good enough for Mother, too."

Delia shrugged. She didn't want to argue with Lily, so she held her tongue.

"You speak as if wickedness were the exclusive prerogative of the *ton*," Lily went on. "The upper ten thousand fancy themselves very exclusive, I know, but they're obliged to share their wickedness with the rest of England. Do you remember old Mrs. Aspley?" she asked suddenly.

"Mrs. Aspley? You mean the old lady who used to throw crab apples at us?"

Lily laughed at the memory. "Oh, my goodness, yes! What an old witch she was, to be sure. I remember being

pelted with crab apples from that twisted tree of hers whenever we dared to approach her door. I always thought she
looked just like that tree, with her gnarled limbs."

"Lily! That's not kind."

"Well, neither was Mrs. Aspley! That is precisely my
point, Delia. I used to hate it when Mother sent us over to
her house. I swear Mrs. Aspley kept a supply of crab apples
in a tub by the door, just so she could throw them at virtuous
young ladies."

Delia frowned. "Lily, why are we discussing old lady
Aspley?"

"Why, only this," Lily said, as if it were obvious. "Mrs.
Aspley was poor as a church mouse, and as far removed
from the *ton* as a person could possibly get, and she was a
wicked old thing. You can't deny it, Delia."

"No, I suppose not." Delia admitted, still not convinced.

"Do you think Charlotte and Eleanor are wicked? Robyn?
Lady Carlisle?"

"No," Delia said, then again with more conviction, "No,
of course I don't, Lily." She paused for a moment, remembering something Alec had said to her a few days ago. "People
are either magnificent or appalling. I suppose that's true
regardless of their station in life."

"Magnificent or appalling, every shade in between, and
sometimes both at once. Well, then," Lily continued with a
satisfied air. "You know, Delia, many people judged Father
harshly because he *wasn't* an aristocrat. Do you really think
Mother would have judged Lord Carlisle harshly because
he *is* one?"

Delia shook her head. She'd never thought of it that way.

"No," Lily said. "She ran from a marriage to Hart Sutherland because he wasn't a good man. She didn't love him.
That was the only reason. Well, that, and because she was
madly in love with Father." Lily was quiet for a moment;
then she added in a subdued voice, "I miss them horribly."

"I know." Delia gave her sister's hand a gentle squeeze. "I do, too."

They were silent for a little while, each lost in her own memories.

"You look tired, Lily," Delia said finally. "I can scarcely keep my eyes open, either. I'm off early tomorrow morning to Surrey, but I'll come see you before I leave, to say good-bye to you and Charlotte and Ellie."

Lily nodded. "You'll travel in one of the Sutherlands' carriages?"

"Yes, as far as Guildford. Hannah will meet me there. James will ride along, too. Eleanor would not hear of me going without him."

"Well, I'm glad of that." Lily rose to leave, but before she passed through the connecting door, she stopped and turned to her sister. "Delia? I'm not ashamed of you. I never could be. You know that, don't you?"

Delia swallowed the sudden lump in her throat. "I do know it, but I adore you for saying so anyway."

"You'll be all right?" Lily still hesitated at the door.

"I will be. I promise. I'm sure I'll feel much better as soon as I get home."

Was she trying to reassure Lily, or herself?

"All right." Lily didn't look convinced. "Good night." She passed into her own room and pulled the door closed behind her.

Delia sat on the bed for a long time after Lily left, thinking; then she got up, removed Eleanor's lovely sky blue gown, and laid it carefully aside. She washed her face, changed into her night rail, and slipped between the cool, soft sheets, but her eyes stayed stubbornly open, her thoughts in turmoil.

What a muddle she'd made of everything. Since the moment she'd crossed the threshold of Bellwood, she'd behaved like one of those hardened gamesters in the scandal sheets, who make one foolish bet after another until they lose everything.

Perhaps Lily wasn't ashamed of her, but she was ashamed of herself.

She frowned a little in the dark, thinking of old Mrs. Aspley and her crab apples. It wasn't the story that struck her; it was what Lily said about their mother having a romantic soul. Delia had always thought her mother so courageous to abandon her privileged life in the *ton*, but it wasn't about bravery. Not really.

As soon as Alec's lips met hers tonight, as soon his arms closed around her and she felt his hair against her fingers, she no longer had a choice. There'd been nothing else for her to do but twine her arms around his neck and hold him against her heart.

She hadn't understood it before, but now she knew it had been the same for her mother, who hadn't been running *away* from something—not Hart Sutherland, or the Chases, or even the *ton*. Millicent had been running *to* something. To someone. To Henry Somerset. It had never been about anything but love, a love for which her mother had risked everything.

I can't bear to see you with him . . . because you're mine.

Alec. Warm, teasing lips and strong, possessive hands. Darkly beautiful.

Odd, the way everything suddenly became very, very simple.

He was flawed, just as she was. Just like every other person. She didn't know if he loved her. She didn't know if he was hers. She knew only that she was his.

And that was all she needed to know.

Chapter Twenty-three

Bellwood had never been so quiet. The soft shuffle of her bare feet as she crept down the hallway was deafening. Her mother wouldn't have approved of what Delia was about to do, but the force that pulled her down the hallway toward Alec's chamber was as inevitable as drawing her next breath, and she was no more able to resist it than she was able to stop breathing. She liked to think her mother would have understood that.

There was no need to count the doors this time. She remembered which one was Alec's. She knocked once, softly but firmly. It felt as if a thousand butterflies fluttered against her rib cage, but underneath their beating wings a thrilling current of excitement thrummed through her.

"What?" Alec barked.

Delia flinched. His harsh tone didn't reassure her, but to turn back now was out of the question. She didn't *want* to turn back. She pushed the door open and slipped inside.

Alec was nowhere to be seen, but she could hear him

moving about in his dressing room. "For God's sake. What now? Do what you need to do, then *go*," he growled, without coming into the room.

Delia stood against the door with her hands clasped in front of her, waiting. When there was no movement and no answer, Alec strode into the room. He froze when he saw her and the papers he'd been carrying in his hand scattered to the floor. There was a stunned pause, then, "Delia. You shouldn't be here."

The butterflies had abandoned her rib cage and fluttered their way into her throat. Alec seemed cold, detached, as if he didn't want her there, and she didn't know how to make him want her. She was no seductress. She didn't have any sensual secrets or tricks to entice him.

They were both silent for a long moment. Their eyes held until gradually the rest of the room began to fade and Delia no longer saw the dresser or the looking glass or the fire burning in the grate. She saw only Alec. He hadn't moved and he hadn't taken his eyes off her. Delia stared back at him, at his shadowy face. She couldn't read his expression or see his eyes, but it didn't matter anymore, because she could feel his hunger. She could feel the way he wanted her, as if he'd brushed his fingers against her skin.

She didn't need tricks or secrets. She didn't need seductive wiles. All she needed was Alec. All she had to do was tell the truth about what she felt in her heart.

"I should be here, Alec." She took a step toward him.

He ran a hand through his thick hair, making it stand on end. Delia watched that hand rake through the dark hair and tried to commit the gesture to memory, so she could take it back with her to her lonely little corner of Surrey.

"Go to bed, Delia." His voice was tense, and he didn't take his eyes off her.

Delia moved as if she were in a dream, farther into the room, toward the fire. She knelt down on the rug in front of the flickering flames and began to pull the pins from her hair.

Alec caught his breath. "Don't."

But she did. She pulled pin after pin until her hair fell around her shoulders and down her back in a shimmering waterfall.

She waited.

With a low, choked sound, Alec crossed the room until he stood behind her where she knelt motionless on the carpet. He took a lock of her hair in his hand and let his fingers slide through the long strands. After a moment Delia leaned her head back so it rested lightly against his thigh.

"You shouldn't be here, Delia," he repeated in a strangled voice. "You should be in your room, behind a locked door, where I can't touch you."

She turned her head against his thigh so she could look up into his shadowy face. "I want you to touch me, Alec."

His fingers flexed in her hair. He released the long lock he'd been caressing and laid it gently on her shoulder. He crossed in front of her, and dropped to his knees before the fire, facing her. He raised his hands to either side of her face and placed his lips against her forehead. He kissed her eyes, her chin, the tip of her nose. Delia swayed, aching for the feel of his lips against her own.

And then they were there, brushing against hers, so lightly, as if he were exploring the shape of them. He continued the teasing strokes until Delia moaned in frustration and grabbed a handful of his shirt to pull him closer.

It was as if a stray spark had set a whole forest ablaze. Alec reacted at once, spreading a large hand against her back, pulling her tightly against his body and closing his mouth ravenously over hers. He swept his tongue across the opening of her lips and she parted with a breathless gasp. He surged inside, stroking against her tongue and the inside of her mouth, demanding she taste him in return. She did, twining her tongue around his and closing her arms around his neck.

She could feel almost to the moment when he began to lose control and surrender to the desire that surged between them. He weaved his fingers tightly into her hair and moved her head to the side so he could taste the skin of her throat. "Yes," he whispered when she arched her neck against his seeking lips. "Yes, just like that. Let me . . ."

His mouth was so sweet against her throat she feared she'd let him do anything. She'd beg him. He began to trace light circles against the sensitive skin under her ear with his thumb, his mouth following his fingers. He nipped her ear-lobe and Delia jerked in his arms, astonished the feel of his teeth against her skin could be so erotic.

"Delia," he murmured. His hands slid from her face to wrap around her waist. For a moment he seemed unaware he gripped her there tightly, but then his hands relaxed and he began to caress her waist and spine in long, seductive strokes. "Are you sure, love?" He tore his mouth from hers even as his hands slipped slowly down her spine to rest on the rounded curve of her bottom. "Are you sure?" he asked again, drawing back so he could look into deep blue eyes gone heavy-lidded with desire. "Tell me now, while I can still stop."

Delia raised herself to her knees and moved toward him until she was nearly sitting in his lap. "Don't stop. I don't want you to stop."

With those whispered words, Alec was lost. He'd tried to stay away from her, tried to resist her even as she knelt in front of the fire, offering herself to him. But now her soft body was pressed against his and she was pleading breath-lessly for him not to stop, and Alec's good intentions fled like seeds scattered into the wind.

Ah, God, he wanted her. He wanted her more than he'd ever wanted anything before. God help him, but he could never give her up. Not even if having her tore him and Robyn apart.

He pushed every other thought away before they could take root and let them fly into the wind along with all his other promises to himself. He cupped the curve of her bottom and fitted her body more closely against him, his desire ratcheting even higher when his hard cock pressing against her made her gasp. His desire for her was a live thing. It breathed and grew inside him, rushing through him and twining around his heart.

Alec's mouth returned to her lips, gentler this time, coaxing, his tongue licking into her mouth with delicate, restrained strokes. He reached up to loosen the buttons of her night rail, surprised to find his hands were shaking. One by one the buttons yielded, and Alec slipped his fingers inside the sagging neck and slid the night rail down her arms. She wore nothing underneath.

"Lovely." His voice was husky, his eyes riveted on her creamy flesh and the rosy pink of her nipples. "I knew you would be." He teased one finger across her collarbone and then brushed it lightly down the center of her chest and under the curve of one breast, watching hungrily as her nipples tightened in response.

His eyes flicked up to her face and he smiled a little wickedly. "Do you want me to touch you, Delia?" His fingers rested under her breast, motionless as he awaited her response.

"Yes," she breathed.

Alec could feel her quick, hectic breaths under the tips of his fingers. "Ask me," he said, his own breath heaving in and out of his chest.

"Please, Alec," she whispered. "Please."

But it was Alec who groaned when the pad of his thumb brushed against her nipple. He circled the rosy tip gently, just once, and then stopped and watched her reaction, astonished he could be so deeply aroused from simply stroking her breasts. After a moment he circled the hard tip again and Delia caught her breath, as if surprised at the sensation.

"Does it feel good, love?" He shook from the effort of holding himself back.

"So good," Delia said with such innocent wonder Alec's tenuous hold on his control began to slip. He cupped both of her breasts in his hands and dragged his thumbs over her nipples, again and again, teasing her mercilessly until her trembling and her low, pleading moans became too much for him and he slid a hand under her back and lifted her toward him, desperate to taste her.

Delia cried out when his hot mouth closed over the tip of her breast. Alec touched just the tip of his tongue to her nipple, but it wasn't enough for him, not nearly enough. He was starved for the taste of her. His tongue flicked against the rosy nub in endless quick, hard strokes. He stopped only long enough to suckle her before his tongue darted out again to torment her. He tried to remind himself to be gentle, to go slowly, but Delia sank her fingers into his hair and arched up to meet his mouth, writhing in his arms, and he couldn't stop. He fastened his mouth onto her other breast to devour it roughly with his lips and tongue.

When he pulled away at last, Delia was panting, her head thrown back and her bottom lip caught between her teeth, her pink nipples proud and erect. The sight was unbearably erotic and Alec felt his cock surge even harder. He needed to calm down. He was behaving like an animal—

"Take off your shirt," Delia demanded breathlessly. When he didn't do so at once, she began to tug and pull at the fabric.

Alec stared at her. Was it possible she was as crazed with desire as he was? She was a virgin, an innocent—

"Hurry! *Now*, Alec."

Alec tore the shirt over his head and threw it carelessly into a corner. Delia stood and pulled her nightdress the rest of the way off and stepped out of the pool of fabric. Alec gazed up at her, amazed and wildly aroused by her eagerness. He wrapped his fingers around her ankles and rose to his knees, running his hands higher and higher up her smooth legs until he grazed the soft, bare skin of her thighs. He stood and in one smooth movement tugged his trousers and smallclothes the rest of the way off and kicked them aside. Then he swept her up into his arms and carried her to his bed.

"Exquisite," Alec murmured when she lay naked before him. He placed one large, warm palm against the flesh of her lower belly and gazed at her, his dark eyes burning.

Delia said nothing, simply held out her arms to him.

Alec stretched out next to her on the bed and gathered her body close against his. He threaded his fingers through her hair and lowered his mouth to hers, kissing her again and again until Delia's breath came in panting gasps and the most maddeningly erotic whimpers and sighs escaped her throat. She strained against him, her body instinctively seeking release. He gently pushed his leg between her knees and pressed his hard thigh against the soft, wet space between her legs.

She was close, and he felt as if he'd explode if he didn't take her *now*. Yet still he hesitated, jaw clenched and body tensed, until he felt her begin to writhe against the leg between her thighs. He spread her legs wider apart then, pinning one of them down under his own, and slipped his hand between her open thighs. He ran his fingers gently through her honey-colored curls and then parted her folds and teased the tip of his finger against the slick cleft, lightly circling her clitoris.

"*Alec.*" Delia's head thrashed from side to side against the bed.

God, she felt incredible. "Tell me what you want, Delia," Alec ground out fiercely. His cock felt ready to explode.

Delia's hips rose and fell with his stroking finger. "*More.*"

Alec slipped one finger into her wet heat, withdrew it, and then began a rhythmic thrusting, groaning when he felt how hot and tight she was. "Say it again." His voice was savage with suppressed desire.

"More, Alec."

God, she was drenched in honey. He couldn't hold out much longer. He added a second finger and began to move them faster inside her, brushing his thumb against her clitoris with every stroke.

"Yes, yes." She struggled to spread her legs wider. *Now.*

Alec moved over her, his arms taking his weight, and pressed his heavy cock against her soft belly. He thrust once, twice against her there, then he took himself in hand and placed his head at her dewy entrance. "It's going to hurt, love." He looked down into her eyes and leaned down to kiss her. "But only for a moment. I promise."

She looked up at him trustingly, and Alec thought he might die, she was so beautiful. He held her hips against the bed and thrust into her, tearing through her tender virginal flesh with one powerful stroke.

Delia gasped and went rigid beneath him. Her tight, wet sheath felt so incredible around his cock, it took every ounce of Alec's control not to keep thrusting into her like a savage, but he forced himself to stay still until he felt her begin to relax underneath him. "All right, love?" he whispered, brushing the hair gently from her face.

After a moment she nodded. "Yes. Don't stop, Alec."

Alec squeezed his eyes shut, struggling to gain control, and then he began to thrust gently, building a rhythm slowly, groaning at the sensation of her surrounding him and pulling him deeper. He was panting as he moved inside her, letting her get accustomed to the feel of his shaft filling her.

After a moment Delia's hands slid down his back and her

fingers curled against his taut buttocks. She moved her hips up to meet his downward thrust. "Oh," she gasped, rising up to meet him again and wrapping her legs around his lean hips. "Oh," she whispered. "Alec. *Yes*."

Alec moved inside her, stroking deep into her over and over again, at once consumed by her and filling her. He gazed down at her, at her closed eyes, her mouth open with passion and wonder, and felt a part of his heart tear away from his chest. "Look at me, Delia," he gasped as he plunged into her writhing body. "*Look at me.*"

Delia opened her eyes and locked gazes with him.

"You are *mine*."

She gazed up at him, her eyes gone stark with passion. "*Please*, Alec." She arched wildly beneath him, urging her hips against his. Then her mouth opened in a silent cry and Alec felt her hot sheath clench around him as she shattered in his arms. Seconds later he cried out, throwing his head back and driving into her in his own devastating release. "Delia," he groaned, pumping into her, shuddering with pleasure as the spasms rocked his body.

For long moments afterward Alec didn't move, but hung suspended above her, his arms shaking with the effort, stunned. Then he kissed her, his lips brushing softly over her forehead before he captured her mouth gently with his own. "Are you all right, love?" His voice was shaking. "Did I hurt you?"

Delia smiled up at him and placed her hand against his cheek. "You didn't hurt me, Alec." She paused; then she said shyly, "I—that was . . . I never knew."

Alec grinned. "I'll take that as a compliment." He rolled to his side and gathered her close against him, twining his legs with hers.

"Oh, it was one." She sighed drowsily and laid her head against his chest.

"Sleep." He threaded his fingers through her hair again, admiring the way the light set the gold strands on fire.

She fell asleep at once, but Alec remained awake for a long time after Delia's eyes had drifted closed. He held her tight against his heart, and thought about how everything in his life had just changed.

Chapter Twenty-four

Delia fell into a deep sleep to the sound of Alec's heartbeat against her ear, wrapped in the warm circle of his arms. At some point in the night he rose and slipped away. He returned a short while later and Delia thought she felt a warm, wet cloth moving gently between her legs, but she was too drowsy to be sure, and far too contented to be embarrassed.

When she did wake an hour or so later, it was to find Alec lying on his side with her head pillowed on his muscular bicep. He gazed at her, his dark eyes dancing wickedly. "You talk in your sleep, you know." He gave her a sly grin as he played with a lock of her hair.

"Oh, no." Delia hid her face in his arm. "Not again." Lily was forever poking fun at her for it.

"There's no reason to hide." Alec took her chin in his hand and turned her face up to his. "You didn't say anything *too* incriminating. I couldn't sleep with all that mumbling going on, though, so I'm afraid I heard every word."

Delia was dying to know what he'd heard, but he looked

so pleased with himself, she was afraid to ask. "Just like my mother. Even in my sleep I can't hold my tongue."

Alec lay next to her. He stroked his fingers lightly along her jaw and traced her cheekbones, his fingers drifting across her face as if he were memorizing it. "Are you very much like your mother? I don't mean the way you look." He smiled faintly. "Obviously, exceptional beauty runs in the family."

"Exceptionally sharp tongues, too," Delia said, even as she blushed with pleasure at his compliment. "I inherited that from her. I do think that trait skipped a few of my sisters, though. Lily and my sister Iris are much more even-tempered, like my father was."

Delia reached up to sweep Alec's dark hair out of his eyes. It was strange, but she didn't mind speaking of her parents with him now. Since their deaths, any mention of them had left her feeling as though she would suffocate with grief, but now she wanted to talk to him about everything.

Alec stroked a warm hand up and down her spine. "You admired her. I can hear it in your voice."

She smiled. "Oh, I did. Very much. I'd like to believe I'm like her. She was . . ." Delia paused, trying to think of a way to put it into words. "She was different. She wasn't afraid of anything, and it was something special to be loved by her, because she loved with her whole heart."

She rolled over on her side and propped her head in her palm. "What was your father like, Alec?"

Alec had been lying on his side facing her, but at this he rolled over onto his back and threw an arm over his eyes. Delia waited. She'd just decided he wasn't going to answer her at all when he said, "He was cold and selfish, utterly controlling. Manipulative. Nasty temper, too. You can't imagine—"

He stopped speaking and for a long time he didn't say anything else, just stared silently at the ceiling, his body rigid. "You can't imagine what it was like living with him when we were children. Robyn and I got the brunt of it, though I doubt it was pleasant for Eleanor and Charlotte, either. He ignored them as if they didn't matter at all."

"How awful," Delia whispered. She said nothing more, but waited for him to continue.

"Sometimes I think I'm just like him." The tension suddenly drained from Alec's body then, as if it had taken all of his energy to hold that secret inside, and now that he'd spoken it aloud, he was finally able to breathe. "I know Robyn thinks so."

Delia felt her own body go rigid with the injustice of it. The old earl had left such a deep and terrible mark on Alec, one he'd carried alone for such a long time. Well, not anymore. She'd likely never see Alec again after today, but at least she could tell him how she felt and what she saw when she looked at him. She could do that much for him.

She shifted until she lay on top of him, and carefully moved his arm away from his face. He stared up at her, expressionless. "But you're not, Alec." Her eyes held his. "To care about your family and try to protect them isn't cold or selfish. It's anything but that. Robyn might not understand it right now, but you're *nothing* like your father was. Nothing at all."

Alec was still underneath her, his eyes searching her face. "I might have been." A small smile lifted one corner of his mouth, and he reached up and cupped her face in his hands. "But perhaps there is hope for me yet."

Delia's foolish heart leapt in her chest. She knew there was no hope for *her*, no hope of a life with Alec. Not with the shameful history between their families. He might believe he cared for her now, but he'd grow to resent her when the *ton* turned their backs on him and his family. No one had informed her thoughtless heart of this, though, and it continued to thud hopefully.

She didn't say any of this to Alec. Instead she said the

first thing that came into her head. "Alec? What did I really say in my sleep?"

He moved under her so she could feel the weight of his hard cock against her thigh. "You cried out for me. You begged me to touch you." His voice became low and husky with mounting desire. "You told me you wanted me again. Do you, Delia?"

Delia stared down at him, transfixed by his smoky voice and the hard, incredibly male body that now arched beneath her, and she knew she'd always want him. "Yes. I want you, Alec."

She placed her hands against his chest and let them rest there for a moment, as if she were touching his beating heart, and then she caressed his arms and shoulders in long, slow, sweeping strokes.

Delia ran her hands across his bare torso, curious about the layers of muscles under all that sleek bronzed skin. She'd never seen a man naked before, but she was quite sure most of them didn't look like Alec. She thought about the first time she'd seen him, with his shirt open, his throat and part of his chest bare. She'd been shocked, and she'd have died before she admitted to it, but even then she'd wanted him.

She raked her fingers through the crisp dark hair on his chest, then shyly circled one of his nipples with a fingertip. Alec drew a sharp breath and Delia hesitated. "Does it feel good?"

"Yes," Alec said huskily, but he closed his eyes as if he were in pain. Curious, she brushed her fingertips across his other nipple. He groaned and his chest heaved as his breathing quickened.

Her palm slipped lower to trace the ridges of his abdomen, but she jerked it away when she felt his muscles tense under her hand. At once Alec took her hand in his and placed it back on his body, a hint of challenge in his eyes. "Don't stop now."

Delia cautiously dipped her fingers back into the grooves of his stomach muscles. "Your body is so hard."

Alec made a choked sound, something between a laugh and a moan. "Sweetheart, you have no idea."

"You have the most alluring trail of hair that begins just here," Delia murmured dreamily, brushing her fingers under his belly button. "It goes all the way down to here"—she followed the trail—"and then disappears"—she drew the blanket down slowly—"under here."

Alec shuddered with pleasure under her seeking fingers. When she drew the blanket slowly over his hard cock, he arched convulsively, and his head tipped back against the pillow.

"Oh, my, Alec," Delia breathed. She paused for a heartbeat and then stroked one tentative finger against his shaft.

"*Yes.*" Alec raised his hips toward her hand.

"I don't know what to do." She desperately wanted to touch him, to learn this most male part of him, but she didn't want to hurt him, and he looked like he was in agony.

"Touch me." Alec took her hand in his and pressed it firmly against him and began to move it, showing her how to stroke him. "Yes," he groaned when Delia continued the caress after he removed his hand. "Just like that, love."

He was soft and hard at once. The skin of his shaft was thin and silky, but underneath the fine skin he was almost impossibly hard, and so *hot*. He pulsed and throbbed in her hand. Delia tightened her grip and stroked just a little harder and Alec gasped. His hips jerked sharply upward and he began to thrust into her hand in a subtle, rhythmic motion.

Delia was stunned she could find his pleasure in her touch so arousing. She watched him, transfixed, as he writhed under her hands. On impulse she leaned down and licked one of his nipples.

"Ah, *God*, Delia," Alec cried out.

He reached out and grasped her wrist to halt the stroking

motion of her hand. "Stop, love. Stop, or this will be over before it begins."

He grasped her around the waist and rolled over so she was sprawled under him with his hips fit snugly between her thighs. She could feel the hard length of him press into her belly. She lifted herself against him and wrapped her legs around his hips with a breathless sigh, eager to feel him move inside her again.

But Alec had other ideas. He slid his arms under her knees to unclasp her legs, keeping her thighs open to him as he slid down her body, tasting her skin. His lips seemed to be on her everywhere at once, trailing hot kisses from her neck to the base of her throat before his mouth closed over the engorged tip of her breast and sucked hard, licking and teasing her nipple.

He nipped lightly against her lower belly, and it dawned on Delia he was still descending, his mouth drawing ever closer to the aching spot between her open legs. Shock penetrated the deep haze of desire that engulfed her. "No, Alec!" She struggled to sit up and close her legs.

Alec's hands tightened on her thighs. "*Yes*, Delia," he hissed softly, holding her open to him. "It's all right." He pressed his hot mouth against the soft skin at the crease of her thigh. "Shhhh," he crooned. "I just want to taste you, love . . . have to taste you . . ."

Then his tongue was between her legs, stroking insistently, and Delia's protest died on her lips. "*Alec*," she moaned, all rational thought fleeing as her entire being focused on the tiny bud of flesh that throbbed under his lashing tongue.

"So sweet," he murmured. "Just like honey."

He brushed his tongue against her slick flesh in slow, lazy, maddening circles. Delia clutched at his hair and arched up to meet his mouth. "Please," she gasped, not even sure what she begged for.

But Alec knew. A low, wicked chuckle escaped him. "Do

you want more, love?" He teased her lightly with the tip of his tongue.

"Yes. *Yes*." Her fingers tightened desperately in his hair.

He pressed her thighs farther apart, devouring her, his strong, deft tongue plunging into her and stroking hard against her wet pink flesh. She rose up to meet his every caress, one hand against her mouth to muffle her cries, the other flung above her head while he worked her. His expert, relentless tongue drove her higher and higher until at last he closed his lips around the tender bud and sucked at her, and she shuddered in his arms as wave after wave of ecstasy swept through her.

For long moments afterward Delia lay still, breathless and trembling. Alec wrapped his arms around her hips and rested his head against her, holding her and pressing gentle kisses against her thighs and belly. When her breath became even and she'd gone limp against him, Alec moved back up her body and rolled them, so she lay on top of him. He closed his eyes, as if savoring the feel of her weight on him.

"Straddle me," he murmured after a moment. He clasped her shoulders and pushed her gently back so she sat on top of him instead of lying down.

Delia's face flamed. It was silly of her to be embarrassed *now*, after he'd seen and touched and even tasted every inch of her body, but . . .

"It's all right. I want to see your face when I touch you. I want to watch you come. You're so beautiful, Delia." He looked up at her, his lids gone heavy over glittering black eyes. His cock pressed insistently against her bottom, so she tightened her knees around his hips and eased backward, moving her body instinctively until the hard length of him rested between her legs, trapped between her warm cleft and his abdomen.

"Delia." Alec jerked his hips helplessly, as if his body was no longer under his control. He laid his hands on her thighs and began to caress them, his warm palms stroking her rhythmically. Then he closed his hands firmly around her waist. "Take me inside you," he whispered. He lifted her with strong hands so she was suspended slightly above him.

Delia hesitated. "I don't know how . . ."

Alec was shuddering now, as if he were crazed with the need to be inside her. "Come up on your knees." He kept his hands on her waist, steadying her while she rose to her knees. "That's it, love," he said when she supported herself above him. Then he took one of her hands, placed it on his stiff cock, and guided it so the head slipped inside her dewy folds. "God, yes." He closed his eyes briefly and arched his back. "Now take me all the way inside."

Delia placed her hands flat against Alec's chest to steady herself and began to lower her body. "Oh." She slid down onto him slowly, savoring every inch of his hard length as he entered her, amazed at the way her body stretched to take him inside.

"Ah, Delia, you feel incredible." He gave one quick, involuntary thrust beneath her, but then he took a deep, shaky breath and his hips stilled. His skin became slick with sweat and his neck muscles corded with strain, but he remained motionless beneath her. "Take all the time you need, love."

Delia felt a surge of pure feminine triumph as he panted beneath her, struggling to control himself as she fed him slowly the rest of the way inside her body. When he was buried deep inside her, she went still, watching him with half-closed eyes as he fought to keep from surging against her. Oh, it was wicked to tease him, wicked to be so terribly excited by her power over him, and yet, and yet . . . "Tell me what you want, Alec," she whispered, running a finger around one of his nipples.

Alec made a strangled sound in his throat, half laugh, half groan. "Tease. You know *exactly* what I want." He grasped her waist and lifted her above him until only the head of his cock remained in her snug passage; then he pulled her back down onto him just as he thrust upward with his hips. His length surged into her, quick and hard, making her gasp. Again and again he thrust into her, setting a powerful rhythm she followed instinctively, riding down on him as he drove his hips upward against her. Delia closed her knees tightly around his waist, urging him to go faster, to plunge deeper.

"Jesus. *Delia*." He gasped, arching his back. He parted her folds to tease at her delicate pink bud with his long, knowing fingers.

Delia felt the elusive bliss slide closer, and she knew she'd come for him again. "Ah, ah, ah," she cried, writhing on him.

"Come for me, Delia," Alec demanded breathlessly, his hips never ceasing their rhythm.

The waves of pleasure crashed over her again and again and she lost herself in them, arching and throwing her head back. Long tendrils of her hair brushed against Alec's thighs and the light caress made him wild. He thrust fiercely into her again, and then again. A harsh groan broke from his lips and his hands closed hard around her thighs as his release took him, his powerful body shuddering beneath her.

Gradually their breathing slowed. Delia stared down at Alec, dazed, stunned into silence by the intensity of their lovemaking. He didn't say a word, either, but gazed back up at her. She couldn't quite read his expression, but his dark eyes were so soft and warm, she was overwhelmed by an absurd urge to cry. She looked away and collapsed on top of him and pressed her face into his neck, her body boneless and slack.

Alec closed his arms around her. He lifted her carefully and settled her against his side, one hand easing her head to his chest. Delia's heavy eyelids closed.

When she awoke, she had no idea how long she'd slept, but the fire had died down and the first faintest fingers of dawn had appeared in the night sky. Alec's body was warm and solid next to hers, his heartbeat reassuring in her ear. Delia remained as perfectly still as she could and closed her eyes tightly. If she didn't move and didn't open her eyes, maybe she could hold on to this moment a little longer.

But then Alec stirred beside her, and Delia's heart sank. She couldn't stop the sun from rising, or stop time, or put off the inevitable any longer. Alec would leave for London this morning, and she'd leave for Surrey, and the memory of this single glorious night with him would have to last her a lifetime.

"Shall we stay here all day?" Alec nibbled her neck, then leaned over and captured her lips with his in a brief kiss. "Let's order a bath," he murmured coaxingly, his lips against her ear.

Delia shivered. "We can't, Alec. What if someone finds us here? Lily will be looking for me." She raised herself onto her elbow, gazed down at him, and felt her heart constrict in her chest. She pressed her forehead to his and forced a smile. "No. You are for London, and I'm—"

"Damn London," Alec interrupted, grinning up at her. "I've never felt less like going there. It's dirty and crowded." He nuzzled against her. The dark beard sprouting on his face tickled her neck. "You're soft and warm, and you smell delicious."

Delia giggled. "You're the Earl of Carlisle." She poked him lightly in the chest with one finger. "The Earl of Carlisle is far too important to linger in bed all day."

Alec captured her hand and pressed a kiss to the tip of her finger. "Is he? Very well, then. But earl or not, nothing could persuade me to leave here if I didn't know I would be with you again in a matter of hours at the London town house."

Delia stared at him, speechless. *Of course.* He didn't realize she'd finalized her plans to leave for Surrey. He must think she'd decided to accompany the family to London this morning. She opened her mouth to tell him the truth, but then closed it again.

Wasn't it better this way? Better if he didn't know? She didn't want to spoil these last precious moments with him, not after what they'd shared last night and this morning. She wanted to remember him as he was now, with his mischievous grin and his sleep-tousled hair and his warm, hard body wrapped around hers.

"Delia?" Alec looked into her eyes and his smile faded a little. "What is it?"

"Nothing. Nothing at all. It's just . . ." She cupped his face in her hand and stroked her thumb across his bristly cheekbone, committing the feel of his skin to memory. "I'll miss you."

"You won't have time to miss me, love. I'll make sure of it." He turned his face and pressed a hard kiss into the center of her palm. But he must have seen something in her eyes still, for he frowned and his brows drew together. "You trust me, don't you, Delia?"

Tears pressed against Delia's eyes and gathered in her throat, choking her. She needed to leave him, before she lost control. "Yes." She touched her mouth to his, the kiss soft and sweet. Fleeting. "Yes, of course I do."

Chapter Twenty-five

Alec didn't have a poetic soul. A little Sir Walter Scott now and again was tolerable, but Blake was a madman and Byron a self-indulgent ass. Still, maybe he should have known it would all end in poetry. If he'd ever doubted the bard's genius before, he didn't anymore.

Love really did make fools of them all.

He would never have admitted it at the time, of course, but he hadn't known Delia for even a single day before he'd been moved to compose flowery verses about her in his head. He'd begun thinking in poems almost instantly. A smile tugged at his lips. Bad poems. Her lips were pink rose petals. Her eyes sparkled like blue fire. The golden strands in her hair outshone the sun. Her bosom was—

Alec shifted uncomfortably in the saddle. Well, never mind her bosom just now. There would be time enough for her bosom later. All the time in the world.

He'd arrived at the Mayfair town house after midday and stayed just long enough to change his clothes before leaving again to conduct his business. It was a damp and blustery day and Alec usually found the ride from Bellwood to London tedious. He should have been in a foul temper by the time he arrived at the outskirts of town, but instead he was absurdly cheerful. The cold water dripping from his hat down his neck all day? Refreshing. The watery ale and bland stew served at the Leaping Hart Inn? Nectar and ambrosia. The mud flying from Ceres's huge hooves and splattering his Hessians? Well, Ceres was a fine, strong beast, and surely that was a good thing? He'd ridden many miles before he realized he'd been smiling the entire way. Anyone who passed him on the road would have thought him a fool. At best. At worst, they'd have thought he'd lost his wits.

Maybe he had, but he didn't give a damn.

Delia would have arrived in London by now. It was nearly five o'clock. The family had still been at Bellwood when he'd left this morning, but if they'd made even decent time . . . He was a besotted fool indeed, for it felt like years had passed since this morning, and the thought of seeing her now made his heart hammer with anticipation. He needed to make her his bride as soon as possible, because there was no way he'd be able to keep his hands off her over a long engagement.

Alec bounded up the steps to the town house. Rylands appeared at the door before he'd reached the top and Alec almost ran over him in his haste to get inside. "Rylands! Please send James out to see to Ceres."

Rylands bowed and took the hat and gloves Alec thrust at him. "James is not yet returned from Surrey, sir, but Thomas can see to the horse."

Alec was halfway across the entrance hall, but he froze at these words. An icy chill shot down his back. "What is James doing in Surrey?" he asked in deadly tones, turning slowly to face Rylands.

The butler blanched at the expression on his master's

face. "H-he's driving Miss Somerset t-to Guildford," Rylands stammered, taking a hasty step backward.

Alec's heart, which had beat with such anticipation only moments ago, pulled in on itself as if wounded, like an open palm closing into a tight fist. It shriveled and contracted until a chasm so deep opened in his chest he feared it would devour him.

"Where is the countess?" His lips had gone so cold and stiff he was surprised the words emerged at all.

Rylands, usually so perfectly impassive, looked stricken. "The whole family and Miss Lily are i-in the drawing room."

Alec turned on his heel without another word. Rylands hurried after him, Alec's gloves and hat still clenched in his hands. When Alec entered the drawing room, his mother looked up with a smile, but it faded the instant she saw his face. "My God, Alec," she cried, going pale. "What's happened?"

"Delia has returned to Surrey. Why?"

Eleanor shot to her feet at the mention of Delia's name. Her hand fluttered nervously at her throat. "Alec—"

But Alec's eyes were fixed on Lily, who sat quietly in a chair in front of the fire, her hands clenched in her lap. "Why?"

Lily paused before answering. "She was needed at home," she said after a moment, but she didn't meet his eyes.

Alec ran a shaking hand down his face. "She's needed here, damn you. *I* need her."

Charlotte gasped at this, but Lily didn't spare her a glance. "I don't believe Delia thought so." She looked directly at him this time. "She seemed to think any fleeting regard you had for her would not outlast the *ton*'s contempt."

Alec stared at Lily until she dropped her gaze. He was silent for a moment, and his hands clenched and unclenched at his sides. "Rylands, have Thomas saddle a horse for me. Not Ceres. A fresh one."

"Alec!" Lady Carlisle cried. Her voice was shaking. "Where are you going?"

"Surrey." He took his hat and gloves out of Rylands's slack fingers and left the room.

"Oh, thank God," Eleanor breathed, collapsing back into her chair. Charlotte sat gaping at the place where Alec had stood just seconds before, stunned. Lily turned back toward the fire, but this time a small, satisfied smile appeared on her lips.

"Alec! Wait a moment." Robyn followed Alec out of the room. He hadn't spoken a word during the entire exchange, but had kept his dark eyes fixed steadily on his brother. "Alec!"

Alec paused at the end of the hallway, his back to Robyn, waiting.

"It's true, then? You're in love with Delia?" Robyn asked.

Alec turned toward his brother, his face drawn. "Robyn. God knows I owe you an explanation. An apology, as well. I hope when I return, you'll allow me to give you both. But please, not now. I need to *go*—"

"Eleanor told me everything," Robyn said, cutting him off. "She said you were in love with Delia." He shook his head. "I didn't believe it at first. I'd begun to think you were a cold fish, brother. Ice in your veins. But your face, just now, when you walked into the drawing room? I've never seen you look so . . ." Robyn paused, then shook his head. "Well, I don't need any further explanation. You can apologize when you return. Who knows? I may even accept it."

A deep sigh tore free from Alec's chest as if the great weight that suffocated him had lifted at last. For a moment the two brothers stood silently in the hallway, staring at each other with nearly identical dark eyes. "So it's true, then?" Robyn asked again after a moment. "You're in love with Delia?"

Alec looked his brother in the eyes. "Madly. Hopelessly."

"Ah. Then there's nothing else for it. Go and get her."

What a fool she was, to be sure.

Delia was bundled into the Sutherlands' coach, alone, on her way back to Surrey. Odd, how just two weeks ago all she'd wished for in the world was to return home. It was all she'd wanted.

Well, that was another lesson learned, she supposed. Be careful what you wish for, or you may just find out what it really means to *want* something. Or someone.

But she didn't want to think about that. Couldn't think about it. So instead she was thinking about young ladies. Young ladies and house parties.

Young ladies attended house parties all the time. These young ladies might dance, or play cards, or sketch or walk. Some of the more daring young ladies might even overindulge in punch and wake up in the morning with the headache, or flirt a touch more than was proper with an inappropriate gentleman. That was the worst of their sins.

But not her. Oh, no. That would be far too sensible. Nothing less would do for her than to go to Bellwood and seduce the lord of the manor. Then she had to fall madly in love with him, as well, and turn the entire house upside down in the process. It was lucky the house party had lasted only a fortnight. She shuddered to think of the damage she might have caused had it lasted a month. At least Bellwood was still standing.

She deserved her fate. To be in a coach on her way back to Surrey, minus one sister, minus her virtue, and missing such a large piece of her heart she was surprised it was able to beat at all.

What a fool she was, to be sure.

She gazed listlessly out the coach window, wondering without interest if she'd ever arrive home. They'd been waylaid in a tiny village outside of Horley when one of the coach horses had thrown a shoe. It had taken hours for James to find the blacksmith, and Delia had been obliged to wait for him at the inn. It wasn't much of a village. The inn, the Rose and something, or the Crown and something, she couldn't quite recall which, wasn't much of an inn, either. The esteemed patrons, all male, had eyed Delia as if they were undecided whether to steal her valise or assault her person first.

She hadn't been much interested in the outcome herself.

Alec would have arrived in London hours ago. He'd have discovered by now she wasn't there.

You trust me, don't you, Delia?

Her heart gave a miserable lurch. She hadn't wanted to deceive him. It hurt her to do it. But it was easier this way, and less painful for both of them. She couldn't have borne it if he'd made her empty promises out of some misplaced sense of duty, just because he thought he'd stolen her virtue. He'd never see the truth—that she'd simply *given* it to him. After a little time had passed, he'd realize it was better this way. Indeed, he'd likely feel a sense of relief. It wasn't as if he loved her, after all.

It wasn't as if he loved her.

Delia clenched her hands into fists. She *hadn't* made a mistake, leaving him, and she would *not* cry. She would not sit here in this coach and weep all the way to Guildford, for she'd known she'd be riding back to Surrey alone. She'd known how it would end.

What she hadn't known was how *alone* being alone would feel.

Yet how could she bring herself to regret making love to Alec? She closed her eyes and thought of his strong, sensuous hands stroking her, his face gilded by the firelight. His voice whispering in her ear. The nearly unbearable pleasure of him as he moved inside her. She could never regret it. It had been the most glorious night of her life.

"Blast it," she whispered weakly when the first tear snaked its way down her cheek. She needed to be at home. Now. She needed to lay her head on Hannah's shoulder and scold her younger sisters and sleep in her own room, even if it was lonely without Lily there. Was it asking too much of this blasted coach that it simply *get her home*?

That thought had no sooner crossed Delia's mind when, incredibly, she felt the coach begin to slow down. Impossible. Surely she was imagining it? She peered out the window. Deep dusk had descended and she couldn't see a thing, but the coach was indeed slowing down, and quickly. A second later Delia heard a distant shout and then James's voice coming from the driver's box, shouting something back. She couldn't make out what he said, but he sounded stunned. A few moments later the coach came to an abrupt stop.

A highwayman. Of course. Delia tried to work up the requisite terror, but the best she could do was a tepid sort of annoyance. She hoped he'd be quick about it. Perhaps if she explained she really was in a tearing hurry to get home . . .

The door to the coach flew open.

Delia gasped. Alec stood there, covered from his boots to his cravat in mud, his hair matted with sweat and rain and his chest heaving with exertion. "Get out of the coach," he gritted through clenched teeth.

His wild appearance was startling enough, but it wasn't what made Delia gasp. It was his eyes. They glittered and flashed with rage. She'd never seen him so angry. "Alec! What—"

That was as far as she got. When she didn't move at once, he reached in, grasped her around her waist, and jerked her from the coach. He set her on her feet, but his hands clutched her shoulders as if he were afraid she was about to disappear into the dusk. "Where the *devil* do you think you're going?"

Delia gaped at him. Her mouth opened and her lips moved but it was some seconds before any words emerged. "Surrey?" she finally managed to squeak.

Alec's hands tightened on her shoulders. "*Why?*" He shook her a little.

Delia tried to twist out of his grasp, but he held her fast. "Um, because I *live* there?"

Alec's mouth was a grim line. He released her shoulders only to grip her upper arm and march her toward his horse. "Not anymore, you don't. Take the coach and horses back to Horley," he said curtly to James, without releasing his hold on Delia's arm. "Wait for us there."

"Yes, my lord," James said, his eyes wide. Within seconds he'd wheeled the coach around, back in the direction of Horley. The coach and horses were quickly swallowed by the night.

Delia began to think she'd prefer a highwayman, especially when Alec clearly intended to throw her over his horse's saddle as if she were a sack of potatoes. She dug her heels into the ground and began to resist him in earnest. "Alec! What do you think you're doing? Stop this!"

But he didn't stop. He only hauled her closer and glared down at her, breathing in harsh, ragged pants. "What am I doing? I'm taking you back to London." He lost his last shred of patience. "Where you should have been in the first place! Why weren't you there, Delia? You lied to me," he added in a low, furious tone.

"I didn't. I didn't lie, Alec."

If anything, this seemed to make him even angrier. He dragged her roughly against him. "All right. Then you neglected to give me a crucial piece of information. Does that make you feel better? No?" he seethed when she looked away from him. "I thought it might not. For it amounts to the same thing as a lie, doesn't it, Delia?"

"I should have told you," she whispered. "I—I'm sorry, Alec."

"Not as sorry as I was when I arrived at the town house to find you weren't there."

Delia heard the break in his voice and all at once the fight went out of her. She'd thought she'd never be in his arms again, and now that she was, all she wanted in the world was to melt against him. She hid her face against his chest, unable to speak.

"Can you imagine how I felt, Delia, when Lily told me you'd left for Surrey? She said you didn't believe my regard for you would outlast the contempt of the *ton*." Some of the anger had drained from his voice, but he grasped her chin in his hand and forced her to face him. "*Look at me.* You told me you trusted me. You lay naked in my arms just this morning, and you told me you trusted me."

"I—" She was about to say she *did* trust him, but she looked into his eyes and the words died on her lips. She *hadn't* trusted him. Not really. She'd told herself she'd risked everything for Alec, but in truth she'd behaved like the worst kind of coward. She'd fled Bellwood as if she were a condemned criminal facing the noose. She'd given him her virtue, but she'd withheld the truth. She'd given him her love, but she hadn't trusted him with it. "I was afraid," she said at last. "The *ton*, and Robyn . . ."

"I don't give a damn about the *ton*, or anyone else. Can't you see? None of that matters anymore. I thought you understood."

Oh, God. She'd made an awful mistake. She had only to look at the anguish that dimmed his dark eyes to see it. She'd been terribly unfair to him, and she wasn't sure she could repair the damage now. Had she hurt him too much? She searched his face, trying to read his expression to see if there was any hope at all.

He stared back at her for a moment without speaking, then, "Why did you make love to me, Delia?"

Was he giving her a second chance? Oh, she didn't know! But maybe he was, and this time she was going to seize it with her bare hands and hold on to it with every part of herself. Just as her mother had done. She placed her hands on either side of his face, took a deep breath, and laid her heart at his feet. "Because I want to give everything I have to you. I love you, Alec."

For a moment he didn't move or speak or even seem to breathe; then his eyes dropped closed, the long dark lashes she loved so well sweeping across his cheekbones. Delia knew she'd never forget the look in his eyes when he opened them again, for they glowed so fiercely they sent a warm tingling heat rushing over her entire body.

He took a deep shuddering breath and clasped her hands in his own. His were shaking. "And why," he asked urgently, pressing one of her hands hard against his chest, over his heart, "would I allow you to give everything to me? Why would I take such a gift from you?"

Delia felt the strong beat of his heart under her palm. She searched the dark pools of his eyes, and what she saw in them thrilled her.

"Because I love you, you maddening woman." He brushed his lips tenderly against hers.

"Enough to chase me all the way to Surrey?" She gave him a tremulous smile.

"Much farther than that." His dark eyes grew serious. "I would chase you to the ends of the earth, Delia."

Then his mouth was on hers in earnest, desperate and demanding, and Delia held him as tightly as she'd ever held anything in her life, her mouth melting under his.

He finally released her lips to press his forehead against

hers. "You'll marry me, of course. You have to." He laid a possessive hand on her belly. "I've compromised you, and since I plan to do it again and again, you'd better become the new Countess of Carlisle as soon as possible."

Delia leaned back in the circle of his arms so she could see his face. "What a scandalous thing to say, my lord. Why, the *ton* would be shocked. They'll gossip for months about us, you know. They'll claim the Somerset women have put a curse on the Sutherland men. They'll say I bewitched you." She wrapped her arms around his waist and laid her head against his chest.

Alec tightened his arms around her. "You *have* bewitched me. I'm utterly and completely in your thrall." He pressed his face into her hair, closed his eyes, and drew in her honey scent. "It must be the eyes of blue fire."

Epilogue

"*Lady Carlisle.*" *Alec strode into the room and came to an* abrupt halt behind Delia, who was seated at her dressing table.

"My lord?" Delia smiled at her husband in the looking glass. Goodness, how handsome he was in his formal evening attire—so handsome she'd like to unwind his cravat, slide his coat from his shoulders, and lure him back to the bed.

If only they could stay hidden in their town house and let London carry on without them for the rest of the season! They'd hardly set a toe outside their bedroom since their marriage several weeks ago, though, and the *ton* would gossip if they didn't make an appearance soon. Besides, she'd promised Lily they'd be there tonight.

She stifled a sigh. Drat Lady Barrow and her musical evening anyway.

"I wonder—" he began, then paused and raised his eyebrows at Alice, Delia's lady's maid. "Leave us."

Delia watched in the glass as Alice, who was putting the last touches on the elaborate arrangement of curls pinned to the back of Delia's head, set aside her tongs, dipped into a hasty curtsy, and fled the room.

"You must stop terrifying poor Alice." Delia twirled one of the curls beside her cheek to smooth it. "Especially when she's not yet completed my coiffure. You do realize the *ton* will titter if my curls are lopsided?"

Alec was frowning down at a paper he held in his hand, but at this he met her eyes in the glass. "They wouldn't dare, for they'd have me to answer to if they did." He swept his gaze over the long curls that brushed her bare shoulders, and he moved closer, so his torso pressed against her back. "They don't look lopsided to me."

Delia heard the husky note in his voice and gave him a saucy little smile. "No? What a relief."

He trailed his fingertips across her back, from one shoulder to the other. "Don't be too relieved, sweet. I fear a total curl collapse is inevitable."

Delia shivered at his touch and at the warmth of his body behind her, but she lowered her eyes with a demure smile and pretended to focus only on her curls. "Oh, no, my lord. That won't do. Not after all of Alice's efforts to coax them into place."

Alec plucked one of her hairpins free. "Alice be damned."

Delia made a grab for the pin. "Alec! What do you think you're doing?"

"What?" He held up his hands in an innocent shrug. "I'm only trying to help. It was lopsided just there, after all." He tossed the hairpin onto the dressing table. "Alice uses too many of these cursed things." He captured one of her curls in his long fingers. "I like your hair loose, so I can run my fingers through it."

Delia drew a deep breath to calm her racing heart. His most casual touch or a glance from his dark, wicked eyes was enough to send her blood rushing through her body. "I'll tell her you think so. Now, what have you there?"

"Here?" Alec pressed closer so she could feel his hard thighs and burgeoning erection against her back. "Shall we see? I believe it's something for you."

A rush of moist heat bloomed between Delia's legs, but she forced a stern frown onto her face. One of them had to be practical, after all, or they'd never get to Lady Barrow's, and she had promised Lily. "And I believe I've married the wickedest man alive. Not *that*. That." She gestured at the paper in his hand.

Alec glanced down at the paper as if he'd forgotten it. "Ah. Yes. Well, my lady, that's what I came to ask you. Why don't you tell me what this is?"

"Is it Iris's last letter?" Delia went back to tweaking her curls. "Read the part about Hannah aloud while I finish my hair, won't you? It's quite funny. Hannah caught Mr. Edward Downing trying to kiss Iris, and she went after him with her broom, and—"

"No, it's not the letter."

Delia darted a glance at him in the glass, surprised to hear an odd, tense note in his voice.

"It's a drawing," he went on, "in Rowlandson's style. Quite a good one, too—good enough so the figures are recognizable. That is"—he turned the paper sideways and studied it—"one of them is. A tiger, I believe. Or wait. Perhaps it's not a tiger, after all, for it looks like a man—a man with wavy dark hair. Perhaps it's an earl?"

Oh, no. Delia's fingers froze in mid-tweak. That blasted drawing! She should get rid of it, but every time she was about to toss it into the fire, she found she couldn't quite let it go, after all, and she'd stuff it back into her writing desk. Alec must have found it there when he went to retrieve Iris's letter.

"Tiger?" She studied him in the mirror, trying to gauge

his expression. He didn't look angry, precisely, but not pleased, either. Or, dear God, had the drawing hurt his feelings? She'd never forgive herself if it had. "Are you sure?"

"Yes. A tiger, or some kind of predatory animal. He has rather sharp teeth, and long, curved claws." Alec continued to turn the paper this way and that, studying it from every angle. "He looks like he's about to ravish this poor, defenseless deer."

Delia twisted her hands in her lap. "It's a gazelle."

"Ah. So it is. A gazelle, with a bow around its neck." Alec lowered the paper, reached over her shoulder, and captured her chin in his fingers. He tilted her face up to the glass, so she was forced to meet his eyes in the mirror. "But this tiger—he's not *just* a tiger, is he?"

Delia saw a red flush climb into her reflection's cheeks. "No. Not quite."

Alec dragged his hand gently down her neck and rested his warm palm against her throat. "No. I didn't think so. He looks unpleasant, to say the least. Who is he?"

Delia closed her eyes. Oh, dear God, he was going to make her say it. She bit her lip with embarrassment and shame, but in the next instant her eyes flew wide open to catch his in the mirror. He was gazing at her mouth, and his erection surged even harder against her back. Her eyes went wider. My goodness. Whatever else Alec was—angry, amused, or hurt—he was also deeply aroused.

He slid his palm lower and dipped his little finger between her breasts. "Lady Carlisle? Who is he?"

Aroused, and persistent. Delia sighed. "He's you. At least, he's who I believed you were at the time. I drew that ages ago, Alec, before I knew you. Before I fell in love with you."

Alec's face softened, but he didn't smile. "But you've kept it all this time. Why? Is there a part of you that still sees me that way?"

His voice was light, but Delia heard it, subtle but unmistakable—a note of doubt. "*No*, Alec." She turned around and looked up at him, then pressed her cheek against his hard stomach and wrapped her arms around his waist. "I don't see you that way at all. I've almost burned that drawing at least a dozen times. I'm not sure myself why I keep it, except it . . . reminds me."

Alec stroked the loose curls away from her face. "What does it remind you of, love?"

For some absurd reason, Delia felt tears press behind her eyes. "It reminds me I judged you harshly, before I even knew you—you see how harshly from that drawing. I keep it because it reminds me never to do so again. I came close to losing you, Alec. The drawing reminds me how fortunate I am to have you, and it reminds me to be grateful for you."

For a moment Alec didn't speak, just continued to stroke her hair, but his hands shook a little now, and his stomach rose and fell against her cheek as he drew one deep breath after another. After a long silence, he unwound her arms from around his waist and dropped to his knees next to her chair. "My love. It's me who's grateful. I don't deserve you, sweet."

Delia shook her head. "That's not true, Alec—"

"Yes, it is. Don't you see, Delia?" He cupped her cheek in his hand. "If not for you, I *would* be the man in that drawing. Or worse. You didn't misjudge me, love. You saved me."

Delia started to speak, but Alec stopped her words with his mouth. He kissed her tenderly at first, his lips soft and gentle, then with growing passion as he opened his mouth over hers and slipped his tongue into her wet warmth. Delia met him eagerly, and when he broke away at last, they were both panting.

Alec traced his fingers over the pulse leaping in her throat. "There is one thing that bothers me about that drawing, though."

"Only one thing?"

He put his hands on her shoulders and turned her away from him, back toward the mirror. "Yes. The bow around the gazelle's neck."

Delia gave a breathless laugh. "The bow? How funny . . ." She trailed off, watching in the mirror as Alec drew a flat, square box from his coat pocket.

He slid his arms around either side of her waist and eased her back, so she was resting against his chest, and placed the box in the center of the dressing table. "Such a beautiful neck," he murmured, his lips close to her ear, "deserves a beautiful ornament." He flipped open the lid of the box with a finger.

Nestled in an ocean of silk was a magnificent sapphire and diamond necklace. The round sapphires were designed to look like flowers, and each of the eight perfect, deep blue stones was set in a bed of diamond petals. From each of the three centermost sapphire blooms hung one long, teardrop-shaped pearl.

Delia gasped. "Oh, my. Oh, Alec."

He lifted the necklace from its silk cocoon, draped it around her neck, and fastened the clasp. "I want you to wear this tonight." His voice was low and husky, and his fingers lingered to stroke the skin at the back of her neck. "The necklace, and nothing else."

Delia was staring at the glittering stones around her neck, but at this her eyes met his in the mirror. "Nothing else?"

Alec pressed his lips against her neck. "There are ear bobs, too." He nipped at one of her earlobes. "I suppose you can wear those if you insist, but they'll only get in the way."

Delia shivered. "Get in the way at Lady Barrow's musical evening?"

Alec was idly toying with one of the pearl drops, but he abandoned it and slid his fingers under the neckline of her gown, into her bodice. "Lady who?"

"Lady . . . Lady . . ." Dear God. *Lady who, indeed?* A quiet moan escaped her as he circled her nipple with maddeningly slow fingers. "Lady Barrow."

"Hmmm. Lady Barrow." He slid the hairpins from her hair one by one, until Alice's elaborate arrangement of curls lay in ruins over her shoulders and down her back. He buried his face in them for a moment, inhaling deeply, then brushed the long locks aside and began to unbutton her gown. "I don't recall inviting her."

Delia watched his other hand move against her breast, mesmerized. His skin was dark against her white flesh, his fingers long and sure as he pinched lightly at her tender pink nipple. "No, she invited us, to her . . . her . . ." Delia let her head fall back against his shoulder.

Alec laughed, the sound soft, teasing. "Her . . . what?" He'd freed each of the tiny buttons from their buttonholes at the back of her gown, and now he tugged the silk down to her waist.

Delia raised her head from his shoulder and tried to gather her thoughts. There was a reason she couldn't melt into her husband's arms, but for the life of her she couldn't remember what . . . Oh, yes. Yes, of course. "Her musical evening. I promised Lily . . ." But her protest was faint, and it faded into oblivion at the look in his hot dark eyes as he watched her nipples stiffen against the thin, white material of her shift, begging for his touch.

"So beautiful, love. Watch me stroke you." His eyes never left her face as he cupped her breasts in his hands and ran his thumbs over her eager nipples. "Watch me in the mirror, sweet." He darted his tongue at the pulse point behind her ear; then he slid his lips down her neck to suck and lick at her throat, the heavy necklace caught between his teeth.

She could do nothing but watch, breathless, as he touched her. Lady Barrow, Lily, the musical evening—each thought fled her head one by one until there was only Alec, his voice soft and wicked in her ear, crooning to her, telling her how much he wanted her, and what he was going to do to her.

When neither of them could stand the teasing touches any longer, he rose to his feet behind her and held out his hand. "Come to bed, sweet."

Delia turned in her chair and looked up at him with a mischievous smile. "Not yet."

"Not yet?" Alec let out a strained laugh. "It's almost too late now, love."

Delia teased her hands slowly up his thighs until she reached his erection, straining at the cloth of his breeches. She caressed him though his clothes until he began to shake with desire; then she unbuttoned his falls, drew out his hard flesh, and stroked her hand over him, her fingers tight against the thin, hot skin. "Not yet, Alec."

His lids went heavy over dark, glittering eyes. "Delia." His voice was a choked whisper.

She ran her cheek against his shaft. "Watch in the mirror, Alec," she murmured, and then she took him in her mouth.

He sank his fingers into her hair. "Dear God. *Delia*."

Delia took him deeper, encouraged by his strangled moans. She looked up at him to find him staring at their reflection in the mirror, a hot flush of color high on his cheekbones. She sank down farther on him, tugging at his hard flesh with her mouth, digging her fingers into his hips when he began to move them.

"Jesus. Stop, love. *Stop*." He tore away from her mouth with a gasp, grabbed her up into his arms, and then nearly sent them both crashing to the floor in his haste to get her to the bed. Delia was giggling as he tossed her onto her back and fell on top of her, one hand scrambling to raise her skirts, the other ripping at his breeches. They both moaned when he slid inside her welcoming heat, and then he began to move, and the elusive bliss slid closer with each powerful thrust until Delia shattered with a scream, and Alec followed her, his body arching against hers as his pleasure took him.

"My God," he said, once he'd caught his breath. "I told you it was almost too late." He rolled onto his back and dragged Delia on top of him. "I think I saw a celestial flash of light at the end."

Delia laughed, braced her elbows on the bed, and reached down to untie his cravat. "That was the diamonds."

He hooked a finger under the necklace and turned it this way and that, watching as it glimmered in the firelight. "They are beautiful, but it's not the diamonds that dazzle me, love. It's you. I want you so much, I can't even manage to get my clothes off first."

"I'll get them off for you." Delia tossed his cravat over the side of the bed, then sat up and surveyed the general ruin of their evening attire. With a shrug, she started on his waistcoat buttons. "No music for us tonight, it seems."

"Oh, I don't know." Alec grinned up at her. "At one point I'm sure I heard a soprano."

Delia threw back her head and laughed. "Did you? Well, my lord, perhaps you'll get to hear her again before the night is done. Was her voice very beautiful?"

He gazed up at her for a moment, and his expression grew serious. "There are none to equal her in voice, beauty, mind, or heart." He lifted her hand and pressed it against the middle of his chest, over his heart. "Here, especially, she is not just unsurpassed. She is *only*."

Delia cupped his face, his beautiful, dear face, in her palm. "Oh, my love. I have no need of musical evenings. You alone can make my heart sing."

TURN THE PAGE FOR A SPECIAL LOOK
AT THE NEXT BOOK IN
THE SUTHERLAND SCANDAL SERIES

The Wickedest Gentleman

COMING IN JUNE 2016 FROM PIATKUS

A high, thin voice floated on the air, audible even through the closed door. The music had begun. Pleyel. Of course. The *Scottish Airs*. What else?

Good God—musical evenings. Of all the bloody dull entertainments the *ton* inflicted on the gentlemen of London, the musical evening was the bloodiest. One stood about in a stifling room and waited for the music to start; then one squeezed one's arse onto a miniature chair and pretended to appreciate the efforts of a screeching soprano. Wait, stand, squeeze, listen, pretend. It was damned tedious.

Robyn rolled his shoulders inside his tight coat. He'd no intention of escorting his sisters all over London this season. That was, unless they wished to forgo their card parties, routs, and balls in favor of a visit to the gaming hells, or a frolic with the Cyprians in Covent Garden.

He tried to imagine his sister Eleanor at a hazard table, her long, elegant fingers wrapped around a pair of dice as every rogue in London breathed down her neck. Or his sister

Charlotte, engaged in a debate with the whores at the Slippery Eel over how low was *too* low when it came to low-cut bodices.

No, he couldn't picture it. Shame, too, because it would be amusing.

Robyn pressed his ear close to the door and listened. Not to Pleyel, but for the soft shuffle of a lady's slippers creeping down the hallway. He preferred petite, dark-haired ladies, especially those of an accommodating nature, to Pleyel.

Ah, dear old London. Wickedness lurked everywhere, even in the unlikeliest places. Another reason to love the old girl.

Where the devil was she? He tapped his foot, his eyes fixed on the door handle, willing it to turn.

It shouldn't be long now.

"Which do you think the handsomest?" Charlotte asked. She tapped Lily's wrist with her fan and nodded her head toward the center of the drawing room.

One couldn't take a step in any direction without tripping over one elegant nobleman or another, but there could be no doubt which group of gentlemen Charlotte referred to. Lily had noticed more than one feminine eyelash batting in that direction.

"My goodness," Eleanor interrupted. "Is Lord Pelkey wearing a pink waistcoat?" She peered over Lily's shoulder at the gentleman in question. "Oh, dear. It *is* pink, with green embroidered butterflies. That leaves him out. No gentleman who wears a pink waistcoat with green butterflies can be considered handsome."

The ladies tittered.

"Better to ask which is the wickedest," said Miss Thurston, a sour young lady with a head full of dull brown hair and a perpetually peeved expression. Her maid had clearly taken pains with the hair, but what had no doubt begun as fashionable ringlets had long since succumbed to the heat of the room. Poor Miss Thurston looked as if she wore a fuzzy brown animal of some sort on her head.

"One of them is as wicked as the next," she declared.

Perhaps the loss of her curls had curdled her temper.

"Mr. Robert Sutherland is the handsomest." As far as Lily was concerned, there was no question. It wasn't that he was so tall or so remarkably well formed, though he was both. It wasn't even his thick dark hair or heavily lashed black eyes.

No, it was his smile. His mouth was just a shade too wide. In another man that mouth might have been a flaw, but Robyn had a slow, suggestive smile, and he wielded it like a pickax. That smile could crack the ice around the coldest feminine heart.

"And the wickedest," put in Frizzle-hair.

Charlotte sighed. "Poor Robyn. How awful, to be the wickedest gentleman in the wickedest city in England."

Lily just stopped herself from rolling her eyes. If she believed half the tales and dire warnings about the wickedness of London, she'd refuse to leave her bedchamber at the Sutherlands' Mayfair town house.

When they'd first arrived, she'd expected to find cutthroats wielding knives in broad daylight, a pickpocket's fingers forever in her reticule, and leering rakes on every street corner. She'd kept a keen eye out for the rakes, as she didn't wish to be caught unawares, but to her knowledge she'd not yet seen one, leering or otherwise, and she'd been here for nearly six weeks already.

It was true she hadn't been out in society much since her arrival. She'd spent most of her time helping her sister Delia prepare for her wedding to Alec Sutherland, but Delia hadn't been the new Lady Carlisle for more than a few days before Eleanor and Charlotte Sutherland, Alec's younger sisters, had whisked Lily off her feet and into London's social whirl. Their mother, the dowager Countess of Carlisle, had graciously offered to sponsor Lily, and all three young ladies anticipated a lively season.

Leering rakes indeed. Handsome, fashionable gentlemen abounded, each more scrupulously polite than the last. Lily had rarely seen such a concentration of impeccable manners. The only thing that had given her a moment's concern was the price of hats on Bond Street.

She was fond of hats.

No matter what Charlotte said, Lily hadn't seen any real evidence of Robyn's wickedness. She prided herself on her fair-mindedness, and she wouldn't dream of condemning a man without evidence.

"What about that one?" Lily gestured with her chin at a tall, golden-haired gentleman. "I can't like the look of him. He has cold eyes."

All four heads swiveled to assess the golden-haired gentleman.

Charlotte craned her neck to see over a large woman wearing a towering purple turban adorned with tall peacock feathers. "Ah," she murmured with a significant look at Lily. "*That* is Lord Atherton."

Lily met Charlotte's eyes. "It is indeed?"

Well, then. That changed everything. Perhaps she *could* like the look of him, after all. It would help if she did, as she planned to marry him.

She glanced back over at the group of gentlemen. Lord Atherton stood just at the edges of it, his back a bit rigid and his air abstracted, as if he were only half listening to their conversation. He wasn't as tall as Robyn, but he was certainly tall enough to satisfy Lily.

Charlotte, who loved a matchmaking caper more than anything, rubbed her hands together in anticipation. "Yes. We'll have Robyn introduce you, and—"

Miss Thurston interrupted her. "He does *not* have cold eyes! Why, how unfair you are!" She looked as though she'd like to slap Lily with her fan. "Lord Atherton is the very model of a refined English gentleman. He has a spotless reputation."

Lily didn't argue this point. His spotlessness wasn't in question. If it had been, she and Charlotte would never have settled upon him, after prolonged discussion, as Lily's perfect mate and the potential future father of her children.

Charlotte didn't entirely agree with Lily's choice. In fact, she'd insisted Lord Atherton was "as dull as a stick of wood." She'd attempted to steer Lily toward a more exciting young gentleman, but Lily wouldn't hear of it.

Excitement wasn't part of her plan.

Perhaps Frizzle-hair had set her cap for Lord Atherton? If so, Lily feared she was destined for disappointment, for that spotless and refined model of English manhood hadn't looked her way once tonight. He hadn't looked Lily's way, either, but he would before the soprano had sung her last note this evening.

"Didn't you just say one of them is as wicked as the next?" Lily asked, turning to Frizzle-hair.

That young lady gave a worldly sniff. "You're from the country, aren't you, Miss Somerset? Perhaps you aren't familiar enough with town gentlemen to venture an opinion, and should defer to those with more knowledge on the subject."

"Perhaps," Lily agreed, all politeness, though she was tempted to laugh aloud at the idea that Frizzle-hair was an expert on gentlemen of either the town or the country variety.

Charlotte gave Lily a sly wink. "How, Miss Thurston, do you judge the degree of a gentleman's wickedness?"

"Well, one does hear things about Mr. Sutherland, you know. Scandalous things." Miss Thurston clamped her lips shut as if to prevent any of these scandalous things from emerging.

Charlotte gasped. "Why, Miss Thurston! Surely you don't rely on gossip to make your determinations?"

"Well, I—" Miss Thurston faltered. Her face flushed. "That is, of course not."

Charlotte took a deep breath and patted her chest with the tips of her fingers. "Oh, I'm *so* relieved to hear it, for the gentleman who escapes gossip's vicious tongue may simply hide his debauchery with greater cunning. That would make him *wickeder* than the others, not less so. Wouldn't it, Miss Thurston?"

Miss Thurston's fountain of wisdom on the vagaries of the English gentleman appeared to have run dry, however. She looked from Eleanor to Charlotte, then from Charlotte to Lily, dipped into a shallow curtsy, and hurried away without another word.

Charlotte watched her scurry off, frizzy curls flying, then snapped open her fan with a quick flick of her wrist. "I enjoyed that."

Lily stifled a giggle. "You're the wicked one, you know, Charlotte."

Charlotte gave her fan a vigorous wave. "Robyn is every bit as bad as Miss Thurston says, but I can't have her say so right to my face, can I? He *is* my brother, after all."

Lily glanced back over at the group of gentlemen, but Robyn was no longer there. She scanned the room for a dark head towering over the rest of the party, but he seemed to have disappeared. "Where did he—"

"Come, let's find a seat," Ellie said. "They're going to start."

Miss Sophia Licari, the soprano, had taken her place at the front of the room.

Lily gathered her skirts in her hand. "Save my seat, won't you? I need to visit the ladies' retiring room. My sash is twisted."

Ellie frowned. "Can't it wait?"

Lily fingered the tiny fold in the green satin sash at her waist. No, it couldn't wait. She couldn't abide a twisted sash under any circumstances.

"Shall I accompany you?" Charlotte asked. "The house is rather confusing—"

"No, no. Just point me in the right direction. I'll find it."

Charlotte made a vague gesture toward the door. "To the right, just there. Down the hallway, the last door on the left. Hurry now, Lily, or you'll miss the best part."

Damn it, his ear had begun to ache from being squashed against the door. If Alicia thought he'd wait all night for her—

A faint sound came from the hallway, just outside the door.

Robyn froze, breath held. *At last.*

A moment later the handle twisted, the door opened a crack, and a dainty, white-gloved hand appeared. He seized her wrist and nearly jerked her off her feet in his haste to get her through the door.

He'd waited long enough.

"What—" she squeaked.

He placed his lips against her ear with a low chuckle. "What took you so long? I was just wondering the same thing myself."

He eased her backward against the door, leaned his body into hers, and released her wrist. He let his fingers brush against her hip as he reached behind her to twist the lock. The bolt slid home with a sharp click.

God, she smelled incredible. He buried his nose in her neck and inhaled. Odd, but he'd never noticed her scent before, and a man didn't often come across a woman who smelled like a meadow. Fresh, like grass warmed by the sun, or like a daisy would smell if it had a scent. He'd have expected a more sophisticated perfume from Alicia, something sweeter, heavier. Less subtle. What a pleasant surprise, this scent. He nuzzled her neck and suppressed a sudden, absurd urge to growl.

Two unsteady hands came up to grasp the lapels of his coat. He expected to feel her arms slide around his neck, but instead she pushed against his chest. "I don't—" she began.

"Of course you do." *Otherwise she wouldn't be here.*

Robyn had no interest in a polite chat, and he'd long since learned the best way to keep a woman quiet was to give her something else to do with her mouth. He dropped a brief kiss on her warm, scented neck but resisted the urge to bury his face in her hair.

A man *should* linger over a scent like hers, but Lord Barrow's study wasn't the place to do it. He could easily be carried away by that scent, and before he knew it, he'd have Alicia flat on her back on what was undoubtedly a very fine carpet.

It wouldn't do to muss his lordship's carpet. It wasn't gentlemanly.

Then again, there was a settee. *Blast*—he should have tested it while he waited for her. But no matter. He'd noticed a desk, as well. A wide, empty desk. Lord Barrow, bless him, was quite tidy. Robyn would have to remember to send the old boy a very fine bottle of brandy to show his gratitude.

Alicia's hands tightened on his lapels. "Please—"

Ah, so eager. He did enjoy it when they begged. "No worries, pet. I'll take care of you."

He lowered his head and crushed his lips against hers. He could have tried for at least a modicum of finesse, but this was by no means Alicia's first time alone in a dark, deserted library with an amorous gentleman. She knew what was coming.

But instead of devouring him as he'd expected, a strangled whimper escaped her and she jerked back, away from him. There was no place for her to go, of course, as she was trapped between the door and his body, but she squirmed to break contact with his mouth.

Alicia, a shy virgin? That was doing it a bit brown, but if she wanted to play games, he'd act the part of the lustful rake to her chaste, innocent young lady. He placed his palms on either side of her face to hold her still and ran his tongue across the dry, closed seam of her lips.

She didn't open them. Robyn swept his tongue insistently against her mouth, but the delectable lips remained closed. What was Alicia playing at? She'd been keen enough to get him in here, and he'd been keen to come in part because he'd expected to get his tongue inside her mouth.

He swept it across her lips again. No luck, but all the same Robyn felt a flutter of desire tickle low in his belly. The moment she denied him the pleasures of her mouth, he found he could think of nothing but how to get his tongue between her lips to surge into her slick heat.

It was something new anyway.

He didn't often have to make an effort to get inside a woman, her mouth or any other part of her. Women made no secret of their attraction to him, and Robyn felt it was impolite to refuse their advances. He took his pleasure where it was offered. Widows, actresses, opera singers, a mistress here and there—they were all delightful diversions in much the same way a visit to Tattersall's or a jaunt down Rotten Row diverted.

Predictable. Simple. Fleeting.

But challenging? No. Women weren't challenging, and hadn't been since he'd been a randy fifteen-year-old lad agonizing over a saucy, buxom maid at his family's seat in Kent. She'd led him a merry chase until at last he'd managed to pin her against a stone wall in a remote part of the rose garden. He'd taken her right there, his breeches around his ankles, the sun on his back, his head swimming with the scent of roses.

He couldn't recall her name now, but to this day the scent of roses and the texture of rough stone still made him hard.

The maid had been the first in a succession of ladies who'd fallen into his arms like pins hitting the turf on a bowling green. Alicia, however, showed not the slightest inclination to hit the turf. She remained stubbornly, temptingly upright.

Christ, he was jaded. Jaded and debauched, because the idea of overcoming her token resistance aroused him. He would *make* her open for him. He would coax her, render her so dizzy with passion she would have no choice but welcome him into her mouth. The flutter of desire he'd felt in his belly unfurled and grew until it became a conflagration.

Robyn slid his tongue away from the seam of her lips. He'd have it inside her before they left this room, but he could take his time getting there. He teased his mouth across hers, nibbling at one corner, then the other. He slipped his tongue deftly across the perfect curve of her lower lip to tease her, then he discovered the faint bow of her upper lip. The tip of his tongue darted into the tiny gap again and again, until he thought he'd go mad if she didn't open her lips.

She made some small sound then, some faint whisper of . . . surrender? He burned with anticipation, but her lips remained closed. Her hands still clutched at his coat, but with each soft touch of his mouth he felt the tension ease from her, one vertebra at a time, until her back relaxed against the door.

Robyn slid his hands between the door and her body to stroke the arch of her lower back, right where it swelled into what promised to be a luscious backside. After a few moments her fists opened and she laid her hands flat on his chest.

Yes. That was it. He smiled against her mouth.

He would not have believed a practiced siren like Alicia could work him into such a frenzy. He'd had dozens of women just like her before. She was no innocent, but damned if she didn't have him imagining she was. He was wild to get into her mouth and find out if she tasted as perfect as she felt. Would she be sweet, like honey, or rich, like new cream?

He'd thought only to have a frolic with her, but perhaps a more permanent arrangement was in order? She was married, of course, but that made no difference to him. He'd had married lovers before.

For God's sake. He hadn't even kissed her properly yet.

He laid his hand against her neck and pressed light, feathery kisses against her cheeks, then another on the tip of her nose. They were gentle, playful kisses—not at all the kind of kisses he'd normally share with a woman like Alicia. Or *any* woman, come to that, since the women he favored were all different versions of her.

At some point he'd begun to pretend it wasn't Alicia at all. Not very gallant of him, but it kept the illusion intact. The innocence of her lips under his, feigned though it was, touched him somehow. He was almost reluctant to end the moment at all.

Almost.

Then, without warning, as if she sensed a change in him, she wrapped her arms around his neck. Robyn froze, afraid she'd retreat again, but then she gave a low, breathy sigh and melted into him. The blood pounded through his body. He wanted to crush her against him and take her mouth roughly then, but he held himself back and instead let just the tip of his tongue graze her lush bottom lip.

Once.

Her lips opened.

Robyn had the strangest urge to sink to his knees, but if he did, he'd take her down to the floor with him, and they no longer had time for *that*. But *this*—he'd been wild to get inside her mouth since she'd opened the door and he'd seen her white-gloved hand.

White gloves? Robyn stilled as he conjured an image of Alicia as she'd looked from across the drawing room. Petite but curvy, dark hair swept on top of her head, gray, catlike eyes aglow with wanton invitation. A dark blue gown and long black gloves fit tightly to her slender arms. Hadn't she had a diamond bauble of some sort on her wrist?

Well, maybe she'd worn the diamond bracelet on the other wrist? The one that hadn't opened the door? Yes, that must be it. And perhaps she'd simply changed into white gloves on her way to meet him in the study? Yes. Yes, of course, she'd want to change her gloves on her way to an illicit assignation.

He was still trying to convince himself this was a perfectly reasonable explanation when a hesitant tongue brushed against his. With that one shy stroke, every thought fled Robyn's head but one.

She tasted like wild strawberries.

"Delicious," he murmured, his voice as rough as a cat's tongue, and so husky he hardly recognized it. He stroked the soft skin of her jaw as his tongue twined with hers, then slipped two fingers under her chin to tilt her mouth up to his to deepen the kiss.

A low, pained groan broke from his chest when at last he was able to take her mouth fully. His tongue touched her everywhere, lost in her sweet, tart taste. She met each glide and stroke and thrust, and he wanted to roar with triumph.

Maybe they did have time for *that*, after all.

He swept her into his arms and backed away from the door. He'd intended to lay her across Lord Barrow's desk, but he only made it as far as the settee. He dropped down onto it, his lips still joined with hers, and dragged her on top of him, across his lap, his throat dry, pulse jumping in his neck, ready to devour her.

Jesus. It's just a kiss. A kiss, like any other kiss he'd shared with countless other women.

But it wasn't the same, and somewhere in his passion-fogged brain, Robyn recognized it. This kiss was different. He hadn't lost control with a woman since he'd turned sixteen, but now his body shook with the need to get inside her.

He cupped her cheek to urge her mouth closer to his and dragged his palm down the front of her neck and over the smooth, warm skin left bare by her low-cut gown. He traced his fingertips to the very edge of the neckline, where the smooth silk met the soft skin of the tops of her breasts.

Oh, God. Such a light touch, but he could feel the faintest throb of her heart under his fingers.

Her pert little backside pressed against his groin, his tongue twined with hers, and he was about to fill his hand with her soft breast. Had this not been the case, Robyn might have noticed it when she stilled on his lap. He might have felt just the merest whisper of a retreat.

As it was, he didn't notice a thing until she withdrew her tongue from his mouth, and then every part of his body howled with the loss. He couldn't fail to notice when she went stiff and unyielding on top of him and began to struggle in earnest to get away. It cooled his ardor just enough to enable him to think clearly.

Damn it. Something was wrong.

The white gloves. He was certain Alicia had been wearing black gloves and a high-necked gown. He'd noted the style because it was an unusual choice for Alicia, whose breasts were forever spilling from her bodices. There was something else, as well. Just now, when he'd swept her into his arms, her head had rested under his chin. Alicia was petite; her head wouldn't have reached farther than his shoulder.

Well, *someone's* head had rested there, for he'd buried his face in her hair to draw in as much as he could of her intoxicating scent. He was damn sure he'd just run his fin-gertips over the bare skin of *someone's* neck and bosom, as well. Even the finest silk wasn't that soft and supple. Or that warm. And her scent—that grass-in-the-sun, daisies-in-a-meadow scent. Alicia was charming in her way, but no woman of her experience could manufacture a scent like that; a scent of such pure, distilled innocence.

He really *wasn't* kissing Alicia. The shyness, the hesita-tion, the reticence—it wasn't feigned. He hadn't the faintest idea who he *was* kissing, but he was quite sure she was an innocent. A responsive, eager, passionate innocent, but an innocent nonetheless.

He'd better stop at once, as kissing and fondling an in-nocent had transformed more than one merry bachelor into a far less merry husband.

At once. That meant *immediately*, or *right now*, as in *this very second*.

She pushed against his chest again, harder this time.

Bloody, bloody, bloody hell.

His innocent temptress was determined to escape him. She writhed and flailed and tried to twist off his lap. She'd flee as soon as he released her; that much was certain. She'd flee and he'd never get a close look at her. He'd never know who she was and he wouldn't be able to find her again.

Unthinkable. Find her he would, innocent or not.

Robyn tightened his arms around her. He had to know who she was.

Then he'd let her go.